The Great
Comic Book Heroes

and Other Essays
by Mordecai Richler

The Great Comic Book Heroes

and Other Essays by Mordecai Richler

Selected and Introduced
by Robert Fulford

General Editor: Malcolm Ross

New Canadian Library No. 152

McClelland and Stewart

ISBN 0-7710-9268-7

The Canadian Publishers
McClelland and Stewart Limited
25 Hollinger Road
Toronto

Printed and bound in Canada

Contents

Acknowledgments

"Maple Leaf Culture Time" appeared first in the *New Statesman*, copyright 1968.

"Etes-vous Canadien?" first appeared in the *New Statesman*, copyright 1969.

"Bond" first appeared in *Commentary*, copyright 1968.

"A Sense of the Ridiculous" first appeared in the *New American Review*, copyright 1968.

"The Catskills" first appeared in *Holiday*, copyright 1965.

"This Year in Jerusalem" first appeared in *Maclean's*, copyright 1961.

"Why I Write" first appeared in *Works in Progress*, copyright 1971, The Literary Guild of America Inc.

The essays in Part One appeared in *Shovelling Trouble* (McClelland and Stewart 1972). Those in Part Two appeared in *Hunting Tigers under Glass* (McClelland and Stewart 1968).

Introduction

Since the late 1960s, Mordecai Richler's essays, articles, and speeches have staked out for him a position as a kind of loyal opposition to the governing ideas of Canadian culture. Richler has during most of this period been variously involved in the making of that culture – he has been a scriptwriter, a Canada Council and Governor-General's Award judge, a Book-of-the-Month Club selector, an enthusiastic encourager of young writers, and above all a novelist who has set the highest standards for his profession. But at the same time, a part of Richler has been standing outside our culture – assessing, judging, criticizing, and occasionally laughing raucously at our pretensions. It is this Richler, the Richler who functions as a kind of conservative cultural anarchist, that we find dominating this collection of essays. It is this Richler who has aroused the scorn and resentment of his contemporaries because he has so often attacked them where they are most vulnerable.

The conflict involved here centres on the word "nationalism" – a word that meant nothing in our literature twenty years ago and means everything now. By certain objective criteria, Richler would seem to be – through act and association – a nationalist. He is clearly concerned about Canada's place in the world, and concerned that its voices, including his own, be heard elsewhere. He publishes his books, including this one, through our most famously nationalist publishing house, McClelland and Stewart. He involves himself in a great many of the activities which seek to promote a national culture in English Canada. Yet he is marked, and possibly would mark himself, as "anti-nationalist."

To understand this, we have to remember Richler's beginnings as a writer in a Canadian literary culture very different from the one we know now. As Richler saw it a quarter of a century ago – so his essays would suggest – Canadian literature was dominated by gentlemen amateurs who believed more in "Canadian" than in "literature." Richler's generation, or some part of it, saw it as their task to reverse this tendency, and to reach beyond Canada towards the literary standards of Britain and the United States. (In the same period, the 1950s, the most accomplished of our painters were making the same attempt, in a vigorous reaction against Post-Group-of-Seven nationalism in art.) Richler's first serious recognition came in England, not Canada, and in the 1950s this must have seemed altogether appropriate to him. He wanted to be part of a larger world, and soon he was. Later his novels came to be admired both in Canada and the United States, and he began to work (as he works now) on the international as well as the Canadian scene. Many of his essays have appeared in *Encounter*, the *New Statesman*, the *New York Review of Books*, and other journals of high quality and international circulation.

It was natural, therefore, for him to see certain developments that began in 1967 as provincial and inward-turning. When a young generation of Canadians struggled to develop new publishing houses and other means of expression, *principally within their own country*, Richler saw this as a turning away from the larger world he had worked so hard to conquer. The possibility that a writer might be satisfied to have a good public in only one country, Canada, seemed to Richler outlandish, and probably still does. Far from joining his fellow writers (and other artists) in their persistent claim that they were neglected in Canada, he came to believe that as a class they enjoyed *too much* attention – the sort of attention that kills through over-praise and over-indulgence. He began to see much writing about Canadian literature as "embarrassingly boosterish" ("O Canada"). He saw all this as a return, in a new way, to the bad old days of complacency and smugness. It was (as he says in "Maple Leaf Culture Time") "our most dangerous Canadian enemy of promise ... "

Whether this statement has in fact proved to be true seems doubtful: in the long view most of our books are trash, as in most countries, but the enthusiasm that has surrounded Canadian literature in the last ten years has helped to draw attention to writers of genuine substance, among them Margaret Atwood, Marian Engel, Margaret Laurence, Richard Wright, Margaret Gibson, and Dennis Lee – writers who in most cases have been reviewed enthusiastically in England and the United States (though not bought in great numbers by British or American readers). These writers and their publishers have received the kind of assistance (from the Canada Council, the Ontario Arts Council, etc.) which Richler a few years ago saw as dangerous.

It's doubtful that Richler would now want to wish away that assistance. But he clearly saw himself acting as a gadfly, an antidote to a glib and easy nationalism.

8

Even the most passionate nationalist would have to admit that in this role he functioned efficiently.

In an introduction to *Hunting Tigers under Glass* (1968), one of the two books from which the present selection is drawn, the other being *Shovelling Trouble* (1972)*, Richler wrote:

> I am not an anti-Canadian or a Jew-baiter. I do, however, deplore many things Jewish and Canadian. Special pleading, whether by Canadian sports writers in Stockholm, kibbutz-niks in Galilee, or proliferating Canada culture boosters, never fails to move me to mockery.

And it is mockery that Richler the essayist handles best: not an easy mockery, at targets far away, but a mockery directed at those close to him, those who are in many ways not entirely different from Richler himself. Richler is a comic essayist with a serious purpose, or a set of serious purposes. He does not claim to set forth a body of ideas; rather he responds, usually as a fairly conservative moralist, to the stimuli he encounters.

Richler seldom sits down to write in praise of a person or an event. A great deal of praise may be found scattered through his writings, but his non-fiction has a persistently negative tone. In this sense it functions as an extension of the viewpoints projected in his satirical fiction, notably *The Incomparable Atuk* (1963), a satire on Canadian nationalism, and *Cocksure* (1968), a satire on the Swinging London of the 1960s, the new sexual permissiveness, and the painfully inoffensive character of Anglo-Canadians. Richler's non-fiction is almost always a response to some phenomenon which has aroused both his interest and his suspicion, and is often presented in the form of a corrective to the general opinion. Are movies becoming an over-rated intellectual fad? Richler provides a corrective in "Writing for the Movies." Is James Bond (a "morally repugnant" figure) becoming a mass idol of depressing proportions? Richler, in "Bond," sets him squarely within the tradition of anti-semitic and anti-foreign heroes, like those of John Buchan.

The stylistic strategy Richler brings to these subjects is an easy mingling of the journalistic and the literary. He has a journalist's ability to describe directly and state bluntly; he has the practised novelist's ability to set a scene carefully and to

---

* Many of the essays had appeared earlier in various magazines and periodicals.

choose dialogue that furthers his theme (see, especially, the dialogue in "The Catskills"). Behind these tools is a persona that is at once aloof and enthusiastic (see "This Year in Jerusalem"), at once detached and personal (see "Why I Write"). This literary persona makes several clear assumptions. One is that he and his views are innately interesting. Another is that his readers share a good many of his prejudices – he writes as if he and his readers were joined in a comfortable brotherhood of opinion, ranged against the uncaring and the thoughtless. A third is that his readers are as intelligent as he is and do not need to be spoken down to.

In his satire Richler does not spare himself or his personal history. In Richler's novels, the Richler-like character who sometimes turns up is seen as, in part, a pathetic and comic figure, given to paranoia and insecurity. In the same way, when Richler shows himself in his essays he depicts himself frequently as baffled, overwhelmed by the phenomena he must face. Richler the satirist seldom spares Richler the distinguished man of letters. The scared little boy who provides so much of the material in *The Apprenticeship of Duddy Kravitz* and other novels is permitted, from time to time, to peek through.

Richler has said often that his essays are not his real work: his real work is fiction, and the essays, like the screenplays, "represent time out." But he has also said that while he writes the screenplays for profit, the essays are written for his own pleasure, and education. As Edmund Wilson once said of literary critics, Richler conducts his education in public, and the essays in this collection are a record of that education. They tell us a great deal about the making of the mind and sensibility that produced *St. Urbain's Horseman*, *The Apprenticeship of Duddy Kravitz*, and *Cocksure* – the mind and sensibility, that is, of the most interesting Canadian writer of his generation.

Robert Fulford
Toronto, 1977

Part One

Maple Leaf Culture Time

Twenty odd years ago, when I was an adolescent zoot-suiter in Montreal, our most revered radio disc jockey's signature tune began, "It's make-believe ballroom time, the hour of sweet romance." Today we are well into an even sweeter hour of Canadian romance, maple leaf culture time, an era at once embarrassingly grandiose, yet charged with promise. We are smitten with an unseemingly hasty tendency to count and codify, issuing definitive anthologies of 100 years of poetry and prose and fat literary anthologies, as if by cataloguing we can make it real, by puffing, meaningful, especially if mere publication is taken as a licence to enshrine the most ephemeral stuff, as witness the following entry in *The Oxford Companion to Canadian History and Literature*[1]:

> Beresford-Howe, Constance Elizabeth (1922 –) Born in Montreal . . . she is the author of several historical romances. These include . . . *My Lady Greensleeves* (1955), based on an Elizabethan divorce case, in which she shows a sound command of historical detail.

What characterises Canadian culture today is not so much energy and talent – though it is there at last, a real but tender shoot – as an astonishing affluence and beneficence. Happily, an enlightened beneficence. But as the British health plan, in its formative years, could be sniped at by reactionaries, for handing out toupées to all comers, so our culture plan is vulnerable to the charge of

[1]Norah Story, *The Oxford Companion to Canadian History and Literature* (Toronto, Oxford University Press, 1967).

staking just about all the alienated kids to committing their inchoate, but modish complaints to paper or canvas. On the other hand, betting on fragile promise is a built-in hazard of art investment and the people who run the Canada Council could hardly be more decent and imaginative. It's a pity, then, that the Council's first eleven years could come to be noted for one conspicuous omission. Morley Callaghan has yet to be presented with its highest award, the Molson Prize.[2]

Which brings me to our ludicrous, newly-minted honours system, an innovation that must be seen as the last snobbish gasp of our eldest generation, the unselective, slavish Anglophiles. Really, in these austerity-minded days it's high time the Queen dismissed her Canadian second-floor maid, the Governor-General, who is of course Chancellor of the Order of the Companions of Canada, which now entitles many a bore to write the initials "CC" after his name, a measure hitherto accorded only to bottles of medicine. But my immediate point is, once more Morley Callaghan was overlooked. And then insulted. For, on second thought it seems, he was asked to accept the also-ran Medal of Canada.

Meanwhile, lesser writers, all of them world-famous in Canada, are blowing the dust off early manuscripts and digging old letters out of the attic, mindful of the burgeoning market in raw Canadiana. Book-length studies of just about everybody in the house are threatened, operas are being commissioned, ballet companies subsidised, and townships sorely in need of tolerable restaurants and bars are being paid to erect theatres instead. If Canada was once loosely stitched together by railroads, such is the force of today's culture-boom that it may be reknit by art palaces coast-to-coast, though there hardly be plays or players, not to mention audiences, to fill them. The promise of a Canadian film industry, backed by ten million dollars, alarms me for other reasons.

Even as in London, the movies have become increasingly, almost insufferably, fashionable among younger Canadian writers, intellectuals, and students. In fact, the sort of student who once

[2]Callaghan was in fact awarded the Molson Prize in 1970.

used to help put out a snarling little magazine, everything in lower-case letters, writing poems about his revolt against crippling poverty, is nowadays more likely to be making a film with a hand-held camera, all about his rebellion against suffocating affluence.

The dizzying prospect of a Canadian film industry frightens me when I dig into my own past experience of Toronto-based production companies. The archetypal Toronto film outfit has made indecently large profits out of TV commercials or has perhaps produced a puerile but money-spinning series about Indians or mounties, and has now set its sights higher, so to speak. They wish to make a "serious, yet commercially viable" film *with Canadian content*. That is to say, if *The Young Wantons* will look yet again at sex (unblinkingly, frankly, outspokenly) this time out it will be set in the palpitating streets of LSD-crazed, hippie-ridden, wife-swapping, transvestite-rich Toronto. Ontary-ary-ary-yo; with French Canadian tits being given equal exposure.

Junk is junk, and there would be no honour in Canada adding to the pile. Given our inexperience it is in the nature of things that our junk would be inferior to the glossy Hollywood or London product. We no more require a film industry for its own sake than the emergent African states need their costly airlines. On the evidence of last year's art film, the appalling *Waiting for Caroline,* co-sponsored by our two worthies, the CBC and the National Film Board, we would be well advised to wait a bit longer before plunging into a programme of feature film production, lest premature activity set us back even further.

If the arts in Canada were neglected, today, such is our longing, they are being rushed into shouldering a significance not yet justi-fied by fulfilment. The proliferating anthologies, summaries, and histories vary enormously in quality. The handsomely produced *Modern Canadian Verse*[3], a bilingual anthology edited by A. J. M. Smith, represents our established poets intelligently and introduces a number of lively young voices. It is a collection for which it would be foolish to make extravagant claims, but it can be offered without

[3]Toronto, Oxford University Press, 1968.

17

apology. Increasingly, Canadian poets (Irving Layton and Leonard Cohen are a case in point) are finding an astonishingly large audience.

Among last year's centennial spill of short story anthologies, *Modern Canadian Stories*[4] promised to be refreshingly different if only because it was edited by foreigners, Giose Rimanelli and Roberto Ruberto. In a foreword, Earle Birney writes of Rimanelli, a new name to me, that he is one of Italy's important men-of-letters, a prize-winning author of novels and short stories, a leading playwright and film writer. But instead of new, yet provocative, judgements, the editors, for the most part, fall back on familiar stories and writers (Leacock, Callaghan, Ethel Wilson, even Mazo de la Roche) for which I do not blame them, as possibilities are still limited. What I do reproach Rimanelli and Ruberto for is a Polonius-like introduction:

> Literature is not a mere word, but the individual expression of man's spirit. Consequently, to study the literature of an epoch means to study the spirit of the man of that epoch. Man lives, thinks, and acts. . . .

Which introduction finally comes unstuck through simple arithmetic ("at least five other Canadian writers deserve mention here: Jack Ludwig, Norman Levine, Dave Godfrey, and Sheila Watson"). More seriously, Mavis Gallant, our most compelling short story writer since Callaghan, is not included.

Neither is Mavis Gallant included among the more than 350 entries in *Canadian Writers/Écrivains Canadiens*[5], a biographical dictionary edited by Guy Sylvestre, Brandon Conron, and Carl F. Klinck, whilst my listing manages a grammatical error and a new, yet provocative judgment in one sentence. "In addition to his novels, Richler . . . worked on the film script for John Osborne's *Room At The Top* and *Life At The Top*."

Norah Story's *Oxford Companion to Canadian History and*

---

[4]Toronto, Ryerson Press, 1968.
[5]Toronto, Ryerson Press, 1968.

Literature, with 2,000 separate articles, 9 pages of maps, 2,300 cross-references, and a list of titles for more than 6,000 books, is at once more scholarly, even definitive. I have no quarrel with it as a historical reference, but as a literary guide it suffers from perfunctory, fact-bound summaries. It honours quantity rather than quality, so that many a dreary lending-library novelist is dealt with at length, but there is no individual entry for Adele Wiseman, author of only one novel, *The Sacrifice.* It's not so much a literary who's who as an all-inclusive directory.

A more ambitious, perceptive study is the *Literary History of Canada*[6], edited by Carl F. Klinck, Claude Bissell, Roy Daniells, Northrop Frye, and others. This volume, eight years in the making, is, in fact, a study of Canadian literature in English and will be followed by a *Histoire de la littérature canadienne-française.* Happily, the *History* is not only comprehensive, but it is informed by wit and sensibility; it dares judgements and strives for critical balance. A balance that is necessarily protective at times, but never tainted by culture-rousing chauvinism. "The book is a tribute," Northrop Frye writes in his 'Conclusion,' "to the maturity of Canadian literary scholarship and criticism, whatever one thinks of the literature."

Non-Canadian readers familiar with Professor Frye's larger body of work are perhaps unaware of his especial Canadian office. Among so many uncritical celebrators, he, like Leavis here, like Trilling in New York, is our keeper of true standards. Had the evaluative view, he writes, based on the conception of criticism as concerned mainly to define and canonise the genuine classics of literature, been the *History's* guiding principle, "this book would, if written at all, have been only a huge debunking project." There is no Canadian writer, he reminds us:

of whom we can say what we can say of the world's major writers, that their readers grow up inside their work without ever being aware of a circumference.

[6]Toronto, University of Toronto Press, 1968.

Yet he allows that the evidence shows "that the Canadian imagination has passed the stage of exploration and has embarked on settlement" and concludes, "the writers featured in this book have identified the habits and attitudes of the country, as Fraser and Mackenzie have identified its rivers. They have also left an imaginative legacy of dignity and high courage."

Professor Frye also notes that such is the obvious and unquenchable desire of the Canadian cultural public to identify itself through its literature that:

> ... there are so many medals offered for literary achievement that a modern Canadian Dryden might well be moved to write a satire on medals, except that if he did he would probably be awarded the medal for satire and humour.

And this, not neglect, it seems to me, is our most dangerous Canadian enemy of promise today.

"Êtes-vous canadien?"

Early in April, 1969, I discovered I was among the year's Governor-General's Award Winners for literature.

"You're accepting it," my Canadian publisher said, astonished.

"Yes."

"You're pleased, you're actually pleased."

"Yes, I am."

Several years earlier, a friend of mine had won the award for a collection of essays. At the reception in Government House, Ottawa, his wife, suddenly distressed, drove him into a corner. "He says he hasn't read it himself, but his maid did and liked it very much."

"No, no," my friend assured her, "his *aide*, he means his *aide*."

Traditionally, the GG, the Queen's very own Canadian second floor maid, stands behind two major horse races: the Queen's Plate and the Governor-General's Awards (never more than six) for the best books of the year. Though one Queen's Plate winner, the fabulous Northern Dancer, also came first in the Kentucky Derby, so far no Governor-General's Award winner has ever been entered in the final heat for the Nobel. The first Governor-General's Awards were presented by Lord Tweedsmuir in 1937 to Bertram Brooker and T. B. Robertson, who, it's safe to say, are now remembered for nothing else. Among others who have officially signed the Canadian literary skies with their honour there are John Murray Gibson, Franklin S. McDowell, Alan Sullivan, Winifred Bambrick, William Sclater and R. MacGregor Dawson. I could go on. I could go on and on, seemingly composing a letterhead with names fit to adorn only the most exclusive Montreal or Toronto law office. But, to be fair, in recent years the awards have also been presented to Morley Callaghan and Gabrielle Roy, Hugh MacLennan, Brian Moore, Rejean Ducharme, George Woodcock, Marshall McLuhan and, posthumously, to Malcolm Lowry.

Until 1959, when the Canada Council took over the administration of the awards, the Governor-General forked out 50 guineas to the horse that won the Queen's Plate, but offered just a handshake (royal only by osmosis since Vincent Massey became the first Canadian-born GG in 1952), and a copy of your book signed in his own hand, to writers. The Canada Council, happily cognisant of the stuff that really excites this country's artistic types, tacked a $1,000 purse to the awards in 1959, raising the ante to $2,500 six years later. What had once been a stigma was now inspiring. It was also made respectable, because the Council saw to it that the judge's panel was literate. A new departure, for in years past the incomparable Canadian Authors' Association adjudicated the awards. "What, who, why, when," asks an editorial in the Association's *Author and Bookman,* "is a Canadian writer?"

> If a writer wants to make big money he will probably stop writing about Canada and almost certainly leave Canada. If a writer wants 'instant fame' he will very likely have to prostitute his talent by such things as writing sex-dripping prose or taking a deliberately shocking stand on a touchy subject.

This year's awards created a small uproar. THE ESTABLISHMENT BEWARE!, ran the headline in the Toronto *Globe and Mail,* THESE AWARDS ARE WITH IT. Winners for 1968 were Hubert Aquin, for his novel, *Trou de mémoires,* Fernand Dumont, for his sociological work, *Le lieu de l'homme,* and Marie-Claire Blais, for her novel, *Les Manuscrits de Pauline Archange.* English-language writers were Leonard Cohen, for his *Selected Poems*; Alice Munro, for her first book of short stories, *Dance of the Happy Shades*; and me, for *Cocksure,* a novel, and *Hunting Tigers Under Glass,* a collection of essays.

Well now, the truth is we were a scurvy lot. Cohen, who enjoys an immense campus following in Canada and the US, is a self-declared pot smoker. Hubert Aquin, a former vice-president of the militantly separatist RIN party, was once arrested and charged with car theft and being in possession of a revolver. My novel, *Cocksure,* had been banned by the rest of the white commonwealth, not to mention W. H. Smith in the mother country. Aquin, as was to be expected, turned down the award instantly, the GG being anathema to him. Fernand Dumont accepted the award, but two weeks later donated his prize money to the separatist Parti Québecois. Cohen, pondering the inner significance of the award in his hotel in the Village, wavered. He told a Toronto *Star* reporter he wasn't sure whether he would accept the award, it would depend on how he felt when he got up that morning. In the end, he didn't wait that long, but instead issued a statement saying there was much in him that would like to accept the award, but the poems absolutely forbid it.

Another reporter caught up with Cohen in Toronto and asked him, yes, yes, but what, exactly, did he mean?

'Well, I mean they're personal and private poems. With any of my other books I would have been happy to accept, but this one is different. I've been writing these poems since I was 15, and they're very private, their meaning would be changed. And there's another reason. I can't see myself standing up there and accepting the award while there's so much unhappiness in the world, so much violence, while so many of my friends are in jail.'

I accepted the award at once, but with mixed feelings. As a writer I was pleased and richer, but as a father of five, mortified. When *Cocksure* was published in Canada, the reviewer in the Montreal *Star* revealed that I had churned out an obvious potboiler with all the lavatory words. The man who pronounces on books in the New Brunswick *Daily Gleaner* put me down for a very filthy fellow and warned parents in Montreal that I would be teaching their children at Sir George Williams University, where I was to be writer-in-residence for a year. Others denounced me as a pornographer. And now the ultimate symbol of correctitude in our country, the GG himself, would actually reward me for being obscene. For the establishment's sake, I couldn't help but be ashamed.

The Governor-General, I was assured, had read and loathed my novel, but unlike Aquin or Cohen, he did turn up for prize-giving day. Which is not to say he didn't protest. "The Governor-General is a patron of all the arts, but has little time to master any," he said. "But I do have my views, literary as well as political, even though, as in the Speech from the Throne, I have to refrain from expressing them."

Many Canadians feel the Governor-General is an anomaly; his office, at best, tiresome, at worst, divisive. Not so old Johnny Diefenbaker, who is fond of complaining that Prime Minister Trudeau is an anti-monarchist. Diefenbaker says that before Trudeau became PM, he was asked how he would have voted on a resolution calling for the abolition of the monarchy, and replied: "If I had been completely logical, I would have abstained because I . . . you know I don't give a damn." Trudeau has denied this in the House, saying, "I believe the monarchy is an important symbol to many people. I think more energy would be lost in Canada by debating this subject than would be gained by our institutions."

My own earliest recollection of the monarchy goes back to the war years when we used to purchase calendars with toothy photographs of Elizabeth and Margaret in their Brownie uniforms. On my way to school every morning I passed another monarchy symbol, the armoury of the Canadian Grenadier Guards and outside, under a funny fur hat, there always stood some tall unblinking *goy*. "If they were ordered to do it," I was told, "they'd march over a cliff. There's discipline for you."

I have, in my time, lived under seven Governors-General. Only one of them, Lord Tweedsmuir, was abhorrent to me, because under the name of John Buchan he wrote thrillers choked with anti-Semitic nonsense.

Our present Governor-General, however, is hardly the sort to arouse strong feelings. Daniel Roland Michener is an upright, compact little man with curly grey hair and a natty moustache; he has, in this age of rock, the manner of the *maitre d'hotel* in a palm court restaurant. Mrs. Michener, a more obdurate figure, is a case of life improving on the art of Grant Wood. She was born to chaperone the dance in the small town high school gym.

All of us assembled in the reception room at Government House on May 13 rose respectfully when the Micheners, preceded by uniformed aides, drifted in, their smiles frozen; but I, for one, would have found Mr. Michener more credible proffering that large black menu than mounting the dais with such confidence. Behind the Governor-General and his lady, bolstering their acquired royalty as it were, hung enormous portraits of Queen Elizabeth and Prince Philip. The portraits were resoundingly awful, not so much poor likenesses as badly proportioned grotesqueries. Roland Michener, rising to address us, seemed distracted, his manner that of a man who had just come from being photographed accepting a gift of snow shoes from an Eskimo child and must push on to award a Brotherhood plaque to a western mayor in a ten gallon hat, rimless glasses, and high-heeled boots.

The speech Mr. Michener read to us from small cards made for some nervous smiles and at least one giggle from the assembled literati. Observing that all but one of the six award winners were from Quebec, he noted that this might not be a coincidence. "Politics in Quebec today are tense . . . social order is in the process of rapid change and upheaval. This is the atmosphere which stirs people to write more and sometimes better, and to produce exciting paintings, sculpture, theatre, and films."

Alas, the writings of Cohen and Marie-Claire Blais are equally non-political. They have been living in the United States for years, and I am normally rooted in London.

Finally, the award winners were summoned to the Governor-General one by one to accept leather-bound copies of their work signed by Mr. Michener. When my turn came, the Governor-General asked me, "*Êtes-vous canadien?*"

Startled, I said, "*Oui.*"

He then went on to congratulate me fulsomely in French. *Is it possible*, I thought, appalled, *that the Governor-General is a covert separatist?* If not, why, when I answered yes to his question, had he assumed I was necessarily French-speaking? The mind boggled. In any event, once he was done, I said, "*Merci.*" I did not correct the Governor-General. In my case, it was *noblesse oblige*.

Bond

1.

Commander James Bond, CMG, RNVR, springs from a long and undoubtedly loyal line of secret service agents and clubland heroes, including William Le Queux's incomparable Duckworth Drew.

> Before I could utter ought save a muffled curse, I was flung head first into an empty piano case, the heavy lid of which was instantly closed on me . . . I had been tricked!

Sapper's Bulldog Drummond. And John Buchan's Richard Hannay.

> He began to snort now and his breath came heavily. "You infernal cad," I said in good round English. "I'm going to knock the stuffing out of you," but he didn't understand what I was saying.

There have been thirteen Bond novels in all, the first coming in 1953, the others appearing at yearly intervals until 1965, after Ian Fleming's fatal heart attack. On his initial appearance in *Casino Royale*, James Bond was thirty-five years old, an age he has more or less maintained over the years. He is some six foot tall, with a lean bronzed face vaguely reminiscent of Hoagy Carmichael, a ruthless set to his mouth, and cold grey-blue eyes with a hint of anger in them. When Bond was eleven years old his parents, Andrew Bond of Glencoe, Scotland, and Monique Delacroix of the canton of Vaud, Switzerland, were killed in a climbing accident;

and so Bond was put in the care of his aunt, Miss Charmian Bond of Pett Bottom, Kent. At the age of twelve, he was sent off to Eton, wherefrom he was removed after two halves, as a result of some alleged trouble with one of the boys' maids. From Eton he went on to Fettes, his father's school. Here Bond flourished as a lightweight boxing champion and judo expert. In 1941, claiming to be nineteen years old, he entered the Ministry of Defence, where he soon became a lieutenant in the Special Branch of the RNVR, reaching the rank of commander by the war's end. In 1954, Bond was awarded a CMG, but nine years later he spurned a knighthood. He has been married once, in 1962, to Tracy, the Corsican countess Teresa di Vicenzo, daughter of the chief of the Unione Corsa, Marc-Ange Draco. Tracy was murdered by Stavro Blofeld two hours after the wedding.

In 1955, Bond earned £1500 a year and had a thousand free of tax on his own. He had a small but comfortable flat off the King's Road, an elderly Scottish housekeeper (a treasure called May) and a 1930 4½ litre Bentley coupé, supercharged, which he kept expertly tuned. In the evenings Bond played cards at Crockford's or made love "with rather cold passion, to one of three similarly disposed married women," and on the weekends he played golf for high stakes at one of the clubs near London.

In the first Bond novel, *Casino Royale*, Bond confides to Mathis, his colleague from the Deuxième Bureau, that in the previous few years he has killed two villains, a Japanese cipher expert and a Norwegian agent who was doubling for the Germans. For these two jobs, he was awarded a double 0 number in the Secret Service, which prefix gave him a licence to kill. Of late, however, he has begun to have qualms. This country-right-or-wrong business, he complains, is getting a little out of date. "History is moving pretty quickly these days and the heroes and villains keep changing parts." Finally, Mathis reassures Bond, explaining that there are still many villains seeking to destroy him and the England he loves. ". . . M will tell you about them. . . . There's still plenty to do. And you'll do it. . . . Surround yourself with human beings, my dear James. They are easier to fight for than principles."

Bond next agonizes over his double 0 prefix in the opening pages of *Goldfinger*, reacting to a dirty assignment.

> . . . What in the hell was he doing, glooming about the Mexican, this capungo who had been sent to kill him? It had been kill or get killed. Anyway, people were killing other people all the time, all over the world. . . . How many people, for instance, were involved in manufacturing H-bombs, from the miners who mined uranium to the shareholders who owned the mining shares?

Bond experiences another crisis (*For Your Eyes Only*) when M recruits him for an act of personal vengeance. To kill Von Hammerstein, "who had operated the law of the jungle on two defenceless old people," friends of M's. To begin with, Bond is sanguine. "I would not hesitate for a minute, sir. If foreign gangsters find they can get away with this kind of thing they'll decide the English are as soft as some other people seem to think we are. This is a case for rough justice – an eye for an eye." But once confronted with the villain in his camp,

> Bond did not like what he was going to do, and all the way from England he had to keep reminding himself . . . Von Hammerstein and his gunmen were particularly dreadful men whom many people around the world would probably be very glad to destroy . . . out of private revenge. But for Bond it was different. He had no personal motives against them. *This was merely his job – as it was the job of a pest control officer to kill rats. He was the public executioner appointed by M to represent the community.* . . . (Emphasis mine)

Bond is not so much an anti-American, as condescending. Contemplating two American gangsters at the Saratoga race track, in *Diamonds Are Forever*, he wonders what these people amount to, set beside ". . . the people in his own Service – the double-firsts, the gay soldiers of fortune, the men who count life well lost for a thousand a year," incidently cutting his salary by a third since *Casino Royale*. Compared with such men, Bond decides, the gangsters "were just teen-age pillow-fantasies." But then, though he professes to enormously admire Allen Dulles, J. Edgar Hoover, and his CIA sidekick in many an adventure, Felix Leiter, he is not uncritical of a country where a fastidious man can't eat a boiled egg. When the villain in *The Hildebrand Rarity,* the coarse American millionaire, Milton Krest, put down England, arguing, nowadays there were only three powers – America, Russia, and China, "That was the big poker game and no other country had either the chips or the cards to come into it," – Bond replies (shatteringly, we are led to believe), "Your argument reminds me of a rather sharp aphorism I once heard about America. . . . It's to the effect that America has progressed from infancy to senility without having passed through a period of maturity."

Reflecting on the Russian *psyche,* in *From Russia, With Love,* Bond says,

> ". . . They simply don't understand the carrot. Only the stick has any effect. Basically they're masochists. They love the knout. That's why they were so happy under Stalin. He gave it to them. I'm not sure how they're going to react to the scraps of carrot they're being fed by Kruschev and Co. As for England, the trouble today is that carrots for all are the fashion. At home and abroad. We don't show teeth any more – only gums."

While Bond risks his neck abroad, a gay soldier of fortune and pest control officer, ungrateful England continues to deteriorate.

James Bond slung his suitcase into the back of the old chocolate-brown Austin taxi and climbed into the front seat beside the foxy, pimpled young man in the black leather windcheater. The young man took a comb out of his breast pocket, ran it carefully through both sides of his duck-tail haircut, put the comb back into his pocket, then leaned forward and pressed the self-starter.The play with the comb, Bond guessed, was to assert to Bond that the driver was really only taking him and his money as a favour. It was typical of the cheap self-assertiveness of young labour since the war. This youth, thought Bond, makes about twenty pounds a week, despises his parents and would like to be Tommy Steele. It's not his fault. He was born into the buyers' market of the Welfare State and into the age of atomic bombs and space flight. For him life is empty and meaningless.

Duckworth Drew, Drummond, Hannay, carried with them on their adventures abroad an innate conviction of the British gentleman's superiority in all matters, a mystique acknowledged by wogs everywhere. Not so James Bond, who in his penultimate adventure, *You Only Live Twice*, must sit through the humiliating criticism of Tiger Tanaka, Head of the Japanese Secret Service.

"Bondo-san, I will now be blunt with you. . . . it is a sad fact that I, and many of us in positions of authority in Japan, have formed an unsatisfactory opinion about the British people since the war. You have not only lost a great Empire, you have seemed almost anxious to throw it away. . . . when you apparently sought to arrest this slide into impotence at Suez, you succeeded only in stage-managing one of the most pitiful bungles in the history of the world. . . . Furthermore, your governments have shown themselves successively incapable of ruling and have handed over effective control of the country to the trade unions, who appear to be dedicated to the principle of doing less and less work for more money. This feather-bedding, this shirking of an honest day's work, is sapping at ever-increasing speed the moral fibre of the British, a quality the world once so much admired. In its place we now see a vacuous, aimless horde of seekers after pleasure – gambling at the pools and bingo, whining at the weather and the declining fortunes of the country, and wallowing nostalgically in gossip about the doings of the Royal Family and your so-called aristocracy in the pages of the most debased newspapers in the world."

Richard Hannay, to be sure, would have knocked the stuffing

out of just such a jabbering Jap. Hannay, in his thumping, roseate time, could boast that in peace and war, by God, there was nothing to beat the British Secret Service, but poor James Bond, after Commander Crabbe, after Burgess and Maclean, after Kim Philby, could not make the same claim without appearing ludicrous even to himself.

If once British commanders sailed forth to jauntily plant the flag here, there, and everywhere, or to put down infernally caddish natives, today they came with order books for Schweppes.

Duckworth Drew, Drummond, and Hannay were all Great Britons; Bond's a Little Englander.

England, England.

James Bond is a meaningless fantasy cut-out unless he is tacked to the canvas of diminishing England. After the war, Sir Harold Nicolson wrote in his diary, he feared his way of life was coming to an end; he and his wife, Victoria Sackville-West, would have to walk and live a Woolworth life. Already, in 1941, it was difficult to find sufficient gardeners to tend to Sissinghurst, and the Travellers' Club had become a battered caravanserai inhabited only by "the scum of the lower London clubs."

In 1945, Labour swept into office with the cry, "We are the masters now." Ten years later, in Fleming/Bond's time, the last and possibly the most docile of the British colonies, the indigenous lower middle and working-class, rebelled again, this time demanding not free medical care and pension schemes, already torn from the state by their elders, but a commanding voice in the arts and letters. Briefly, a new style in architecture. So we had Osborne, Amis, Sillitoe, and Wesker, among others.

The gentleman's England, where everyone knew his place in the natural order, the England John Buchan, Sir Harold Nicolson, Bobbety[1], Chips[2], and Boofy[3] had been educated to inherit – "Good God," Hannay says, "what a damn task-mistress duty is!" – was

[1] The 5th Marquess of Salisbury
[2] Sir Henry Channon
[3] The Earl of Arran

indeed a war victim. Come Ian Fleming, there has been a metamorphosis. We are no longer dealing with gentlemen, but with a parody-gentleman.

Look at it this way. Sir Harold Nicolson collected books because he cherished them, Ian Fleming amassed first editions because, with Britain's place unsure and the pound wobbly, he grasped their market value. Similarly, if the Buchan's Own Annual cry of God, King, and Empire, was now risible, it was also, providing the packaging was sufficiently shrewd, very, very salable.

Sir Harold Nicolson was arrogantly anti-American, but after World War II a more exigent realism began to operate. Suddenly, an Englishman abroad had to mind his manners. Just as Fleming could not afford to be too overtly anti-Semitic, proffering a sanitized racism instead, so it wouldn't do for Bond to put down all things American. Ian Fleming was patronizing (Bond says of America, it's "a civilized country. More or less."), but whatever his inner convictions, there is an admixture of commercial forelock touching. Where once Englishmen bestrode the American lecture circuit with the insolence of Malcolm X, they now came as Sir Stepin Fetchits. The Bond novels were written for profit. Without the American market, there wouldn't be enough.

Little England's increasingly humiliating status has spawned a blinkered romanticism on the left and the right. On the left, this yielded CND (the touching assumption that it matters morally to the world whether or not England gives up the Bomb unilaterally) and anti-Americanism. On the right, there is the decidedly more expensive fantasy that this off-shore island can still confront the world as Great Britain. If the brutal facts, the familiar facts, are that England has been unable to adjust to its shrivelled island status, largely because of antiquated industry, economic mismanagement, a fusty civil service, and reactionary trade unions, then the comforting right-wing pot dream, a long time in the making, is that virtuous Albion is beset by disruptive communists within and foreign devils and conspirators without.

"(If you) get to the real boss," John Buchan writes in *The Thirty-Nine Steps*, "then the one you are brought up against is a little white-faced Jew in a bathchair with an eye like a rattlesnake."

In Buchan's defence, his biographer, Janet Adam Smith, has observed that some of his best and richest friends were Jews. Yes, indeed. Describing a 1903 affair in Park Lane, Buchan wrote, "A true millionaire's dinner – fresh strawberries in April, plovers' eggs, hooky noses and diamonds." Elsewhere, Buchan went so far out on a limb as to write that it would be unfair to think of Johannesburg as 'Judasburg.' "You will see more Jews in Montreal or Aberdeen, but not more than in Paris; and any smart London restaurant will show as large a Semitic proportion as a Johannesburg club." Furthermore, like many another promising young anti-Semite, Buchan mellowed into an active supporter of Zionism, perhaps in the forelorn hope that hooky-nosed gourmets would quit Mayfair for the Negev.

Alas, they still abounded in London in Sir Henry Channon's time. On January 27, 1934, Chips wrote in his diary, "I went for a walk with Hore-Belisha, the much advertised Minister of Transport. He is an oily man, half a Jew, an opportunist, with the Semitic flare for publicity." Then, only two months later, on March 18, Chips golfed with Diana Cooper at Trent, Sir Philip Sassoon's Kent house. "Trent is a dream house, perfect, luxurious, distinguished with the exotic taste to be expected in any Sassoon Schloss. But the servants are casual, indeed, almost rude; but this, too, often happens in a rich Jew's establishment."

Sir Harold Nicolson's Jewish problem bit deeper. On June 18, 1945, he wrote in his diary, "I do not think that anybody of any Party has any clear idea of how the election will run. The Labour people seem to think the Tories will come back . . . the Tories feel that the Forces will all vote for Labour, and that there may be a land-slide towards the left. They say the *Daily Mirror* is responsible for this, having pandered to the men in the ranks and given them a general distrust of authority. The Jewish capacity for destruction is really illimitable. Although I loathe anti-Semitism, I do dislike Jews."

In a scrupulous, if embarrassed, footnote Nigel Nicolson, who edited his father's diaries, wrote, "H. N. had the idea that the Board of the *Daily Mirror* was mainly composed of Jews."

If Sir Harold Nicolson saw destructive Jews manipulating Churchill's defeat, then Ian Fleming, an even coarser spirit, sniffed plotters, either coloured or with Jewish blood, perpetually scheming at the undoing of the England he cherished. This, largely, is what James Bond is about.

Kingsley Amis, Bond's most reputable apologist, argues, in *The James Bond Dossier*, that in all the Bond canon ". . . there's no hint of anti-semitism, and no feeling about colour more intense than, for instance, Chinese Negroes make good sinister minor-villain material. (They do, too.)" Okay; let's take a look at the evidence.

The sketchy villain of the first Bond novel, *Casino Royale*, is one Le Chiffre, alias Herr Ziffer, first encountered as a displaced person, inmate of Dachau DP camp. Le Chiffre, a dangerous agent of the USSR, is described as probably a mixture of Mediterranean with Prussian or Polish strains and some Jewish blood. He is a flagellant with large sexual appetites. According to the Head of Station S of the British Secret Service, Le Chiffre's Jewish blood is signalled by small ears with large lobes, which is a new one on me.

The next villain Bond tackles, Mr. Big (*Live And Let Die*) is – says M, weighing his words – probably the most powerful Negro criminal in the world.

"I don't think," says Bond, "I've ever heard of great Negro criminals before."

M replies that the Negro races are just beginning to throw up geniuses in all the professions, and so it's about time they turned up a great criminal. "They've got plenty of brains. . . . And now Moscow's taught one of them the technique."

The comedy soon thickens. In New York, Lieutenant Binswager of Homicide suggests to Bond that they pull in Mr. Big for tax evasion "or parkin' in front of a hydrant or sumpn." Here Captain Dexter of the FBI intervenes. "D'you want a race riot? . . . If he wasn't sprung in half an hour by that black mouthpiece of his, those Voodoo drums would start beating from here to the Deep South. When they're full of that stuff we all know what happens. Remember '35 and '43? You'd have to call out the militia."

To be on the safe side, Sir Hugo Drax, the arch-villain of *Moonraker,* is not a Jew. Instead he is cunningly endowed with all the characteristics the anti-Semite traditionally ascribes to a Jewish millionaire. He is without background, having emerged out of nowhere since the war. A bit loud-mouthed and ostentatious. Something of a card. People feel sorry for him, in spite of his gay life, although he's a multi-millionaire. He made his money on the metal market by cornering a very valuable ore called Columbite. Sir Hugo's broker and constant bridge companion is a man called Meyer. ("Nice chap. A Jew.") Sir Hugo made his fortune in the City by operating out of Tangier – free port, no taxes, no currency restrictions. He throws his money about. "Best houses," Bond says, "best cars, best women. Boxes at the Opera, at Goodwood. Prize-winning Jersey herds." Alas, he has also thrust his way into exclusive clubland, Blades specifically, where, in partnership with the nice Jew, Meyer, he cheats at bridge.

If Drax is not a Jew, he comes within an ear lobe of it. A bullying, boorish, loud-mouthed vulgarian, Bond decides on first meeting. *He has a powerful nose, he sweats, he's hairy,* but – but – "he had allowed his whiskers to grow down to the level of the lobes of his ears," and so, *pace* the Head of Station S, a chap couldn't tell for sure. In the end, Sir Hugo Drax is unmasked as . . . Graf Hugo von der Drache, *Sturmer*-caricature-transmogrified-into-Nazi-ogre-turned-commie-agent.

In *Diamonds Are Forever* it is a smart Jewish girl who opens the door to 'The House of Diamonds,' a swindle shop. On the same page, we read,

> . . . There was a click and the door opened a few inches and a voice with a thick foreign intonation expostulated volubly: "Bud Mister Grunspan, why being so hard? Vee must all make a liffing, yes? I am tell you this vonderful stone gost me ten tousant pounts. Ten tousant! You ton't belieff me? But I svear

it. On my vort of honour." There was a negative pause and the voice made its final bid. "Bedder still! I bet you fife pounts!"

Goldfinger begins to rework familiar ground. Goldfinger is clearly a Jewish name. Like Drax, he floats his gold round the world, manipulating the price, and naturally he cheats at cards. And golf.

"Nationality?" Bond asks Mr. Du Pont.

"You wouldn't believe it, but he's a Britisher. Domiciled in Nassau. You'd think he'd be a Jew from the name, but he doesn't look it. . . ."

Like Drax, Goldfinger has red hair, but, significantly, in the lengthy physical description on page 30 *there is no mention of his ear lobe size*. All the same, Bond, on his first meeting with Goldfinger, muses, "What could his history be? Today he might be an Englishman. What had he been born? Not a Jew – though there might be Jewish blood in him. . . ."

Next we come to a real Jew, Sol Horowitz, one of the two hoods in *The Spy Who Loved Me*. Horowitz is described as skeletal, his skin grey, the lips thin and purplish like an unstitched wound, his teeth cheaply capped with steel. And the ears? This is ambiguous. Jewy possibly, but assimilated. "The ears lay very flat and close to the bony, rather box-shaped head. . . ."

The Fleming Ear Syndrome reaches its climax with Blofeld. Blofeld, again not Jewish in spite of the name and easily the archetypal Fleming villain, has one hell of an ear problem. Blofeld, with old age encroaching, wishes to have a title, and so he applies to the British College of Arms, asking to be recognized as Monsieur le Comte Balthazar de Bleuville. Not so easy. According to Sable Basilisk, at the College of Arms, the Bleuvilles, through the centuries, have shared one odd characteristic. Basilisk tells Bond, "Now, when I was scratching around the crypt of the chapel at Blonville, having a look at the old Bleuville tombs, my flashlight, moving over the stone faces, picked out a curious fact that I tucked away in my mind but that your question has brought to the surface.

None of the Bleuvilles, as far as I could tell, and certainly not through a hundred and fifty years, had lobes to their ears.

"Ah," said Bond, running over in his mind the Identicast picture of Blofeld and the complete printed physiognometry of the man in Records. "So he shouldn't by right have lobes to his ears. Or at any rate it would be a strong piece of evidence for his case if he hadn't?"

"That's right."

"Well, he *has* got lobes," said Bond annoyed. "Rather pronounced lobes as a matter of fact. Where does that get us?"

Where does that get us? Jimmy, Jimmy, I thought, as I read this for the first time, use your loaf. Remember the Head of Station S, *Casino Royale*, Le Chiffre, LARGE LOBES, SMALL EARS. Blofeld has J——— blood!

Even more significant, Blofeld is head of an international conspiracy. Bond's most pernicious enemies head, or work for, hidden international conspiracies, usually SMERSH or SPECTRE.

SMERSH, first described in *Casino Royale,* is the conjunction of two Russian words: 'Smyert Shpionam,' meaning roughly: "Death to Spies!" It was, in 1953, under the general direction of Beria, with headquarters in Leningrad and a sub-station in Moscow, and ranked above the MVD (formerly NKVD).

SPECTRE is The Special Executive for Counterintelligence, Terrorism, Revenge, and Extortion, a private enterprise for private profit, and its founder and chairman is Ernst Stavro Blofeld. SPECTRE's headquarters are in Paris, on the Boulevard Haussmann. Not the Avenue d'Iéna, the richest street in Paris, Fleming writes, because "too many of the landlords and tenants in the Avenue d'Iéna have names ending in 'escu,' 'ovitch,' 'ski,' and 'stein,' and these are sometimes not the ending of respectable names." If you stopped at SPECTRE's headquarters, at 136 *bis* Boul. Haussmann, you would find a discreetly glittering brass plate that says 'FIRCO' and, underneath, *Fraternité Internationale de la Résistance Contre l'Oppression*. FIRCO's stated aim is to keep alive the ideals that flourished during the last war among members of all resistance groups. It was most active during International Refugee Year.

Looked at another way, just as we have learned that Mr. Big may be forking out Moscow gold to pay for race riots in the United States, so a seemingly humanitarian refugee organization examined closely may be a front for an international conspiracy of evil-doers.

SMERSH and SPECTRE are both inclined to secret congresses, usually called to plot the political or financial ruin or even the physical destruction of the freedom-loving west. As secret organizations go, SMERSH is growth stuff. As described in *Casino Royale,* in 1953, it was "believed to consist of only a few hundred operatives of very high quality," but only two years later, as set out in *From Russia, With Love,* SMERSH employed a total of 40,000 men and women. Its headquarters had also moved from Leningrad to a rather posh set-up in Moscow, which I take to be a sign of favour. In *Goldfinger*, there is a SMERSH-inspired secret congress of America's leading mobsters brought together with the object of sacking Fort Knox. The initial covert meeting of SPECTRE, elaborately described in *Thunderball,* reveals a conspiracy to steal two atomic weapons from a NATO airplane and then threaten the British prime minister with the nuclear destruction of a major city unless a ransom of 100 million pounds sterling is forthcoming. SPECTRE next conspires against England in *On Her Majesty's Secret Service.* Blofeld, the organization's evil genius, has retired to a Swiss plateau and hypnotized some lovely British girls, infecting them with deadly crop and livestock diseases which they are to carry back to England, spreading pestilence.

Earlier, John Buchan, 1st Lord Tweedsmuir of Elsfield, Governor-General of Canada, and author of *The Thirty-Nine Steps* and four other Richard Hannay novels, was also obsessed with vile plots against Albion, but felt no need to equivocate. We are barely into *The Thirty-Nine Steps,* when we are introduced to Scudder, the brave and good spy, whom Hannay takes to be "a sharp, restless fellow, who always wanted to get down to the roots of things." Scudder tells Hannay that behind all the governments and the armies there was a big subterranean movement going on, engineered by a very dangerous people. Most of them were the sort of educated anarchists that make revolutions, but beside them there were financiers who were playing for money. It suited the books of both classes of conspirators to set Europe by the ears.

When I asked Why, he said that the anarchist lot thought it would give them their chance . . . they looked to see a new world emerge. The capitalists would . . . make fortunes by buying up the wreckage. Capital, he said, had no conscience and no fatherland. Besides, the Jew was behind it, and the Jew hated Russia worse than hell.

"Do you wonder?" he cried. "For three hundred years they have been persecuted, and this is the return match for the *pogroms*. The Jew is everywhere, but you have to go far down the backstairs to find him. Take any big Teutonic business concern. If you have dealings with it the first man you meet is Prince *von und zu* Something, an elegant young man who talks Eton-and-Harrow English. But he cuts no ice. If your business is big, you get behind him and find a prognathous Westphalian with a retreating brow and the manners of a hog. . . . But if you're on the biggest kind of job and are bound to get to the real boss, ten to one you are brought up against a little white-faced Jew in a bathchair with an eye like a rattlesnake. Yes, sir, he is the man who is ruling the world just now, and he has his knife in the Empire of the Tzar, because his aunt was outraged and his father flogged in some one-horse location on the Volga."

The clear progenitor of these conspiracies against England is the notorious anti-Semitic forgery, *The Protocols of the Elders of Zion*, which first appeared in western Europe in 1920 and had, by 1930, been circulated throughout the world in millions of copies. The *Protocols* were used to incite massacres of Jews during the Russian civil war. Earlier, they were especially helpful in fomenting the pogrom at Kishinev in Bessarabia in 1903. From Russia, the

Protocols travelled to Nazi Germany. Recently, they were serialized in a Cairo newspaper.

The history of the *Protocols,* and just how they were tortuously evolved from another forgery, *Dialogue aux Enfers entre Montesquieu et Machiavel,* by a French lawyer called Maurice Joly, in 1864, has already been definitely traced by Norman Cohn in his *Warrant For Genocide*; and so I will limit myself to brief comments here.

Editions of the *Protocols* are often preceded by an earlier invention, *The Rabbi's Speech,* that could easily serve as a model for later dissertations on the glories of power and evil as revealed to Bond by Goldfinger, Drax, and Blofeld.

Like Auric Goldfinger, the Rabbi believes gold is the strength, the recompense, the sum of everything man fears and craves. "The day," he says, "when we shall have made ourselves the sole possessors of all the gold in the world, the real power will be in our hands." Like Sir Hugo Drax, the Rabbi understands the need for market manipulation. "The surest means of attaining [power] is to have supreme control over all industrial, financial, and commercial operation. . . ." SMERSH would envy the Rabbi's political acumen. "So far as possible we must talk to the proletariat. . . . We will drive them to upheavals, to revolutions; and each of these catastrophes marks a big step forward for our . . . sole aim – world domination."

The twenty-four protocols purport to be made up of lectures delivered to the Jewish secret government, the Elders of Zion, on how to achieve world domination. Tangled and contradictory, the main idea is that the Jews, spreading confusion and terror, will eventually take over the globe. Like SPECTRE, they will use liberalism as a front. Like Mr. Big, they will foster discontent and unrest. The common people will be directed to overthrow their rulers and then a despot will be put in power. As there are more evil than good men in the world, force – the Elders have concluded – is the only sure means of government. Underground railways – a big feature in all versions of the *Protocols* – will be constructed in major cities, so that the Elders could counter any organized rebellion by blowing capital cities to smithereens – a recurring threat in the Bond novels (*Moonraker, Thunderball*).

In fact, the more one scrutinizes the serpentine plots in Ian Fleming's novels, the more it would seem that the Elders *are* in conspiracy against England. Not only are they threatening to blow up London, but they would seize the largest store of the world's gold, back disruptive labour disputes, run dope into the country ('Risico') and infect British crops and livestock with deadly pests.

In our time, no books, no films, have enjoyed such a dazzling international success as the James Bond stories, but the impact was not instantaneous. When *Casino Royale* appeared in 1953 the reviews were good, but three American publishers rejected the book and sales were mediocre, which was a sore disappointment to Bond's unabashedly self-promoting author, Ian Fleming, then forty-three years old.

By the spring of 1966 the thirteen Bond novels had been translated into twenty-six different languages and sold more than forty-five million copies. The movie versions of *Doctor No, From Russia, With Love, Goldfinger,* and *Thunderball,* had been seen by some hundred million people and were in fact among the most profitable ever produced. Bond has spawned a flock of imitators, including Matt Helm, Quiller, and Boysie Oakes. More than two hundred commercial products, ranging from men's toiletries to bubble gum, have been authorised to carry the official Bond trademark. Only recently, after a fantastic run, has the boom in Bond begun to slump.

The success of Bond is all the more intriguing because Ian Fleming was such an appalling writer. He had no sense of place that scratched deeper than Sunday supplement travel articles or route maps, a much-favoured device. His celebrated use of insider's facts and O.K. brand names, especially about gunmanship and the international high life, has been faulted again and again. Eric Ambler and Graham Greene (in his entertainments) have written vastly superior spy stories and when Fleming ventured into the American underworld, he begged comparison with Mickey Spillane rather than such original stylists as Dashiel Hammett and Raymond Chandler. He had a resoundingly tin ear, as witness a Harlem black man talking, vintage 1954 (*Live And Let Die*).

'Yuh done look okay yoself, honeychile . . . an' dat's da troof. But Ah mus' spressify dat yuh stays close up tuh me an keeps yo eyes offn dat lowdown trash'n his hot pants. 'N Ah may say . . . dat ef Ah ketches yuh makin' up tah dat dope Ah'll jist nacherlly whup da hide off'n yo sweet ass.'

Or, as an example of the recurring American gangster, Sol 'Horror' Horowitz (*The Spy Who Loved Me*).

'The lady's right. You didn't ought to have spilled that java, Sluggsy. But ya see, lady, that's why they call him Sluggsy, on account he's smart with the hardware.'

As Fleming was almost totally without the ability to create character through distinctive action or dialogue, he generally falls back on villains who are physically grotesque. So Mr. Big has "a great football of a head, twice the normal size and very nearly round," hairless, with no eyebrows and no eyelashes, the eyes bulging slightly and the irises golden round black pupils. Doctor No's head "was elongated and tapered from a round, completely bald skull down to a sharp chin so that the impression was of a reversed raindrop – or rather oildrop, for the skin was a deep almost translucent yellow."

Each Bond novel, except for *The Spy Who Loved Me*, follows an unswerving formula, though the sequence of steps is sometimes shuffled through the introduction of flashbacks.

1. Bond, bored by inactivity, is summoned by M and given a mission.
2. Bond and villain confront each other tentatively.
3. A sexy woman is introduced and seduced by Bond. If she is in cahoots with the villain, she will find Bond irresistible and come over to his side.
4. The villain captures Bond and punishes him (torture, usually), then reveals his diabolical scheme. "As you will never get out of

this alive. . . ." or "It is rare that I have the opportunity to talk to a man of your intelligence. . . ."

5. Bond escapes, triumphs over villain, destroying his vile plot.
6. Bond and sexy woman are now allowed their long-delayed tryst.

This basic formula is usually tarted-up by two devices.

1. We, the unwashed, are granted a seemingly knowledgable, insider's peek at a glamorous industry or institution. Say, diamond or gold smuggling; the Royal College of Arms, Blades, and other elegant clubs. This makes for long chapters of all but unbroken exposition, rather like fawning magazine articles. Sometimes, as with the description of Blades (*Moonraker*), the genuflection is unintentionally comic.

> It was a sparkling scene. There were perhaps fifty men in the room, the majority in dinner-jackets, all at ease with themselves and their surroundings, all stimulated by the peerless food and drink, all animated by a common interest – the prospect of high gambling, the grand slam, the ace pot, the key throw in a 64 game at backgammon. There might be cheats amongst them, men who beat their wives, men with perverse instincts, greedy men, cowardly men, lying men; but the elegance of the room invested each with a kind of aristocracy.

2. We are taken on a Fleming guided tour of an exotic locale. Las Vegas, Japan, West Indies. This also makes for lengthy, insufferably knowing expositional exchanges, rather thinly disguised travel notes, as, for example, when Tiger Tanaka educates Bond to Japanese mores (*You Only Live Twice*).

Not surprisingly, considering Fleming's boyish frame of mind, competitive games figure prominently in the Bond mythology, as do chases in snob cars or along model railways. The deadly card game, Bond against the villain, is another repeated set piece. *Casino Royale, Moonraker, Goldfinger*.

A recurring character in the Bond adventures is the American Felix Leiter, once with the CIA, then with Pinkertons. Leiter, an impossibly stupid and hearty fellow, is cut from the same cloth as comic strip cold war heroes *Buzz Sawyer* and *Steve Canyon*. A born gee whiz, gung ho type.

If Fleming's sense of character was feeble and his powers of invention limited, the sadism and heated sex I was led to expect turned out to be tepid. But at least one torture scene is worth noting, if only because its connotations are so glaringly obvious. In *Casino Royale*, Le Chiffre pauses from beating the naked Bond with a carpet beater to say,

> "My dear boy" Le Chiffre spoke like a father, "the game of Red Indians is over, quite over. You have stumbled by mischance into a game for grown-ups and you have already found it a painful experience. You are not equipped, my dear boy, to play games with adults and it was very foolish of your nanny in London to have sent you out here with your spade and bucket. Very foolish indeed and most unfortunate for you."

A roll-call of Bond's girls yields Vesper Lynd, Solitaire, Gala Brand, Tiffany Case, Honeychile Rider, Pussy Galore, Domino Vitali, Kissy Syzuki, Mary Goodnight. As the perfume brand type labels indicate the girls are clockwork objects rather than people. The composite Bond girl, as Kingsley Amis has already noted, can be distinguished by her beautiful firm breasts, each, I might add, with its pointed stigma of desire. The Bond girls are healthy, out-door types, but they are not all perfectly made. Take Honeychile Rider, for instance. *Café au lait* skin, ash blonde hair, naked on first meeting except for a broad leather belt round her waist with a hunting knife in a leather sheath, she suffers from a badly broken nose, smashed crooked like a boxer's. Then there's the question of Honeychile's behind, which was "almost as firm and rounded as a boy's." A description which brought Fleming a letter from Noel Coward. "I was slightly shocked," Coward wrote, "by the lascivious announcement that Honeychile's bottom was like a boy's. I know we are all becoming progressively more broadminded nowadays but really, old chap, what *could* you have been thinking of?"

Descriptions of clad Bond girls tend to focus on undergarments. Jill Masterson, on first meeting in *Goldfinger*, was naked except for a black bra and briefs. Tatiana, in *From Russia, With Love*, is discovered "wearing nothing but the black ribbon round her neck and black silk stockings rolled above her knees." Not that I object to a word of it. After all, sexy, unfailingly available girls are a legitimate and most enjoyable convention of thrillers and spy stories. If I find Fleming's politics distasteful, his occasional flirtation with ideas embarrassing, I am happy to say I am in accord with him in admiring firm, thrusting, beautiful breasts.

Unlike Harold Robbins, Ian Fleming does not actually linger overlong on sexual description. Or perversion. He is seldom as brutalized as Mickey Spillane in page after page. If anything, he's something of a prude. The closest he comes to obsenity is "———you" in *Dr. No*. Mind you, this fastidiousness is followed hard by a detailed description of a black man punishing a girl by squeezing her Mount of Venus between his thumb and forefinger, until his knuckles go white with the pressure. "She's Love Moun' be sore long after ma face done get healed." Other, more exquisite tortures of women follow in further adventures, usually enforced when the girls are deliciously nude, but James Bond's language never degenerates beyond an uncharacteristic imprecation in *You Only Live Twice*. "Freddie Uncle Charlie Katie," he says, meaning fuck, I take it.

The Bond novels are not so much sexy as they are boyishly smutty. James Bond's aunt, for instance, lives "in the quaintly named hamlet of Pett Bottom." There's a girl called Kissy and another named Pussy. Not one of the Bond girls, however, lubricates as sexily as does Tracy's Lancia Flaminia Zagato Spyder, "a low, white two-seater . . . (with) a sexy boom from its twin exhausts."

Ian Fleming was frightened of women. "Some," he wrote, "respond to the whip, some to the kiss. . . ." A woman, he felt, should be an illusion; and he was deeply upset by their bodily functions. Once, in Capri, according to his biographer, John Pearson, Fleming disowned a girl he had liked the looks of after she retired for a few moments behind a rock. "He had," a former girl friend told Pearson, "a remarkable phobia about bodily things. . . . I'm certain he would never have tied a cut finger for me. I feel he would also have preferred me not to eat and drink as well." Fleming once told Barbara Griggs of the London *Evening Standard* "that women simply are not clean – absolutely filthy, the whole lot of them. Englishwomen simply do not wash and scrub enough." So, added to the image of James Bond, never travelling without an armoury of electronic devices, the latest in computorized death-dealing gadgetry, one now suspects his fastidious creator also lugged an old-fashioned douche bag with him everywhere.

Bond is well worth looking at in juxtaposition to his inventor, Ian Fleming.

In *Casino Royale*, Bond, staked by British Intelligence, plays a deadly game of baccarat at Royale-les-Eaux with Le Chiffre of SMERSH, and wins a phenomenal sum, thereby depriving the USSR of its budget for subversion in France. This adventure, Fleming was fond of saying, was based on a war-time trip to Lisbon with Admiral Godfrey of Naval Intelligence. At the casino, Fleming said, he engaged in a baccarat battle with a group of Nazis, hoping to strike a blow at the German economy. Alas, he lost.

Actually, John Pearson writes, "It was a decidedly dismal evening at the casino – only a handful of Portuguese were present, the stakes were low, the croupiers were bored." Fleming whispered to the unimpressed Admiral, "Just suppose those fellows were German agents – what a coup it would be if we cleaned them out entirely."

Fleming, raised as he was on Buchan and Sapper, had other imaginative notions whilst serving with British Naval Intelligence during the war, among them the idea of sinking a great block of concrete with men inside it in the English Channel, just before the Dieppe raid, to keep watch on the harbour with periscopes. Or to freeze clouds, moor them along the coast of southern England, and use them as platforms for anti-aircraft guns.

Fleming's trip with Admiral Godfrey did not terminate in Lisbon, but carried on to New York. Armed, for the occasion, with a small command fighting knife and a fountain pen with a cyanide cartridge, as well as his Old Etonion tie, Fleming (and the Admiral) was supposed to slip into New York anonymously. "But as they went ashore from the flying boat," Pearson writes, "press photographers began to crowd around them. Although they soon realized that it was the elegant, sweet-smelling figure of Madame Schiaperelli who was attracting the cameras, the damage was done. That evening the chief of British Naval Intelligence was to be seen in the background of all the press photographs of the famous French couturière arriving in New York."

Fleming said he wrote his first novel, *Casino Royale*, at Goldeneye, his Jamaica home, in 1952, to "take his mind off the shock of getting married at the age of forty-three." It seems possible that the inspiration for his villain, Le Chiffre, was The Great Beast 666, necromancer Aleister Crowley, who, like Mussolini, had the whites of his eyes completely visible round the iris. Crowley, incidently, was also the model for the first novel by Fleming's literary hero, Somerset Maugham.

M, also initially introduced in *Casino Royale*, was arguably a composite figure based on Admiral Godfrey and Sir Robert Menzies, Eton and the Life Guards. M remains an obstinately unsympathetic figure even to Bond admirers. ". . . it may be obvious," Amis writes, "why M's frosty, damnably clear eyes are damnably clear. No thought is taking place behind them." Whilst John Pearson writes of Bond's relationship with M, "never has such cool ingratitude produced such utter loyalty." If Bond's father-figure of a villain, Le Chiffre, threatens him with castration in his first adventure, then Bond, last time out (*The Man With The Golden Gun*) is discovered brainwashed in the opening pages and attempts to assassinate M. The unpermissive M. "In particular," Amis writes, "M disapproves of Bond's 'womanizing,' though he never says so directly, and would evidently prefer him not to form a permanent attachment either. He barely conceals his glee at the news that Bond is after all not going to marry Tiffany Case. This is perhaps more the attitude of a doting mother than a father."

A really perceptive observation, for Fleming, as a boy, was

frightened of his stern and demanding mother and did in fact call her M.

Pearson writes in *The Life of Ian Fleming:*

> Apart from Le Chiffre, M, and Vesper Lynd, the minor characters in *Casino Royale* are the merest shadows with names attached. The only other character who matters is Ian Fleming himself. For James Bond is not really a character in this book. He is a mouthpiece for the man who inhabits him, a dummy for him to hang his clothes on, a zombie to perform the dreams of violence and daring which fascinate his creator. It is only because Fleming holds so little of himself back, because he talks and dreams so freely through the device of James Bond, that the book has such readability. *Casino Royale* is really an experiment in the autobiography of dreams.

Without a doubt Fleming's dream conception of himself was James Bond, gay adventurer, two-fisted soldier of fortune, and, in the Hannay tradition, ever the complete gentleman.

Bond renounces his occasionally vast gambling gains, donating his winnings to a service widows' fund; he is self-mocking about his heroics, avoids publicity, and once offered a knighthood, in *The Man With The Golden Gun*, he turns it down bashfully because, "He has never been a public figure and did not wish to become one . . . there was one thing above all he treasured. His privacy. His anonymity."

Yet even as Hannay's creator, John Buchan, was a man of prodigious drive and ambition, so Ian Fleming was a chap with his eye always resolutely on the main chance.

"Most authors, particularly when they begin," Pearson writes dryly, "leave details of publication to their agents or to the goodwill of the publisher." Not so Fleming, who instantly submitted a plan for 'Advertising and Promotion' to Jonathan Cape. Copies of *Casino Royale* were ready by March 1953. Without delay, Fleming wrote a letter to the editors of all Lord Kemsley's provincial newspapers, sending it off with an autographed copy of his book. "Dr. Jekyll has written this blatant thriller in his spare time, and it may amuse you. If you don't think it too puerile for Sheffield (or Stockport, Macclesfield, Middlesborough, Blackburn, etc.) it would be wonderful if you would hand a copy with a pair of tongs to your reviewer."

This jokey little note, properly read, was an order from the bridge to the chaps on the lower-deck, for Fleming was a known intimate of Lord Kemsley's as well as foreign news manager of the *Sunday Times*, then the Kemsley flagship, so to speak.

Fleming also astutely sent a copy of his novel to Somerset Maugham, who replied, "It goes with a swing from the first page to the last and is really thrilling all through. . . . You really managed to get the tension to the highest possible pitch." If James Bond would have cherished such a private tribute from an old man, Ian Fleming immediately grasped its commercial potential, and wrote back, "Dear Willie, I have just got your letter. When I am 79 shall I waste my time reading such a book and taking the trouble to write to the author in my own hand? I pray so, but I doubt it. I am even more flattered and impressed after catching a glimpse of the empestered life you lead at Cap Ferrat, deluged with fan mail, besieged by the press, inundated with bumpf of one sort or another. . . . Is it bad literary manners to ask if my publishers may quote from your letter? Please advise me – as a 'parain' not as a favour to me and my publishers."

Maugham replied, "Please don't use what I said about your book to advertise it."

As the sales of *Casino Royale* were disappointing, Fleming turned to writing the influential Atticus gossip column in the *Sunday Times*, which provided him with a convenient platform to flatter those whose favours he sought. After Lord Kemsley refused to run a *Sunday Times* Portrait Gallery puff of Lord Beaverbrook on his seventy-sixth birthday, he did allow Fleming, following some special pleading, to celebrate Beaverbrook in his column. "History will have to decide whether he or Northcliffe was the greatest newspaperman of this half century. In the sense that he combines rare journalistic flair, the rare quality of wonder . . . with courage and vitality . . . the verdict may quite possibly go to Lord Beaver-brook. . . ."

Beaverbrook, who had an insatiable appetite for flattery, bought the serial rights to the next Bond novel and later ran a Bond comic strip in the *Daily Express*.

Once Macmillans undertook to publish *Casino Royale* in America, the Fleming self-advertisement campaign accelerated. Fleming wrote to a friend asking him to influence Walter Winchell into plugging the book. He wrote to Iva Patcevitch, saying, "If you can possibly give it a shove in *Vogue* or elsewhere, Anna and I will allow you to play Canasta against us, which should be ample reward." He also wrote to Fleur Cowles and Margaret Case. "You will soon be fed up with this book as I have sent copies around to all our friends asking them to give it a hand in America, which is a very barefaced way to go on. . . . I know Harry Luce won't be bothered with it, or Clare, but if you could somehow prevail upon *Time* to give it a review you would be an angel."

In 1955, the sales of his books still dragging, Fleming met Raymond Chandler at a dinner party. At the time, Chandler was an old and broken man, incoherent from drink. "He was very nice to me," Fleming wrote, "and said he liked my first book, *Casino Royale*, but he didn't really want to talk about anything except the loss of his wife, about which he expressed himself with a nakedness that embarrassed me while endearing him to me."

If the battered old writer, whom Fleming professed to admire, was tragically self-absorbed, he was, all the same, instantly sent a copy of Fleming's forthcoming *Live And Let Die*. "A few days later," Pearson writes, "Chandler telephoned Fleming to say how much he had enjoyed it, and went on to ask the author – vaguely, perhaps – if he would care for him to endorse the book for the benefit of his publishers – the kind of thing he was always refusing to do in the United States and a subject on which in his published letters, he displays such ferocious cynicism. "Rather unattractively," Fleming wrote later, "I took him up on his suggestion."

Chandler was as good as his word, Pearson goes on to say, "although it sounds as if it was rather a struggle. On May 25 he wrote

51

pathetically to Fleming apologizing for taking so long – 'in fact, lately I have had a very difficult time reading at all.'" But a week later he came through for Fleming, his blurb beginning, "Ian Fleming is probably the most *forceful* and *driving* writer of what I suppose still must be called thrillers in England. . . ." (Emphasis mine.) Chandler's letter of praise ended, somewhat ambiguously, "If this is any good to you, would you like me to have it engraved on a slab of gold?"

Fleming was also able to find uses for a burnt-out prime minister. In November 1956, twelve days after the Suez cease fire, it was announced that Prime Minister Anthony Eden was ill from the effects of severe overstrain. It became necessary to find a secluded spot where Eden could recuperate, and so Alan Lennox-Boyd, then Secretary of State for Colonial Affairs and a friend of Ian Fleming, approached Fleming about Goldeneye, his home in Jamaica. Fleming, flattered by the choice, neglected to say there were only iron bedsteads at Goldeneye, there was no hot water in the shower and there was no bathroom, but there were bush rats in the roof. He did not advise Lennox-Boyd that Noel Coward's home nearby, or Sir William Stephenson's, would have been more commodious for an ailing man. He did not even say that the Prime Minister would be without a telephone at Goldeneye. "The myth of Goldeneye was about to enter history," John Pearson writes, "it was too much to expect its creator to upset it."

Sir Anthony and Lady Eden set off for Goldeneye and Fleming sat back in Kent to write to Macmillans. "I hope that the Edens' visit to Goldeneye has done something to my American sales. Here there have been full-page spreads of the property, including Violet emptying ash trays and heaven knows what-all. It has really been a splendid week and greatly increased the value of the property until Anne started talking to reporters about barracuda, the hardness of the beds, and curried goat. Now some papers treat the place as if it was a hovel and others as if it was the millionaire home of some particularly disgusting millionaire tax dodger. . . ." Two weeks later the bush rats caught up with Fleming. The London *Evening Standard* reported that Sir Anthony, troubled by rats during the night, had organized a hunt. Fleming, distressed, wrote to a friend, "The greatly increased rental value was brought down sharply by a completely dreamed-up report to the effect that Goldeneye was over-run by rats and that the Edens and the detectives had spent the whole night chasing them. . . ."

The Prime Minister's stay at Goldeneye brought Fleming to the attention of a public far wider than his books had so far managed for him. It was now, Pearson writes, that Fleming's public began to change. "Up to then he had been 'the Peter Cheyney of the carriage trade'. . . . After Eden's visit . . . many people were interested . . . (and) began to read him. After five long years the 'best-seller stakes' had begun in earnest. . . . if Fleming with his flair for self-promotion had planned the whole thing himself it could hardly have been better done."

Fleming continued to type out his dream-life at Goldeneye, visualising himself as gentlemanly James Bond, but the self-evident truth is he had infinitely more in common with his pushy, ill-bred foreign villains, and one is obliged to consider his sophisticated racialism as no less than a projection of his own coarse qualities.

Two final points.

It is possible to explain the initial success of the Bond novels in that they came at a time when Buchan's vicious anti-Semitism and Sapper's neo-fascist xenophobia were no longer acceptable; nevertheless a real need as well as a large audience for such reading matter still existed. It was Fleming's most brilliant stroke to present himself not as an old-fashioned, frothing wog-hater, but as an ostensibly civilized voice which offered sanitized racialism instead. The Bond novels not only satisfy Little Englanders who believe they have been undone by dastardly foreign plotters, but pander to their continuing notion of self-importance. So, when the Head of SMERSH, Colonel General Grubozaboychikov, known as 'G,' summons a high level conference to announce that it has become necessary to inflict an act of terrorism aimed at the heart of the Intelligence apparatus of the west, it is (on the advice of General Vozdvishensky) the British Secret Service that he chooses.

'. . . I think we all have to respect (England's) Intelligence Service,' General Vozdvishensky looked around the table. There were grudging nods from everyone present, including General G. '. . . Their Secret Service . . . agents are good. They pay them little money. . . . They are rarely awarded a decoration until they retire. And yet these men and women continue to do this dangerous work. It is curious. It is perhaps the Public School and University tradition. The love of adventure. But it is odd they play this game so well, for they are not natural conspirators.'

Kingsley Amis argues, in *The Bond Dossier*, that "To use foreigners as villains is a convention older than literature. It's not in itself a symptom of intolerance about foreigners. . . ."

Amis's approach is so good-natured, so ostensibly reasonable, that to protest no, no, is to seem an entirely humourless left-wing nag, a Hampstead harpie. I am not, God help me, suing for that boring office. I do not object to the use of foreigners *per se* as villains. I am even willing to waive moral objections to a writer in whose fictions no Englishman ever does wrong and only Jewy or black or yellow men fill the villain's role. However, even in novels whose primary purpose is to entertain, I am entitled to ask for a modicum of plausibility. And so, whilst I would grudgingly agree with Amis that there is nothing wrong in choosing foreigners for villains, I must add that it is – in the context of contemporary England – an inaccuracy. A most outrageous inaccuracy. After all, even on the narrow squalid level of Intelligence, the most sensational betrayals have come from men who, to quote General G of SMERSH, were so admirably suited to their work by dint of their Public School and University traditions. Guy Burgess, Donald Maclean, and Kim Philby. It should be added, hastily added, that these three men, contrary to the Fleming style, were not ogres and did not sell out for gold. Rightly or wrongly, they acted on political principle. Furthermore, their real value to the KGB (the final insult, this) was not their British information, but the American secrets they were a party to.

Kingsley Amis and I, the people he drinks with, the people I drink with, are neither anti-Semitic nor colour prejudiced, however divergent our politics. We circulate in a sheltered society. Not so my children, which brings me to my primary motive for writing this essay.

The minority man, as Norman Mailer has astutely pointed out, grows up with a double-image of himself, his own and society's. My boys are crazy about the James Bond movies, they identify with 007, as yet unaware that they have been cast as the villains of the dramas. As a boy I was brought up to revere John Buchan, then Lord Tweedsmuir, Governor-General of Canada. Before he came to speak at Junior Red Cross Prize Day, we were told that he stood for the ultimate British virtues. Fair play, clean living, gentlemanly conduct. We were not forewarned that he was also an ignorant, nasty-minded anti-Semite. I discovered this for myself, reading *The Thirty-Nine Steps*. As badly as I wanted to identify with Richard Hannay, two-fisted soldier of fortune, I couldn't without betraying myself. My grandfather, *pace* Buchan, went in fear of being flogged in some one-horse location on the Volga, which was why we were in Canada. However, I owe to Buchan the image of my grandfather as a little white-faced Jew with an eye like a rattlesnake. It is an image I briefly responded to, alas, if only because Hannay, so obviously on the side of the good, accepted it without question. This, possibly, is why I've grown up to loathe Buchan, Fleming, and their sort.

In his preface to *The Bond Dossier*, Amis writes "quite apart from everything else, I'm a Fleming fan. Appreciation of an author ought to be *sine qua non* for writing at length about him." Well, no. It is equally valid to examine an author's work in detail if you find his books morally repugnant and the writer himself an insufferably self-satisfied boor.

A Sense of the Ridiculous

Notes on Paris 1951 And After
For Mason Hoffenberg and Joe Dughi

In the summer of 1967, our very golden EXPO summer, I was
drinking with an old and cherished friend at Montreal airport,
waiting for my flight to London, when all at once he said, "You
know, I'm going to be forty soon."

At the time, I was still a smug thirty-six.

"Hell," he added, whacking his glass against the table, outraged,
"it's utterly ridiculous. Me, forty? My father's forty!"

Though we were both Montrealers, we had first met in Paris
in 1951, and we warmed over those days now, *our* movable feast,
until my flight was called.

A few days later, back in London, where I had been rooted
for more than ten years, I sat sipping coffee on the King's Road,
Chelsea, brooding about Paris and watching the girls pass in their
minis and high suede boots. Suddenly, hatefully, it struck me that
there was a generation younger than mine. Another bunch. And
so we were no longer licenced to idle at cafés, to be merely promising
as we were in Paris, but were regularly expected to deliver the
goods, books and movies to be judged by others. At my age,
appointments must be kept, I thought, searching for a taxi.

Time counts.

As it happened, my appointment was with a Star at the Dorchester. The Star, internationally-known, obscenely overpaid, was attended in his suite by a bitch-mother private secretary, a soothing queer architect to keep everybody's glasses filled with chilled Chevalier Montrachet, and, kneeling by the hassock on which big bare feet rested, a chiropodist. The chiropodist, black leather tool box open before him, scissor-filled drawers protruding, black bowler lying alongside on the rug, was kneading the Star's feet, pausing to reverently snip a nail or caress a big toe, lingering whenever he provoked an involuntary little yelp of pleasure.

"I am ever so worried," the chiropodist said, "about your returning to Hollywood, Sir."

"Mmmnnn." This delivered with eyes squeezed ecstatically shut.

"Who will look after your feet there?"

The Star had summoned me because he wanted to do a picture about the assassination of Leon Trotsky. Trotsky, my hero. "The way I see it," he said, "Trotsky was one of the last really, really great men. Like Louis B. Mayer."

I didn't take on the screenplay. Instead, on bloody-minded impulse, I bought air tickets and announced to my wife, "We're flying to Paris tomorrow."

Back to Paris to be cleansed.

As my original left bank days had been decidedly impecunious, this was something like an act of vengence. We stayed on the right bank, eating breakfast in bed at the Georges V, dropping into the Dior boutique, doing the galleries, stopping for a fin de maison here and a Perrier there, window-shopping on the rue du Rivoli, dining at Lapérouse, le Tour d'Argent, and le Méditerranée.

Fifteen years had not only made for changes in me.

The seedy Café Royale, on Boul. St. Germain, the terrace once spilling over with rambunctious friends until two in the morning, when the action drifted on to the Mabillion and from there to the notorious Pergola, had been displaced by the sickeningly mod, affluent le Drugstore. In Montparnasse, the Dôme was out of favour again, everybody now gathering at the barn-like La Coupole.

Strolling past the Café le Tournot, I no longer recognized the abundantly confident *Paris Review* bunch (the loping Plimpton in his snapbrim fedora, Eugene Walter, Peter Mathiessen) either conferring on the pavement or sprawled on the terrace, dunking croissants into the morning café au lait, always and enviably surrounded by the most appetizing college girls in town. Neither was the affable Richard Wright to be seen any more, working on the pinball machine.

Others, alas, were still drifting from café to café, cruelly winded now, grubbiness no longer redeemed by youth, bald, twitchy, defensive, and embittered. To a man, they had all the faults of genius. They were alienated, of course, as well as being bad credit risks, rent-skippers, prodigious drinkers or junkies, and reprobates, and yet – and yet – they had been left behind, unlucky or not sufficiently talented. They made me exceedingly nervous, for now they appeared embarrassing, like fat bachelors of fifty tooling about in fire-engine red MGs or women in their forties flouncing their mini-skirts.

The shrill, hysterical editor of one of the little magazines of the Fifties caught up with me. "I want you to know," he said, "that I rejected all that crap Terry Southern is publishing in America now."

Gently, I let on that Terry and I were old friends.

"Jimmy Baldwin," he said, "has copied all my gestures. If you see him on TV, it's me," he shrieked. "It's me."

On balance, our weekend in Paris was more unsettling than satisfying. Seated at the Dôme, well-dressed, consuming double scotches rather than nursing a solitary beer on the lookout for somebody who had just cashed his GI cheque on the black market, I realized I appeared just the sort of tourist who would have aroused the unfeeling scorn of the boy I had been in 1951. A scruffy boy with easy, bigoted attitudes, encouraging a beard, addicted to t-shirts, the obligatory blue jeans and, naturally, sandals. Absorbed by the Tarot and trying to write in the manner of Céline. Given to wild pronouncements about Coca-Cola culture and late nights listening to Sydney Bechet at the Vieux Colombier.

We had not yet been labelled beats, certainly not hippies. Rather, we were taken for existentialists by *Life*, if not by Jean-Paul Sartre, who had a sign posted in a jazz cellar warning he had nothing whatsoever to do with these children and that they hardly represented his ideas.

I frequently feel I've lost something somewhere. Spontaneity maybe, or honest appetite. In Paris all I ever craved for was to be accepted as a serious novelist one day, seemingly an impossible dream. Now I'm harnessed to this ritual of being a writer, shaking out the morning mail for cheque-size envelopes – scanning the newspapers – breakfast – then upstairs to work. To try to work.

If I get stuck, if it turns out an especially sour, unyielding morning, I will recite a lecture to myself that begins, Your father had to be out at six every morning, driving to the junk yard in the sub-zero dark, through Montreal blizzards. You work at home, never at your desk before nine, earning more for a day's remembered insults than your father ever made, hustling scrap, in a week.

Or I return, in my mind's eye, to Paris.

Paris, the dividing line. Before Paris, experience could be savoured for its own immediate satisfactions. It was total. Afterwards, I became cunning, a writer, somebody with a use for everything, even intimacies.

I was only a callow kid of nineteen when I arrived in Paris in 1951, and so it was, in the truest sense, my university. St. Germain des Prés was my campus, Montparnasse my frat house, and my two years there are a sweetness I retain, as others do wistful memories of McGill or Oxford. Even now, I tend to measure my present conduct against the rules I made for myself in Paris.

The first declaration to make about Paris is that we young Americans, and this Canadian, didn't go there so much to discover Europe as to find and reassure each other, who were separated by such vast distances at home. Among the as yet unknown young writers in Paris at the time, either friends or nodding café acquaintances, there were Terry Southern, Alan Temko, Alfred Chester,

Herbert Gold, David Burnett, Mavis Gallant, Alexander Trocchi, Christopher Logue, Mason Hoffenberg, James Baldwin, and the late David Stacton.

About reputations.

A few years ago, after I had spoken at one of those vast synagogue-cum-community plants that have supplanted the pokey little *shuls* of my Montreal boyhood, all-pervasive deodorant displacing the smell of pickled herring, a lady shot indignantly out of her seat to say, "I'm sure you don't remember me, but we were at school together. Even then you had filthy opinions, but who took you seriously? Nobody. *Can you please tell me,*" she demanded, "*why on earth anybody takes you seriously now?*"

Why, indeed? If only she knew how profoundly I agreed with her. For I, too, am totally unable to make that imaginative leap that would enable me to accept that anybody I grew up with – or, in this case, cracked peanuts with at the Mabillion – or puffed pot with at the Old Navy – could now be mistaken for a writer. A reputation.

In 1965, when Alexander Trocchi enjoyed a season in England as a sort of Dr. Spock of pot, pontificating about how good it was for you on one in-depth TV discussion after another, I was hard put to suppress an incredulous giggle each time his intelligent, craggy face filled the screen. I am equally unconvinced, stunned even, when I see Terry Southern's or Herb Gold's picture in *Time*.

I also find it disheartening that, in the end, writers are no less status-conscious than the middle-class they – we, I should say – excoriate with such appetite. As my high school friends, the old Sunday morning scrub team, has been split by economics, this taxi driver's boy now a fat suburban cat, that tailor's son still ducking bailiffs in a one-man basement factory, so we, who pretended to transcend such matters, have, over the demanding years, been divided by reputations. If our yardstick is more exacting, it still measures without mercy, coarsening the happy time we once shared.

Paris.

It would be nice, it would be tidy, to say with hindsight that we were a group, knit by political anger or a literary policy or even an aesthetic revulsion for all things American, but the truth was we recognized each other by no more than a shared sense of the ridiculous. And so we passed many a languorous, pot-filled afternoon on the terrace of the Dôme or the Selecte, improvising, not unlike jazz groups, on the hot news from America, where Truman was yielding to Eisenhower. We bounced an inanity to and fro, until, magnified through bizarre extension, we had disposed of it as an absurdity. We invented obscene quiz shows for television, and ad-libbed sexual outrages that could be interpolated into a John Marquand novel, a Norman Rockwell *Post* cover, or a June Allyson movie. The most original innovator and wit amongst us was easily the deceptively gentle Mason Hoffenberg, and one way or another we all remain indebted to him.

Oddly, I cannot recall that we ever discussed "our stuff" with each other. In fact, a stranger noting our cultivated indifference, the cool café posture, could never have guessed that when we weren't shuffling from café to café, in search of girls – a party – any diversion – we were actually labouring hard and long at typewriters in cramped, squalid hotel rooms, sending off stories to America, stories that rebounded with a sickening whack. The indifference to success was feigned, our café cool was false, for the truth is we were real Americans, hungering for recognition and its rewards, terrified of failure.

The rules of behaviour, unwritten, were nevertheless, rigid. It was not considered corrupt to take a thousand dollars from Girodias to write a pornographic novel under a pseudonym for the tourist trade, but anybody who went home to commit a thesis was automatically out. We weighed one another not by our backgrounds or prospects, but by taste, the books we kept by our bedside. Above all, we cherished the unrehearsed response, the zany personality, and so we prized many a bohemian dolt or exhibitionist, the girl who dyed her hair orange or kept a monkey for a pet, the most defiant queen, or the sub-Kerouac who wouldn't read anything because it might influence his style. Looked at another way, you were sure to know somebody who would happily bring on an abortion with a hat pin or turn you on heroin or peddle your passport, but nobody at all you could count on to behave decently if you were stuck with your Uncle Irv and Aunt Sophie, who were "doing Europe" this summer.

Each group its own conventions, which is to say we were not so much non-conformists as subject to our own peculiar conformities or, if you like, anti-bourgeois inversions. And so, if you were going to read a fat Irwin Shaw, a lousy best-seller, you were safest concealing it under a Marquis de Sade jacket. What I personally found most trying was the necessity to choke enthusiasm, never to reveal elation, when the truth was I was out of my mind with joy to be living in Paris, actually living in Paris, France.

My room at the Grand Hotel Excelsior, off the Boul' Mich, was filled with rats, rats and a gratifyingly depraved past, for the hotel had once functioned as a brothel for the Wehrmacht. Before entering my room, I hollered, and whacked on the door, hoping to scatter the repulsive little beasts. Before putting on my sweater, I shook it out for rat droppings. But lying on my lumpy bed, ghetto-liberated, a real expatriate, I could read the forbidden, outspoken Henry Miller, skipping the windy cosmic passages, warming to the hot stuff. Paris in the fabled twenties, when luscious slavering American school teachers came over to seek out artists like me, begging for it. Waylaying randy old Henry in public toilets, seizing him by the cock. Scratching on his hotel room door, entering to gobble him. *Wherever I travel I'm too late. The orgy has moved elsewhere.*

My father wrote, grabbing for me across the seas to remind me of my heritage. He enclosed a Jewish calendar, warning me that Rosh Hashonnah came early this year, even for me who smoked hashish on the sabbath. Scared even as I smoked it, but more terrified of being put down as chicken-shit. My father wrote to say that the YMHA *Beacon* was sponsoring a short story contest and that the *Reader's Digest* was in the market for 'Unforgettable Characters.' Meanwhile, the *New Yorker* wouldn't have me, neither would the *Partisan Review*.

Moving among us, there was the slippery, eccentric Mr. Soon.

He was, he said, the first Citizen of the World. He had anticipated Gary Davis, who was much in the news then. Mussolini had deported Mr. Soon from Italy, even as he had one of our underground heroes, the necromancer Alistair Crowley, The Great Beast 666, but the Swiss had promptly shipped Mr. Soon back again. He had no papers. He had a filthy, knotted beard, a body seemingly fabricated of mecanno parts, the old clothes and cigarettes we gave him, and a passion for baclavas. The police were always nabbing him for questioning. They wanted to know about drug addiction and foreigners who had been in Paris for more than three months without a *carte d'identité*. Mr. Soon became an informer.

"And what," he'd ask, "do you think of the poetry of Mao Tse Tung?"

"Zingy."

"And how," he'd ask, "does one spell your name?"

My American friends were more agitated than I, a non-draftable Canadian, about the Korean War. We sat on the terrace of the Mabillion, drunkenly accumulating beer coasters, on the day General Ridgeway drove into Paris, replacing Eisenhower at SHAPE. Only a thin bored crowd of the curious turned out to look over the general from Korea, yet the gendarmes were everywhere, and the boulevard was black with Gardes Mobiles, their fierce polished helmets catching the sun. All at once, the Place de l'Odeon was clotted with communist demonstrators, men, women and boys, squirting out of the backstreets, whipping out broomsticks from inside their shapeless jackets and hoisting anti-American posters on them.

"RIDGEWAY," the men hollered.

"*A la porte,*" the women responded in a piercing squeal.

Instantly the gendarmes penetrated the demonstration, fanning out, swinging the capes that were weighed down with lead, cracking heads, and smashing noses. The once disciplined cry of *Ridgeway, à la porte*!, faltered, then broke. Demonstrators retreated, scattering, clutching their bleeding faces.

A German general, summoned by NATO, came to Paris, and

French Jews and socialists paraded in sombre silence down the Champs Elysées, wearing striped pyjamas, their former concentration camp uniforms. A Parisian Jewish couple I had befriended informed me at dinner that their new-born boy would not be circumcised, "Just in case." The Algerian troubles had begun. There was a war on in what we then called Indo-China. The gendarmes began to raid left bank hotels one by one, looking for Arabs without papers. Six o'clock in the morning they would pound on your door, open it, and demand to see your passport. "I am a c-c-c-itizen of the world," said Greenblatt, at that time something called a non-figurative poet, now with Desilu Productions.

One night the virulently anti-communist group, Paix et Liberté, pasted up posters everywhere that showed a flag, the Hammer and Sickle, flying from the top of the Eiffel Tower. HOW WOULD YOU LIKE TO SEE THIS? the caption read. Early the next morning the communists went from poster to poster and pasted the Stars and Stripes over the Russian flag.

With Joe Dughi, a survivor of Normandy and the Battle of the Bulge, who was taking the course on French Civilization at the Sorbonne, I made the long trip to a flaking working-class suburb to see the Russian propaganda feature film, *Meeting on the Elbe*. In the inspiring opening sequence, the Russian army is seen approaching the Elbe, orderly, joyous soldiers mounted on gleaming tanks, each tank carrying a laurel wreath and a portrait of Stalin. Suddenly, we hear the corrupt, jerky strains of Yankee Doodle Dandy, and the camera swoops down on the opposite bank, where the unshaven behemoths who make up the American army are revealed staggering toward the river, soldiers stumbling drunkenly into the water. On the symbolically lowered bridge, the white-uniformed Russian colonel, upright as Gary Cooper, says, "It's good to see the American army – even if it's on the last day of the war." Then he passes his binoculars to his American counterpart, a tubby pig-eyed Lou Costello figure. The American colonel scowls, displeased to see his men fraternizing with the Russians. Suddenly, he grins slyly. "You must admit," he says, lowering the binoculars, "that the Germans made excellent optical equipment."

The Russian colonel replies: "These binoculars were made in Moscow, comrade."

In the Russian zone, always seen by day, the Gary Cooper colonel has set up his headquarters in a modest farm house. Outside, his adorable orderly, a Ukrainian Andy Devine, cavorts with sandyhaired German kids, reciting Heine to them. But in the American zone, seen only by night, the obese, cigar-chomping American colonel has appropriated a castle. Loutish enlisted men parade enormous oil paintings before him, and the colonel chalks a big X on those he wants shipped home. All the while, I should add, he is on the long distance line to Wall Street, asking for quotations on Bavarian forest.

Recently, I have been reading John Clellon Holmes's *Nothing More To Declare,* a memoir which makes it plain that the ideas and idiom, even some of the people, prevalent in the Village during the Fifties were interchangeable with those in Paris. The truculent Legman, once a *Neurotica* editor, of whom he writes so generously, inevitably turned up in St. Germain des Prés to produce his definitive edition of filthy limericks on rag paper and, incidently, to assure us gruffly that the novel was dead. Absolutely dead.

Even as in the Village, we were obsessed by the shared trivia and pop of our boyhood, seldom arguing about ideas, which would have made us feel self-conscious, stuffy, but instead going on and on about Fibber McGee's closet, Mandrake's enemies, Warner Brothers' character actors like Elisha Cook Jr., the Andrew Sisters, and the Katzenjammer Kids. To read about such sessions now in other people's novels or essays doesn't make for recognition so much as resentment at having one's past broadcast, played back as it were, a ready-to-wear past, which in retrospect was not peculiar to Paris but a Fifties commonplace.

At times it seems to me that what my generation of novelists does best, celebrating itself, is also discrediting. Too often, I think, it is we who are the fumblers, the misfits, *but unmistakably lovable,* intellectual heroes of our very own fictions, triumphant in our vengeful imaginations as we never were in actuality. Only a few contemporaries, say Brian Moore, live up to what I once took to be the novelist's primary moral responsibility, which is to be the loser's advocate. To tell us what it's like to be Judith Hearne. Or a pinched Irish school teacher. The majority tend to compose paeans of disguised praise of people very much like themselves. Taken to an extreme, the fictional guise is dropped and we are revealed cheering ourselves. And so George Plimpton is the pitcher and hero of *Out of My League* by George Plimpton. Norman Podhoretz, in *Making It*, is the protagonist of his own novel. And most recently, in *The Armies of the Night*, Norman Mailer writes about himself in the third person.

This is not to plead for a retreat to social realism or novels of protest, but simply to say that, as novelists, many of us are perhaps too easily bored, too self-regarding, and not sufficiently curious about mean lives, bland people. The unglamorous.

All at once, it was spring.

One day shopkeepers were wretched, waiters surly, concierges mean about taking messages, and the next, the glass windows encasing café terraces were removed everywhere, and Parisians were transmogrified: shopkeepers, waiters, concierges actually spoke in dulcet tones.

Afternoons we took to the Jardins du Luxembourg, lying on the grass and speculating about Duke Snider's arm, the essays in *The God That Failed*, Jersey Joe Walcott's age, whether Salinger's *The Catcher in the Rye* could be good *and* a Book-of-the-Month, how far Senator Joe McCarthy might go, was Calder Willingham over-rated, how much it might set us back to motorcycle to Seville, was Alger Hiss lying, why wasn't Nathaniel West more widely read, could Don Newcombe win thirty games, and was it disreputable of Max Brod to withhold Kafka's 'Letter To My Father.'

Piaf was big with us, as was Jacques Prévert's *Paroles*, the song *Les Feuilles mortes,* Trenet, and the films of Simone Signoret.

Anything by Genet, or Samuel Beckett was passed from hand to hand. I tried to read *La Nausée* in French, but stumbled and gave it up.

Early one Sunday morning in May, laying in a kitbag filled with wine, *paté,* hardboiled eggs, guiches and salamis and cold veal from the charcuterie, cheeses, a bottle of armagnac and baguettes, five of us squeezed into a battered Renault quatre-chevaux and set off for Chartres and the beaches of Normandy. 1952 it was, but we soon discovered that the rocky beaches were still littered with the debris of war. Approaching the coast we bumped drunkenly past shelled-out, crumbling buildings, VERBOTEN printed on one wall and ACHTUNG! on another. This moved us to incredulous laughter, evoking old Warner Brothers films and dimly recalled hit parade tunes. But, once on the beaches, we were sobered and silent. Incredibly thick pill boxes, split and shattered, had yet to be cleared away. Others, barely damaged, clearly showed scorch-marks. Staring into the dark pill boxes, through gun slits that were still intact, was chilling, even though gulls now squawked reassuringly overhead. Barefoot, our trousers rolled to the knees, we roamed the beaches, finding deep pits and empty shell cases here and there. As the tide receded, concrete teeth were revealed still aimed at the incoming tanks and landing craft. I stooped to retrieve a soldier's boot from a garland of sea weed. Slimy, soggy, already sea-green, I could still make out the bullet-hole in the toe.

Ikons.

We were not, it's worth noting, true adventurers, but followers of a romantic convention. A second *Aliyah*, so to speak. "History has not quite repeated itself," Brian Moore wrote in a review of *Exile's Return* for the *Spectator*. "When one reads of the passionate, naïve manifestos in Malcolm Cowley's 'literary odyssey of the 1920s,' the high ambitions and the search for artistic values which sent the 'lost generation' to Paris, one cannot help feeling a touch of envy. It would seem that the difference between the American artists' pilgrimage to Europe in the Twenties and in the Sixties is the difference between first love and the obligatory initial visit to a brothel.

"Moneyed by a grant from Fulbright, Guggenheim, or Ford, the American painter now goes to France for a holiday: he knows that the action is all in New York. Similarly, the young American writer abroad shows little interest in the prose experiments of Robbe-Grillet, Sarraute, and Simon; he tends to dismiss Britain's younger novelists and playwrights as boring social realists (*we finished with that stuff twenty years ago*), and as for Sartre, Beckett, Genet, or Ionesco, he has dug them already off-Broadway. It seems that American writers, in three short generations, have moved from the provincial (*we haven't yet produced any writing that could be called major*) to the parochial (*the only stuff worth reading nowadays is coming out of America*)."

Our group, in the Fifties, came sandwiched between, largely unmoneyed, except for those on the GI Bill, and certainly curious about French writing, especially Sartre, Camus, and, above all, Céline. We were also self-consciously aware of the Twenties. We knew the table at the Dôme that had been Hemingway's and made a point of eating at the restaurant on rue Monsieur le Prince where Joyce was reputed to have taken his dinner. Not me, but others regularly sipped tea with Alice Toklas. Raymond Duncan, swirling past in his toga, was a common, if absurd, sight. *Transition* still appeared fitfully.

Other connections with the Twenties were through the second-generation. David Burnett, one of the editors of *New-Story*, was the son of Whit Burnett and Martha Foley, who had brought out the original *Story*. My own first publication was in *Points*, a little magazine that was edited by Sinbad Vail, the son of Lawrence Vail and Peggy Guggenheim. It wasn't much of a magazine, and though Vail printed 4,000 copies of the first issue, he was only able to peddle 400. In the same issue as my original mawkish short story there was a better one by Brendan Behan, who was described as "27, Irish . . . Has been arrested several times for activities in the Irish Republican Army, which he joined in 1937, and in all has been sentenced to 17 years in gaol, has in fact served about 7 years in Borstal and Parkhurst Prison. Disapproves of English prison system. At present working as a housepainter on the State Railways."

Among other little magazines current at the time there were *Id* and *Janus*. ("An aristocrat by his individualism, a revolutionary against all societies," wrote Daniel Mauroc, "the homosexual is both the Jew and the Negro, the precursor and the unassimilable, the terrorist and the *raffiné*. . . .") and *Merlin*, edited by Trocchi, Richard Seaver, Logue, and John Coleman, who is now the *New Statesman's* film critic. *Merlin's* address, incidently, was the English Bookshop, 42 rue de Seine, which had once belonged to Sylvia Beach.

In retrospect, I cannot recall that anybody, except Alan Temko, perhaps, was as yet writing fantasy or satire. Mostly, the stories we published were realistic and about home, be it Texas, Harlem, Brooklyn, or Denver. Possibly, just possibly, everything can be stripped down to a prosaic explanation. The cult of hashish, for instance, had a simple economic basis. It was easy to come by and cheap, far cheaper than scotch. Similarly, if a decade after our sojourn in Paris a number of us began to write what has since come to be branded black humour, it may well be that we were not so much inspired as driven to it by mechanics. After all, the writer who opts out of the mainstream of American experience, self-indulgently luxuriating in bohemia, the pleasure of like-minded souls, is also cutting himself off from his natural material, sacrificing his sense of social continuity; and so when we swung round to writing about contemporary America, we could only attack obliquely, shrewdly settling on a style that did not betray knowledge gaps of day to day experience.

For the most part, I moved with the *New-Story* bunch, David Burnett, Terry Southern, Mason Hoffenberg, Alan Temko, and others. One afternoon, Burnett told me, a new arrival from the States walked into the office and said, "For ten thousand dollars, I will stop in front of a car on the Place Vendôme and say I did it because *New-Story* rejected one of my stories. Naturally, I'm willing to guarantee coverage in all the American newspapers."

"But what if you're hurt?" he was asked.

"Don't worry about me, I'm a paraphrase artist."

"A what?"

"I can take any story in *Collier's*, rewrite it, and sell it to the *Post*."

New-Story, beset by financial difficulties from the very first issue, seldom able to fork out the promised two bucks a page to contributors or meet printer's bills, was eventually displaced by the more affluent *Paris Review*. But during its short and turbulent life *New-Story* was, I believe, the first magazine to publish Jean Genet in English. Once, browsing at George Whitman's hole-in-the-wall bookshop near Notre-Dame, where Bernard Frechtman's translation of *Our Lady of the Flowers* was prominently displayed, I overheard an exasperated Whitman explain to a camera-laden American matron, "No, no, it's not the same Genet as writes for the *New Yorker*."

Possibly, the most memorable of all the little magazines was the French publication, *Ur, Cahiers Pour Un Dictat Culturel*. *Ur* was edited by Jean-Isador Isou, embattled author of *A Reply To Karl Marx*, a slender riposte hawked by gorgeous girls in blue jeans to tourists at right bank cafés – tourists under the tantalizing illusion that they were buying the hot stuff.

Ur was a platform for the Letterists, who believed that all the arts were dead and could only be resurrected by a synthesis of their collective absurdities. This, like anything else that was seemingly new or outrageous, appealed to us. And so Friday nights, our pockets stuffed with oranges and apples, pitching cores into the Seine, scuffling, singing *Adon Olam*, we passed under the shadows of Notre Dame and made our way to a café on the Ile St. Louis to listen to Isador Isou and others read poems composed of grunts and cries, incoherent arrangements of letters, set to an anti-musical background of vacuum cleaners, drills, car horns, and train whistles. We listened, rubbing our jaws, nodding, looking pensive.

– *Ça, alors.*

– *Je m'en fous.*

– *Azoi,* Ginsberg. *Azoi.*

Ginsberg was the first to go home. I asked him to see my father and tell him how hard up I was.

"Sometimes," Ginsberg told him, "your son sits up all night in his cold room, writing."

"And what does he do all day?"

Crack peanuts on the terrace of the Café Royale. Ruminate over the baseball scores in the *Herald-Tribune*.

We were all, as Hemingway once said, at the right age. Everybody was talented. Special. Nobody had money. (Except of course Art Buchwald, the most openly envied ex-GI in Paris. Buchwald, who had not yet emerged as a humourist, had cunningly solved two problems at once, food and money, inaugurating a restaurant column in the *Herald-Tribune*.) We were all trying to write or paint and so there was always the hope, it's true, of a publisher's advance or a contract with a gallery. There was also the national lottery. There was, too, the glorious dream that today you would run into the fabled lady senator from the United States who was reputed to come over every summer and, as she put it, invest in the artistic future of five or six promising, creative youngsters. She would give you a thousand dollars, more sometimes, no strings attached. But I never met her. I was reminded of the days when as a kid in Montreal I was never without a Wrigley's chewing gum wrapper, because of that magic man who could pop up anywhere, stop you, and ask for a wrapper. If you had one with you, he gave you a dollar. Some days, they said, he handed out as much as fifty dollars. I never met him, either.

Immediately before Christmas, however, one of my uncles sent me money. I had written to him, quoting Auden, Kierkegaard, *The Book of Changes*, Maimonides, and Dylan Thomas, explaining we must love one another or die. "I can hear that sort of crap," he wrote back, "any Sunday morning on the Manischewitz Hour," but a cheque for a hundred dollars was enclosed, and I instantly decided to go to Cambridge for the holidays.

Stringent rationing – goose eggs, a toe-nail size chunk of meat a week – was still the depressing rule in England and, as I had old friends in Cambridge, I arrived laden with foodstuffs, my raincoat sagging with contraband steaks and packages of butter. A friend of a friend took me along to sip sherry with E. M. Forster at his rooms in King's College.

Forster immediately unnerved me by asking what I thought of F. Scott Fitzgerald's work.

Feebly, I replied I thought very highly of it indeed.

Forster then remarked that he generally asked visiting young Americans what they felt about Fitzgerald, whose high reputation baffled him. Forster said that though Fitzgerald unfailingly chose the most lyrical titles for his novels, the works themselves seemed to him to be without especial merit.

Unaccustomed to sherry, intimidated by Forster, who in fact couldn't have been more kind or gentle, I stupidly knocked back my sherry in one gulp, like a synagogue schnapps, whilst the others sipped theirs decorously. Forster waved for my glass to be refilled and then inquired without the least condescension about the progress of my work. Embarrassed, I hastily changed the subject.

"And what," he asked, "do you make of Angus's first novel?"

Angus being Angus Wilson and the novel, *Hemlock and After*.

"I haven't read it yet," I lied, terrified lest I make a fool of myself.

I left Forster a copy of Nelson Algren's *The Man With The Golden Arm*, which I had just read and enormously admired. A few days later the novel was returned to me with a note I didn't keep, and so quote from memory. He had only read as far as page 120 in Algren's novel, Foster wrote. It had less vomit than the last American novel he had read, but. . . .

At the time, I was told that the American novel Forster found most interesting was Willard Motley's *Knock On Any Door*.

Cambridge, E. M. Forster, was a mistake; it made me despair for me and my friends and our shared literary pretensions. In the rooms I visited at King's, St. Mary's, and Pembroke, gowned young men were wading through the entire *Faerie Queene*, they had absorbed *Beowulf*, Chaucer, and were clearly heirs to the tradition. All at once, it seemed outlandish, a grandiose *chutzpah*, that we, street corner bohemians, kibbitzers, still swapping horror stories about our abominable Yiddish mommas, should even presume to write. Confirmation, if it were needed, was provided by John Lehmann, who returned my first attempt at a sub-Céline novel with a printed rejection slip.

"Hi, keed," my brother wrote, "How are things in Gay Paree?", and there followed a list of the latest YMHA basketball scores.

Things in Gay Paree were uncommonly lousy. I had contacted scurvy, of all things, from not eating sufficient fruit or vegetables. The money began to run out. Come midnight, come thirst, I used to search for my affluent friend, Armstrong, who was then putting me up in his apartment in Étoile. I would seek out Armstrong in the homosexual pits of St. Germain and Montparnasse. The Montana, the Fiacre, l'Abbaye, the Reine Blanche. If Armstrong was sweetening up a butch, I would slip in and out again discreetly, but if Armstrong was alone, alone and sodden, he would comfort me with cognacs and ham rolls and take me home in a taxi.

Enormous, rosycheeked, raisineyed Armstrong was addicted to acquired Yiddishisms. He'd say, "Oy, bless my little. I don't know why I go there, Mottel."

"Uh huh."

"Did you catch the old queen at the bar?"

"I'm still hungry. What about you?"

"*Zut.*"

"You know, I've never eaten at Les Halles. All this time in Paris. . . ."

"I don't care a tit if you ever eat at Les Halles. We're going home, you scheming *yenta.*"

Armstrong and I had sat next to each other in Political Science 101 at Sir George Williams College. SYSTEMS OF GOVERNMENT, the professor wrote on the blackboard,

a. monarchy   c. democracy
b. totalitarianism   d. others

Canada is a ————————

Armstrong passed me a note. "A Presbyterian twat."

At Sir George, Armstrong had taken out the most desirable girls, but I could never make out. The girls I longed for longed for the basketball players or charmers like Armstrong and the only one who would tolerate me had been the sort who read Penguins on streetcars or were above using make-up. Or played the accordion at parties, singing about Joe Hill and *Los Quatro Générales*. Or demonstrated. Then, two years ago, Armstrong had tossed up everything to come to Paris and study acting. Now he no longer put up with girls and had become an unstoppable young executive in a major advertising company. "I would only have made a mediocre actor," he was fond of saying to me as I sat amidst my rejection slips.

Once more I was able to wrangle money from home, three hundred dollars and this time I ventured south for the summer, to Haut-de-Cagnes. Here I first encountered American and British expatriates of the Twenties, shadowy remittance men, coupon-clippers, who painted a bit, sculpted some, and wrote from time to time. An instructive but shattering look, I feared, at my future prospects. Above all, the expatriates drank prodigiously. Twenties flotsam, whose languid, self-indulgent, bickering, party-crammed life in the Alpes-Maritimes had been disrupted only by World War II.

Bit players of bygone age, they persisted in continuing as if it were still burgeoning, supplying the *Nice-Matin*, for instance, with guest lists of their lawn parties; and carrying on as if Cyril Connelly's first novel, *The Rockpool*, were a present scandal. "He was only here for three weeks altogether, don't you know," a colonel told me.

"I'm only *very* thinly disguised in it," a lady said haughtily.

Extremely early one morning I rolled out of bed in response to a knock on the door. It was Mr. Soon.

"I have just seen the sun coming up over the Mediterranean," he said.

In spite of the heat, Mr. Soon wore a crushed greasy raincoat. Terry Southern, if I remember correctly, had given it to him. He had also thoughtfully provided him with my address. "Won't you come in?" I asked.

"Not yet. I am going to walk on the Promenade des Anglais."

"You might as well leave your coat here, then."

"But it would be inelegant to walk on the Promenade in Nice without a coat, don't you think?"

Mr. Soon returned late in the afternoon and I took him to Jimmy's Bar, on the brim of the steep grey hill of Haut-de-Cagnes.

"It reminds me most of California here," Mr. Soon said.

"But I had no idea you had ever been to California."

"No. Never. Have you?"

I watched, indeed, soon everyone on the terrace turned to stare, as Mr. Soon, his beard a filthy tangle, reached absently into his pocket for a magnifying glass, held it to the sun, and lit a Gauloise. Mr. Soon, who spoke several languages, including Chinese, imperfectly, was evasive whenever we asked him where he had been born in this his twenty-third reincarnation. We put him down for Russian, but when I brought him along to Marushka's she insisted that he spoke the language ineptly.

Marushka, now in her sixties, had lived in Cagnes for years. Modigliani had written a sonnet to her and she could recall the night Isadora had danced in the square. Marushka was not impressed by Mr. Soon. "He's a German," she said, as if it was quite the nastiest thing she could think of.

I took Mr. Soon home with me and made up a bed for him on the floor, only to be awakened at two a.m. because all the lights had been turned on. Mr. Soon sat at my table, writing, with one of my books, *The Guide For The Perplexed*, by his side. "I am copying out the table of contents," he said.

"But what on earth for?"

"It is a very interesting table of contents, don't you think?

A week later Mr. Soon was still with me. One afternoon he caught me hunting mosquitoes with a rolled newspaper and subjected me to a long, melancholy lecture on the holy nature of all living things. Infuriated, I said, "Maybe *I* was a mosquito in a previous incarnation, eh?"

"No. You were a Persian Prince."

"What makes you say that?" I asked, immensely pleased.

"Let us go to Jimmy's. It is so interesting to sit there and contemplate, don't you think?"

I was driven to writing myself a letter and opening it while Mr. Soon and I sat at the breakfast table. "Some friends of mine are coming down from Paris the day after tomorrow. I'd quite forgotten I had invited them to stay with me."

"Very interesting. How long will they be staying?"

"There's no saying."

"I can stay at the Tarzan Camping and return when they are gone."

We began to sell things. Typewriters, books, wristwatches. When we all seemed to have reached bottom, when our credit was no longer good anywhere, something turned up. An ex-GI, Seymour, who ran a tourist office in Nice called SEE-MOR TOURS, became casting director for extra parts in films and we all got jobs for ten dollars a day.

Once more, Armstrong tolerated me in his Paris flat. One night, in the Montana, Armstrong introduced me to an elegant group of people at his table, including the Countess Louise. The next morning he informed me, "Louise, um, thinks you're cute, boychick. She's just dumped Jacques and she's looking for another banana."

Armstrong went on to explain that if I were satisfactory I would have a studio in Louise's flat and an allowance of one hundred thousand francs monthly.

"And what do I have to do to earn all that?"

"Oy-vey. There's nothing like a Jewish childhood. Don't be so provincial."

Louise was a thin wizened lady in her forties. Glittering earrings dripped from her ears and icy rings swelled on the fingers of either hand. "It would only be once a week," Armstrong said. "She'd take you to first nights at the opera and all the best restaurants. Wouldn't you like that?"

"Go to hell."

"You're invited to her place for drinks on Thursday. I'd better buy you some clothes first."

On Thursday I sat in the sun at the Mabillion consuming beer after beer before I risked the trip to the Countess's flat. I hadn't felt as jumpy or been so thoroughly bright and scrubbed from the skin out since my bar-mitzvah. A butler took my coat. The hall walls were painted scarlet and embedded with precious stones. I was led into the drawing room where a nude study of a younger Louise, who had used to be a patroness of surrealists, hung in a lighted alcove. Spiders and bugs fed on the Countess's ash-grey bosom. I heard laughter and voices from another room. Finally a light-footed American in a black antelope jacket drifted into the drawing room. "Louise is receiving in the bedroom," he said.

Possibly, I thought, I'm one of many candidates. I stalked anxiously round an aviary of stuffed tropical fowl. Leaning against the mantelpiece, I knocked over an antique gun.

"Oh, dear." The young American retrieved it gently. "This," he said, "is the gun Verlaine used in his duel with Rimbaud."

At last Louise was washed into the room on a froth of beautiful boys and girls. She took my hand and pressed it. "Well, hullo," I said.

We sped off in two black Jaguars to a private party for Cocteau. All the bright young people, except me, had some accomplishment behind them. They chatted breezily about their publishers and producers and agents. Eventually one of them turned to me, offering a smile. "You're Louise's little Canadian, aren't you?"

"That's the ticket."

Louise asked me about Montreal.

"After Paris," I said, swaying drunkenly, "it's the world's largest French-speaking city."

The American in the black antelope jacket joined me at the bar, clapping me on the shoulder. "Louise will be very good to you," he said.

Azoi.

"We all adore her."

Suddenly Louise was with us. "But you must meet Cocteau," she said.

I was directed to a queue awaiting presentation. Cocteau wore a suede windbreaker. The three young men ahead of me, one of them a sailor kissed him on both cheeks as they were introduced. Feeling foolish, I offered him my hand and then returned to the bar and had another whisky, and yet another, before I noticed that all my group, including my Countess, had gone, leaving me behind.

Armstrong was not pleased with me, but then he was a troubled man. His secretary, a randy little bit from Guildford, an ex-India Army man's daughter, was eager for him, and Armstrong, intimidated, had gone so far as to fondle her breasts at the office. "If I don't screw the bitch," he said to me, "she'll say I'm queer. Oy, my poor *tuchus*."

Armstrong's day-to-day existence was fraught with horrors. Obese, he remained a compulsive eater. Terrified of blackmailers and police *provocateurs*, he was still driven to cruising Piccadilly and Leicester Square on trips to London. Every day he met with accountants and salesmen, pinched men in shiny office suits who delighted in vicious jokes about queers, and Armstrong felt compelled to prove himself the most ferocious queer-baiter of them all.

"Maybe I should marry Betty. She wants to. Well, boychick?"

In the bathroom, I looked up to see black net bikini underwear dripping from a line over the tub. Armstrong pounded on the door. "We could have kids," he said.

The medicine cabinet was laden with deodorants and sweetening sprays and rolls of absorbent cotton and vaseline jars.

"I'm capable, you know."

A few nights later Armstrong brought a British boy home. A painter, a taschist. "Oy, Mottel," he said, easing me out of the flat. "*Gevalt*, old chap."

The next morning I stumbled into the bathroom, coming sharply awake when I saw a red rose floating in the toilet bowl.

After Armstrong had left for work, the painter, a tall fastidious boy with flaxen hair, joined me at the breakfast table. He misunderstood my frostiness. "I wouldn't be staying here," he assured me, "but Richard said your relationship is platonic."

I looked up indignantly from my newspaper, briefly startled, then smiled and said, "Well, you see I could never take him home and introduce him to my family. He's not Jewish."

Two weeks later my father sent me enough money for a ticket home and, regretfully, I went to the steamship office at l'Opéra. An advertisement in the window read:

"liked Lisbon, loved Tahiti. But when it comes to
getting the feel of the sea . . ."
give me the crashing waves and rugged rocks
give me the gulls and nets and men and boats
give me the harbours and homes and spires and quays
GIVE ME NEW BRUNSWICK
                    CANADA

I had been away two years.

Why I Write

As I write, October 1970, I have just finished a novel of intimidating length, a fiction begun five years ago, on the other side of the moon, so I am, understandably enough, concerned by the state of the novel in general. Is it dead? Dead *again*. Like God or MGM. Father McLuhan says so (writing, 'The Age of Writing has passed') and Dylan Thomas's daughter recently pronounced stingingly from Rome, "Nobody reads novels any more."

I'm soon going to be forty. Too old to learn how to teach. Or play the guitar. Stuck, like the blacksmith, with the only craft I know. But brooding about the novel, and its present unmodishness, it's not the established practitioner I'm grieving for, it's the novice, that otherwise effervescent young man stricken with the wasting disease whose earliest symptom is the first novel. These are far from halcyon days for the fledgling novelist.

Look at it this way. Most publishers, confronted with a rectal polyp, hold on to hope, tempting the surgeon with a bigger advance. They know the score. What's truly terminal. Offered a first novel or worse news – *infamy* – a short story collection, they call for the ledgers which commemorate last season's calamities. The bright new talents nobody wanted to read. Now more to be remaindered than remembered, as *Time* once observed.

I know. Carting off my cumbersome manuscript to be xeroxed, it was my first novel that was uppermost in my mind, *The Acrobats*, published in 1954, when I was twenty-three years old. At the time, I was living in Montreal, and my British publisher, André Deutsch, urged me to visit his Canadian distributor before sailing for England. So I caught the overnight Greyhound bus to Toronto, arriving at 7 a.m. in a city where I knew nobody and walking the sweltering summer streets until 9.30, when offices would open.

The Canadian distributor, bracingly realistic, did not detain me overlong with *recherché* chitchat about style, content or influences. "Have you written a thick book or a thin book?" he demanded.

A thin one, I allowed.

"Thick books sell better than thin ones here."

A slow learner, I published five more before I at last surfaced with a thick one, *St. Urbain's Horseman,* which was all of 180,000 words. And retrieving my seven xeroxed copies, I couldn't help but reflect that the £80 I forked out for them was only slightly less than the British advance against royalties I was paid for my first novel sixteen years ago. The American publisher, G. P. Putnam's Sons, was more generous; they sent me 750 dollars. But I was disheartened when I received their catalogue. Putnam's was, at the time, trying a new experiment in book selling. If you didn't enjoy one of their books, your bookseller would return you the money, no questions asked. Only two books listed in the autumn catalogue conspicuously failed to carry this guarantee, mine, and another young writer's.

The Acrobats ultimately sold some 2,000 copies in England and less than a 1,000 in the U.S., but it was – as I pointed out to my aunt, on a visit to Montreal – translated into five foreign languages.

"There must," she said, smoothing out her skirt, "be a shortage of books."

My uncle, also a critic, was astonished when he computed my earnings against the time I had invested. I would have earned more mowing his lawn, and, furthermore, it would have been healthier for me.

The novel, the novel.

Write a study of the Pre-Columbian butterfly, compose an account of colonial administration in Tongo, and Nigel Dennis, that most perspicacious and witty of British reviewers, might perversely enshrine it in a 1,000 word essay in the *Sunday Telegraph*. Or Malcolm Muggeridge might take it as the text for a lengthy sermon, excoriating once more that generation of younger vipers who will continue to enjoy, enjoy, after he has passed on to his much-advertised rest. But novels, coming in batches of twenty weekly, seldom rate a notice of their own in England. Sixteen are instant losers. Or, looked at another way, payola from the literary editor. Badly-paid reviewer's perks. The reviewer is not even expected to read them, but it is understood he can flog them for half-price to a buyer from Fleet Street. Of the four that remain, comprising the typical novel column, one is made especially for skewering in the last deadly paragraph, and two are destined for the scales of critical balance. On the one hand, somewhat promising, on the other, ho-hum. Only one makes the lead. But it must lead in four of the five influential newspapers, say, the *Sunday Times*, *Observer*, *Times* and *Guardian*, if anybody's to take notice. Some even buying.

"Basically," a concerned New York editor told me, "the trouble is we are trying to market something nobody wants. Or needs."

The novel has had its day, we are assured, and in the Age of Aquarius, film, man, film's the stuff that will do more than fiction can to justify God's way to man. Given any rainy afternoon who wants to read Doris Lessing fully-clothed for forty bob when, for only ten, you can actually see Jane Fonda starkers, shaking it for you and art, and leaving you with sufficient change for a half-bottle of gin?

To be fair, everything has (and continues) to be tried. Novels like decks of playing cards. Shuffle, and read it anyway it comes up. Novels like jokes or mutual funds. You cut your potential time-investment loss by inviting everybody in the office to pound out a chapter. *Naked Came The Stranger. I Knew Daisy Smutten.* Or instead-of-sex. Why weary yourself, performing badly perhaps when, if only you lose yourself in *The Adventurers*, you can have better-hung Dax come for you? And, sooner or later, somebody's bound to turn to the cassette. No need to bruise your thumbs turning pages. You slip the thing into a machine and listen to Racquel Welch read it. "The latest Amis as read by. . . ."

On a recent visit to Canadian university campuses, I found myself a creature to be pitied, still writing novels when anybody could tell you that's no longer "where it's at." But I've tried the logical alternative, screen writing, and though I still write for the films from time to time, it's not really for me.

The trouble is, like most novelists, I am conditioned to working for years on material I discuss with nobody. To adjust from that to script writing is too much like what Truman Capote once described as group sports. Even so, five years in a room with a novel-in-progress can be more than gruelling. If getting up to it some mornings is a pleasure, it is, just as often, a punishment. A self-inflicted punishment. There have been false starts, wrong turns, and weeks with nothing to show except sharpened pencils and bookshelves rearranged. I have rewritten chapters ten times that in the end simply didn't belong and had to be cut. Ironically, even unforgivably, it usually seems to be those passages over which I have laboured most arduously, nurtured in the hot-house, as it were, that never really spring to life, and the pages that came too quickly, with utterly suspect ease, that read most felicitously.

Riding into my second year on *St. Urbain's Horseman*, disheartened by proliferating school bills, diminished savings, and only fitful progress, I finally got stuck so badly that there was nothing for it but to shove the manuscript aside. I started in on another novel, a year's heat, which yielded *Cocksure*. Anthony Burgess clapped hands in *Life*, *Time* approved, *Newsweek* cheered, and the British notices were almost uniformly fulsome. Encouraged and somewhat solvent again, I resolved to resume work on *Horseman*. After twelve years in London, I was to return to Montreal for a year with my wife and five children, to report for duty as writer-in-residence at Sir George Williams University, my *alma mater*. Or, put plainly, in return for taking a "creative writing" seminar one afternoon a week, I could get on with my novel, comparatively free of financial worry.

Ostensibly, conditions were ideal, winds couldn't be more favourable, and so I started in for the ninth time on page one of *St. Urbain's Horseman*. I didn't get much further before, my stomach crawling with fear, I began to feel I'd lost something somewhere.

I got stuck. Morning after morning, I'd switch to an article or a book review, already long overdue. Or compose self-pitying letters to friends. Or dawdle until eleven a.m., when it was too late to make a decent start on anything, and I was at last free to quit my room and stroll downtown. St. Catherine Street. Montreal's Main Stem, as the doyen of our gossip columnists has it. Pretending to browse for books by lesser novelists, I could surreptitiously check out the shops on stacks of the paperback edition of *Cocksure*.

Or take in a movie maybe.

Ego dividends. I could pick a movie that I had been asked to write myself, but declined. Whatever the movie, it was quite likely I would know the director or the script writer, maybe even one of the stars.

So there you have it. Cat's out of the bag. In London, I skitter on the periphery of festooned circles, know plenty of inside stories. Bomb-shells. Like which cabinet minister is an insatiable pederast. What best-selling novel was really stitched together by a cunning editor. Which wrinkled Hollywood glamour queen is predisposed toward gang shags with hirsute Neapolitan waiters from the Mirabelle. Yes, yes, I'll own up to it. I am, after eighteen years as a writer, not utterly unconnected or unknown, as witness the entry in the indispensable *Oxford Companion to Canadian Literature*.

Richler, Mordecai (1931—) Born in Montreal, he was educated at Sir George Williams College and spent two years abroad. Returning to Canada in 1952, he joined the staff of the Canadian Broadcasting Corporation. He now lives in England, where he writes film scripts, novels, and short stories. The key to Richler's novels is . . .

After eighteen years and six novels there is nothing I cherish so much as the first and most vulnerable book, *The Acrobats*, not only because it marked the first time my name appeared in a Canadian newspaper, a prescient Toronto columnist writing from London,

"You've not heard of Mordecai Richler yet, but, look out, she's a name to watch for"; but also because it was the one book I could write as a totally private act, with the deep, inner assurance that nobody would be such a damn fool as to publish it. That any editor would boot it back to me, a condescending rejection note enclosed, enabling me to quit Paris for Montreal, an honourable failure, and get down to the serious business of looking for a job. A real job.

I did in fact return to Montreal, broke, while my manuscript made the rounds. My father, who hadn't seen me for two years, took me out for a drive.

"I hear you wrote a novel in Europe," he said.

"Yes."

"What's it called?"

"*The Acrobats*."

"What in the hell do you know about the circus?"

I explained the title was a symbolic one.

"Is it about Jews or ordinary people?" my father asked.

To my astonishment, André Deutsch offered to publish the novel. Now, when somebody asked me what I did, I could reply, without seeming fraudulent to myself, that I was indeed a writer. If, returned to Hampstead once more, I still tended to doubt it in the early morning hours, now *The Acrobats*, in shop windows here and there, was the proof I needed. My novel on display side by side with real ones. There is no publication as agonizing or charged with elation as the first.

Gradually, you assume that what you write will be published. After the first book, composing a novel is no longer self-indulgent, a conceit. It becomes, among other things, a living. Though to this day reviews can still sting or delight, it's sales that buy you the time to get on with the next. Mind you, there are a number of critics whose esteem I prize, whose opprobrium can sear, but, for the most part, I, in common with other writers, have learned to read reviews like a market report. This one will help move the novel, that one not.

Writing a novel, as George Orwell has observed, is a horrible, exhausting struggle. "One would never undertake such a thing if one were not driven by some demon whom one can neither resist nor understand." Something else. Each novel is a failure, or there would be no compulsion to begin afresh. Critics don't help. Speaking as someone who fills that office on occasion, I must say that the critic's essential relationship is with the reader, not the writer. It is his duty to celebrate good books, eviscerate bad ones, lying ones.

When I first published, in 1954, it was commonly assumed that to commit a film script was to sell out (Daniel Fuchs, Christopher Isherwood, Irwin Shaw), and that the good and dedicated life was in academe. Now, the inverse seems to be the Canadian and, I daresay, American case. The creative young yearn to be in films, journeymen retire to the universities: *seems* to be the case, because, happily, there are exceptions.

All of us tend to romanticize the world we nearly chose. In my case, academe, where instead of having to bring home the meat, I would only be obliged to stamp it, rejecting this shoulder of beef as Hank James derivative, or that side of pork as sub-Jimmy Joyce. I saw myself no longer a perplexed free-lancer with an unpredictable income, balancing this magazine assignment, that film job, against the time it would buy me. No sir. Sipping Tio Pepe in the faculty club, snug in my leather winged-back armchair and the company of other disinterested scholars, I would not, given the assurance of a monthly cheque, chat about anything so coarse as money.

– Why don't you, um, write a novel yourself this summer, Professor Richler?

– Well, Dr. Lemming, like you, I have too much respect for the tradition to sully it with my own feeble scribblings.

– Quite.

– Just so.

Alas, academe, like girls, whisky, and literature, promised better than it paid. I now realize, after having ridden the academic gravy train for a season, that vaudeville hasn't disappeared or been killed by TV, but merely retired to small circuits, among them, the universities. Take the Canadian poets, for instance. Applying for Canada Council grants today, they no longer catalogue their publications (the obsolete accomplishments of linear man) but, instead, like TV actors on the make, they list their personal appearances, the campuses where they read aloud. Wowsy at Simon Fraser U., hotsy at Carleton. Working wrinkles out of the act in the stix, with a headliner coming up in the veritable Palace of the Canadian campus circuit, the University of Toronto.

If stand-up comics now employ batteries of gag writers because national TV exposure means they can only use their material once, then professors, playing to a new house every season, can peddle the same oneliners year after year, improving only on timing and delivery. For promos, they publish. Bringing out journals necessary to no known audience, but essential to their advancement.

Put plainly, these days everybody's in show business, all trades are riddled with impurities. And so, after a most enjoyable (and salaried) year in academe – a reverse sabbatical, if you like – I returned to the uncertain world of the free-lance writer, where nobody, as James Thurber once wrote, sits at anybody's feet unless he's been knocked there. I returned with my family to London, no deeper into *St. Urbain's Horseman* than when I had left.

Why do you write?

Doctors are seldom asked why they practise, shoemakers how come they cobble, or baseball players why they don't drive a coal truck instead, but again and again writers, like housebreakers, are asked why they do it.

Orwell, as might be expected, supplies the most honest answer in his essay, "Why I Write."

"1. Sheer egoism. Desire to seem clever, to be talked about, to be remembered after death, to get your own back on grownups who snubbed you in childhood, etc. etc." To this I would add egoism informed by imagination, style, and a desire to be known, yes, *but only on your own conditions*.

Nobody is more embittered than the neglected writer and, obviously, allowed a certain recognition, I am a happier and more generous man than I would otherwise be. But nothing I have done to win this recognition appals me, has gone against my nature. I fervently believe that all a writer should send into the marketplace to be judged is his own work; the rest should remain private. I deplore the writer as a personality, however large and undoubted the talent, as is the case with Norman Mailer. I also do not believe in special licence for so-called artistic temperament. After all, my problems, as I grudgingly come within spitting distance of middle age, are the same as anybody else's. Easier maybe. I can bend my anxieties to subversive uses. Making stories of them. When I'm not writing, I'm a husband and a father of five. Worried about pollution. The population explosion. My sons' report cards.

"2. Aesthetic enthusiasm. Perception of beauty in the external world, or, on the other hand, in words and their right arrangement." The agonies involved in creating a novel, the unsatisfying draft, the scenes you never get right, are redeemed by those rare and memorable days when, seemingly without reason, everything falls right. Bonus days. Blessed days when, drawing on resources unsuspected, you pluck ideas and prose out of your skull that you never dreamt yourself capable of.

Such, such are the real joys.

Unfortunately, I don't feel that I've ever been able to sustain such flights for a novel's length. So the passages that flow are balanced with those which were forced in the hothouse. Of all the novels I've written, it is *The Apprenticeship of Duddy Kravitz* and *Cocksure* which come closest to my intentions and, therefore, give me the most pleasure. I should add that I'm still lumbered with the characters and ideas, the social concerns I first attempted in *The Acrobats*. Every serious writer has, I think, one theme, many variations to play on it.

Like any serious writer, I want to write one novel that will last, something that will make me remembered after death, and so I'm compelled to keep trying.

"3. Historical impulse. Desire to see things as they are. . . ."

No matter how long I continue to live abroad, I do feel forever rooted in Montreal's St. Urbain Street. That was my time, my place, and I have elected myself to get it right.

"4. Political purpose – using the word 'political' in the widest possible sense. Desire to push the world in a certain direction, to alter other people's idea of the kind of society that they should strive after."

Not an overlarge consideration in my work, though I would say that any serious writer is a moralist and only incidently an entertainer.

After a year on the academic payroll, I returned to London in August 1969, abysmally depressed, because after four years *St. Urbain's Horseman* was no nearer to completion and, once more, my savings were running down. I retired to my room each morning, ostensibly to work, but actually to prepare highly impressive schedules. Starting next Monday, without fail, I would write three pages a day. Meanwhile, I would train for this ordeal by taking a nap every afternoon, followed by trips to the movies I simply had to see, thereby steeling myself against future fatigue and distractions. Next Monday, however, nothing came. Instead, taking the sports pages of the *International Herald-Tribune* as my text, I calculated, based on present standings and won-lost ratios, where each team in both major baseball leagues would end the season. Monday, falling on the eighth of the month, was a bad date, anyway. Neither here nor there. I would seriously begin work, I decided, on the 15th of the month, writing *six* pages daily. After all, if Simenon could write a novel in a week, surely. . . . When I failed to write even a paragraph on the 15th, I was not upset. Finally, I grasped the real nature of my problem. Wrong typewriter. Wrong colour ribbon. Wrong texture paper. I traded in my machine for one with a new type face, bought six blue ribbons, and three boxes of heavy bond paper, but still nothing came. Absolutely nothing.

Then, suddenly, in September, I began to put in long hours in my room, writing with ease, one day's work more gratifying than the next, and within a year the novel was done, all 550 typewritten pages.

The first person to read the manuscript, my wife, was, like all writers' wives, in an invidious position. I depend on my wife's taste and honesty. It is she, unenviably, who must tell me if I've gone wrong. If she disapproved, however diplomatically, there would be angry words, some things I would have to say about her own deficiencies, say her choice of clothes, her cooking, and the mess she was making of raising our children. I would also point out that it was gratuitously cruel of her to laugh aloud in bed, reading *Portnoy's Complaint,* when I was having such a struggle with my own novel. All the same, I would not submit the manuscript. If she found it wanting, I would put it aside for six months to be considered afresh. Another year, another draft. And yet – and yet – even if she proclaimed the manuscript a masterpiece, radiating delight, I would immediately discount her praise, thinking she's only my wife, loyal and loving, and therefore dangerously preju-diced. Maybe a liar. Certainly beyond the critical pale.

After my wife had pronounced, foolishly saying *St. Urbain's Horseman* was the best novel I'd written by far (making me resentful, because this obviously meant she hadn't enjoyed my earlier work as much as she should have done) I submitted the manuscript to my editors. Another hurdle, another intricate rela-tionship. I deal with editors who are commonly taken to be among the most prescient in publishing – Robert Gottlieb at Knopf and, in England, Tony Godwin at Weidenfeld & Nicolson – but once I had sent them my manuscript, and they had obviously not dropped everything to read it overnight, wakening me with fulsome cables long distance calls, champagne and caviar, I began to arm myself with fancied resentments and the case that could be made against their much-advertised (but as I had reason to suspect) over-rated acumen. As each morning's mail failed to yield a letter, and the telephone didn't ring, I lay seething on the living room sofa, ticking off, in my mind's eye, all the lesser novelists on their lists, those they flattered with larger ads, bigger first prints, more generous advances, more expensive lunches, than they had ever allowed me. In fact I had all but decided it was time to move on to other, more appreciative publishers when, only a week after I had submitted the manuscript, both editors wrote me enthusiastic letters. Enthusi astic letters, that is, until you have scrutinized them for the ninth time, reading between the lines, and grasp that the compliments are forced, the praise false, and that the sour truth hidden beneath the clichés is that they don't really like the novel. Or even if they did, their taste is demonstrably fallible, and corrupted by the fact that they are personal friends, especially fond of my wife.

Put plainly, nothing helps.

Part Two

o canada

Last year (L.B.J. willing, French Canada permitting) Canada was a hundred years old and this, *The Unknown Country, The Golden Hinge, The Uneasy Neighbour, The Giant of the North*, was transmogrified, albeit along decent Presbyterian lines, into a Disneyland that rocked'n'rolled from coast to coast. Put plainly, there was not a township so small or a city so cynical that it could risk being caught without a centennial project. Some of the schemes, like Montreal's Expo 67, were grand, indeed, even if the freshness of conception ("The theme of Expo 67 will be: 'MAN AND HIS WORLD'") didn't exactly hit you bang in the eye. Other municipal projects, among the 2000 approved, included a centennial salmon-spawning channel. And just in case the sapients on your town council failed to come up with something sufficiently fetching, then, waiting to guide you in Toronto, rather like glorified bar-mitzvah caterers, there was a centennial advisory company. Among hotsy projects undertaken, one, by the Federated Women's Institutes of Canada, sponsored a competition for a centennial poem and another, this from our very own Imperial Order of the Daughters of the Empire (I.O.D.E.), announced a contest for the best novel or play "set in one of Canada's provinces as it is today or was in the past." *Canadian Municipal Utilities*, a trade journal, suggested "it would be a very fitting Birthday Present for a municipality to have a water system or sewage treatment plant in 1967 ... Canada's people in 1967 may not think of the Fathers of Confederation each time they wash their hands or flush a toilet, but. . . ."

Meanwhile Canada remains a loosely-knit, all but unmanageable confederation. There is trouble, trouble everywhere. "There is no Canadian nation," Marcel Chaput, a French-Canadian separatist leader, has written. "There is a Canadian state (which is) a purely political and artificial entity. . . ." French Canada, quiescent for years, is in a turmoil. John Diefenbaker's inept, but comic, federal government has been displaced by an equally inept and scandal-ridden government, this one led by Lester Pearson, of whom so much was hoped. Industry and natural resources everywhere are too often American-owned. And sadly it is not only our iron and copper ore that is going down to the States, but also, at the alarming rate of 50,000 a year, some of the people most crucial to Canada's development. Scientists, engineers, doctors, and businessmen, too many of whom are understandably drawn to what Morley Callaghan has called "the sources of light."

This is the climate then in which Canadians have become increasingly anxious to discover within themselves a culture-cum-national identity that amounts to something less nebulous than being nicer than Americans and not as snobby as the British; and the protracted search has made for many changes since I first left Canada in 1954.

At the time, it seemed to many observers, myself included, that the country was starved for culture, and nothing could be worse. How foolish we were. For now that the country is culture-crazed and more preoccupied than ever before with its own absence of a navel, how one yearns for Canada's engaging buckeye suspicion of art and artists of not so long ago. I was brought up in a folksy Canada. I remember the bad old days when it was necessary to come to the defence of artistic youngsters, and we suffered a wave of enlightened CBC radio and TV plays which educated the public to the fact that we were not all notoriously heavy drinkers, like William Faulkner, or queers, like Jean Genet. We strung words together sort of, but we were regular fellers: Canadians. In a typical play a sensitive little twerp named David or Christopher, usually son of a boorish insurance agent, roused his dad's ire because he wouldn't play hockey or hit back. Instead he was studying piano with an effeminate Frenchman or painting with a tricksy Hungarian Jew ("A piece of blank paper! Mit a brush und paints, vot an opportunity for beauty!") and in the end made dad eat his words by winning the piano competition in Toronto or, if the writer was inclined to irony, by being commissioned to paint a mural for the new skyscraper being built by the insurance company dad worked for.

– That's some kid you've got there, Henry. When it comes to splashing paint on walls he's a real home-run hitter.

– Gosh.

When I was a student there was actually a course on Can. lit. at Sir George Williams U., but the text was mimeographed and a typical assignment was for a student to list all the books ever written about the Hudson's Bay Co., noting the dimensions, number of pages, and photographs. Now there are a number of books, most of them embarrassingly boosterish, about Canadian writing, and there is at least one serious quarterly, the bi-lingual *Canadian Literature*, edited by George Woodcock, that is exclusively – no, quixotically – devoted to the study of Canadian writing past and present. In the very first issue Dwight Macdonald, asked to appraise a number of Canadian little magazines, was left with the impression of "a starved, pinched version of our own culture." Canada, he felt, was "a mingy version of the United States." That was 1959. Since then a real Canadian book club has been formed, with monthly selections that run from Malcolm Lowry's *Ultramarine* to *Love and Peanut Butter* ("Lesley Conger's warm and lively account of the trials of being a wife, mother and writer in a wild Vancouver household."); and there is a worthy and useful paperback library of Canadian, um, classics. Blue chip Leacocks, some good Callaghans, and rather too many of our frontier day

97

unreadables indecently exhumed. In fact today the cultural heat is such that the shrewd downtown grocer who has survived supermarket competition must now live through another crisis: the spadebearded entrepeneur who wants to buy out the lease and convert the premises into an art gallery. Instead of Libby's soup and Kellogg's Super "K", pictures of Libby's soup and Kellogg's Super "K". If when I was a student there was something shamefully un-Presbyterian in admitting you were a writer, today to merely let on that you're "creative" is to stand back and duck a shower of prizes and offers, and to enjoy a nice little side income in supplying radio and tv stations with your outspoken opinions on divorce, household pets, masturbation, and the Bomb (a shadow we live under).

There are rather more art than harvest festivals in Canada these days and variations on a seminar I attended in Toronto in 1961 ("to measure Canada's national cultural development in relation to other nations") are plentiful. A recent edition of the Entertainments supplement to the Saturday edition of the Montreal *Star* lists no less than fifty art galleries in its calendar of events. The calendar also informs readers that this is "Liberal Judaism Week" and afficionados can hear Rabbi H. Leonard Poller discuss "Count Up, Count Down, What Does the Liberal Jew Count?" An ad in the same edition runs,

SOMETHING MISSING?

What do Vancouver, Winnipeg, Toronto, Ottawa (soon) and Halifax have that Montreal hasn't. A professional English language theatre, that's what! Want to do something to help change this terrible situation? Send your name to ....

All of which goes to prove that Canadian culture, and criticism thereof, is clearly a growth industry, though it always seemed to me to be one of the few that was proof against an American takeover bid. Then, in 1960, Edmund Wilson wrote in the *New Yorker* that Morley Callaghan "is today perhaps the most unjustly neglected novelist in the English-speaking world" and that here was a writer "whose work may be mentioned without absurdity in association with Chekhov's and Turgenev's." A shot that ricochetted through all the universities on the northerly side of the world's largest unarmed frontier and sent critics scrambling after the Callaghan novels . . . only to report back that they still found them wanting.

Then it was rumoured that Mr. Wilson was in Montreal, he had actually been seen in Toronto, and was working on a book about Canadian writing. (Canadian writing, for Christ's sake! Edmund Wilson!) Now *O Canada: An American's Notes on Canadian Culture* has at last been published. *O CANADA, O EDMUND WILSON, O NUTS,* ran a review headline in the Toronto *Telegram,* which now reports on books as well as axe-murders, and underneath somebody called Michael Bawtree wrote, "not quite my idea of criticism." H.L.M. of the Windsor *Star* agreed. Taking issue with Mr. Wilson's evaluation of Callaghan, he wrote, "Much more can be learned about Canada from the writings of Thomas Costain, who isn't mentioned." H.L.M. also did not concur with Mr. Wilson's opinion that Canadian criticism tended to be provincial. "In the main it probably doesn't go along with the presumption that if a book is dirty enough, it's good enough, in fact superior."

Well, well. But this is really no more bumpkinish than reviews in too many American newspapers and the truth is not all Canadian criticism comes off the cob. Some of our most discerning critics (George Woodcock, Robert Fulford) found much to admire in Mr. Wilson's book, but they were also troubled by other aspects of it. Speaking for myself, I'm more than an admirer of Mr. Wilson, I've been a grateful addict for years, but I felt let down by *O Canada.* Maybe the trouble was I approached the book too much in the spirit of the hero of Walker Percy's *The Movie-Goer,* who could not feel his district was real until it was put on the silver screen. Unfortunately, not even Mr. Wilson could make Can. lit. real for me. *O Canada,* especially in its discussion of the French, is acute, even illuminating at times, but elsewhere it is too often cursory, and Edmund Wilson's approach to Canadian culture suffers from being filtered through a romantic American lens, a nostalgia for things past. I will return to this point later. Meanwhile, some notes on Mr. Wilson's notes.

MORLEY CALLAGHAN. It is Mr. Wilson's opinion that Callaghan has been unjustly neglected by his compatriots, possibly because it is difficult for them to imagine a writer of such stature living amongst them, and also because "literary mediocrity is predisposed to be spiteful to talent." Yes, yes, but it is not Canadians who have for so long neglected Callaghan, surely our most talented writer, but rather the Americans and the British. Years ago Malcolm Cowley wondered (in *Exile's Return*, I think) whatever became of Morley Callaghan, and Mr. Wilson himself observes that after Callaghan returned to Canada in the late thirties he was "quickly forgotten in the United States . . . and almost unknown in England." In all that time, Canadian publishers continued to keep Callaghan's novels and collected stories in print and serious Canadian critics continued to regard him very highly indeed. During Mr. Callaghan's lean period the c.b.c. helped to sustain him with non-literary work (panel shows, interview programmes) and *Maclean's* awarded him a $5,000 prize for an early version of *The Many-Coloured Coat*. This is not neglect. "The fact is," George Woodcock recently wrote in the *New Leader*, "that Callaghan has, if anything, been overpraised in Canada, and that, if critics there were mildly annoyed at Wilson's somewhat inapt comparisons, it was not because, as he suggests, mean spirits were trying to martyr an artist, but because the time has come to look honestly at the very uneven work of a novelist who has produced some of the best Canadian writing – and also some of the worst.

I tend, for once, to agree with the Canadian point of view. I have found many of Callaghan's novels heavy going, but I think his short stories are superb and add up to the best work ever to have come out of Canada.

HUGH MACLENNAN. Canadian intellectuals are inclined to be patronizing about MacLennan because he is a culture-hero to the Canadian middle-class. That is to say, those Canadians who find Yousuf Karsh artistic, CBC-TV documentaries about homosexuals thought-provoking, and the need for a Canadian theatre urgent, tend to be among MacLennan's most ardent readers. Mr. Wilson writes that MacLennan is a "writer strongly to be recommended to anyone who wanted to understand Canada," and I would emphatically agree with this as well as the implied criticism that he can't be recommended on purely literary grounds. He can be read with enjoyment by those who look forward to the next Morris West novel or find Stanley Kramer's movies stimulating. But there is something else. MacLennan genuinely loves Canada, he worries over it, and writes about the country with intelligence and sympathy. "He has set out," as Mr. Wilson observes, "to render in his fiction some systematic dramatization of the life of eastern Canada." Unfortunately, the upshot is often mechanical. MacLennan's characters seem to be fabricated of points-of-view rather than flesh and blood.

Mr. Wilson has not tried to be comprehensive, and so there is no consideration of the novels of Ethel Wilson or Robertson Davies, but what a pleasure it was to find Mavis Gallant's fiction deservedly praised for once. Mrs. Gallant, possibly because she has never run with the Can. lit. hounds, is generally overlooked in such studies. However, it is a pity that Mr. Wilson has not gone into the special relationship of the CBC to Canadian writing. For years, in the absence of literary magazines of quality, CBC radio (as distinct from CBC-TV which is largely imitative and inferior to American TV has run a little magazine of the air, *Anthology*; and has broadcast on one programme or another the first stories, poems, plays, and criticism of our liveliest young writers. On the other hand, it was not surprising that on the first page of *O Canada* Mr. Wilson does acknowledge a debt to Robert

Weaver, who was the originator of *Anthology* and is the editor of our most reputable literary magazine, *The Tamarack Review*.

Mr. Wilson notes the hostility among Canadians "of taste (to) the ever-increasing addiction of the popular audience to (American) popular entertainments: magazines, movies, and jazz. In the case of (American) magazines, the Canadian publishers have a serious grievance that, by bringing out special Canadian editions, such periodicals as *Time* and *Reader's Digest* divert from the Canadian magazines a good part of the national advertising. . . ." All of which, I'm afraid, only adds up to a partial truth. For, as Mr. Wilson notes elsewhere, *Maclean's*, Canada's national magazine, which flourished all too briefly under Ken Lefolii's editorship, has reverted to fight its circulation battle in a sentimental quagmire abandoned by *Sat Eve Post* long ago. Other Canadian magazines are either well-intentioned but boring, like the pathetic *Canadian Forum*, or second-rate versions of American magazines, and most Canadians of taste would rather do without all Canadian magazines, than their *Statesman*, *Esquire*, *Time*, *New Yorker*, *Spectator*, or what have you. And if Canadians were shut off from American mass culture – if, as Richard Rovere once wrote, the border was sealed tight against American junk – then the country would happily set out to produce inferior junk of its own. It must also be clearly stated that the best, as well as the worst, cultural influences on Canada, are American. We have always looked to New York, not Toronto, for our standards of excellence. New York is our cultural capital.

Finally, my fundamental quarrel with Mr. Wilson is he does not seem to have journeyed north so much to discover a country as to rediscover a vanished America. We Canadians, as I wrote in the *Spectator* years ago, are the English-speaking world's elected squares. To the British, we are the nicest, whitest Americans. To Americans, we represent a nostalgia for the unhurried horse and buggy age. In his youth, Mr. Wilson writes, he tended to imagine Canada as a vast hunting preserve, and even now he gets the impression in Canada of less worry and more leisure. Canadians, he feels, listen to one another, instead of "shooting off their faces." So it is not surprising, in this context, that Mr. Wilson found in Hugh MacLennan's book of essays, *Scotchman's Return*, "a point of view surprisingly and agreeably different from anything else" he knew in English. Let's look at just one of the essays, *Portrait of a Year*:

"The year 1955 was surely one of the loveliest years any living person can remember. Like a woman of perfect tact, she let her moods follow her natural growth in harmonious sequence. . . Through January and February she was bright, flashing and thoughtless, in March she turned teenager and dumped four feet of snow on our sidewalks. . . In June she married the countryside and at once began to produce a family. . . ."

Is this so different, I wonder, from what Mr. Wilson surely would have mocked had it appeared in the *Reader's Digest*?

In *O Canada*, Mr. Wilson has justifiably accused Canadian critics of sometimes overpraising their own writers, but hasn't he, possibly in a generous mood, applied rather less severe standards to Canadian writing than he once memorably put to Somerset Maugham's work?

Having said this much, let me add that I agree with Professor Neil Compton who wrote in *Commentary* that Edmund Wilson "wrong" still makes better reading than most critics right. And in setting out the grievances and reviewing the literature of French Canada, Mr. Wilson has written the most lucid account of a sad history for the non-specialist that I have read anywhere.

expo 67

I am an obsessive reader of fringe magazines: DOGS in Canada (" 'If people were as nice as their dogs we'd have the finest sport in the world,' observed the Old Timer."); *Police Review*, Weekly Journal of the British Police ("Ex-Supt. Arthur Williams," begins a short story by 'Flatfoot', "had served for thirty years in a provincial city Force and was now in retirement. He had never considered himself to be a sentimentalist but now, each evening, seated comfortably before the television set, puffing gently on his pipe, he invariably found his mind wandering back . . ."). I also take Manchester *Jewish Life*, *Men in Vogue*, *Toronto Life* ("As winter-time became ensconced in Toronto, party began to follow party. . . ."), and many, many more. But in 1967, in the months before I planned to return to Canada for the first time in three years, the magazine that afforded me the most pleasure was *the stage in Canada*, published monthly by the Canadian Theatre Centre in Toronto. The January issue, vintage stuff, featured the report of the Theatre Centre's professional ethics committee, a group that met under the chairmanship of one Malcolm Black. Among the ten articles in the proposed code of ethics, the ones I found the most stirring were:

2. *Observe the Golden Rule:* . . . Members ought to treat each other as they prefer to be treated. Members ought to observe the golden rule.

7. *Enhance the professional images:* Whether or not we of the Theatre continue to be viewed as "rogues and vagabonds" depends on us, and our sincere attempts to enhance our professional image.

10. *Use imagination:* As artists, we include imagination as part of our stock-in-trade . . . Members are urged, at all times, in all situations, to use imagination.

Canada, Canada. Older than Bertrand Russell. A hundred years old in 1967. "A nation like no other," begins the Centennial Library brochure, "larger than the entire continent of Europe, second in size only to Russia . . . Canada is unique."

IN MONTREAL, I read in the New York *Times*, COMPLETE ASSURANCE SPEAKS IN 2 LANGUAGES. Mrs. Charles Taschereau told the *Times* that she found it difficult to keep still. "If I have nothing else to do," she said, "I might paint a wall." Mrs. Hartland Molson described my Montreal as a city of "living within the home," except for hockey games and visiting friends, whilst Mrs. Samuel Bronfman said, "I love people, but my husband is a better judge of them." Such nice, simple people, the Canadian rich, but I found the new personalities and events baffling. On arrival, for instance, what should my attitude be toward Judy LaMarsh, the minister responsible for culture? Who was Peter Reilly? What was psychedelic TV? I wished EXPO the best, the very best, but where were they going to find enough fellow-travellers to fill the Expo Theatre for The Popular Stars of Prague on September 1st? Hungering for more information about home, I devoured the Canadian magazines, especially the intellectual ones, like *The Canadian Forum*. One month I read, "In 1965, 73,980 Canadians died of heart disease, 63,000 were seriously or totally crippled by arthritis, and 25,637 died of cancer. There were 670 who died of TB, half of them people over 70 years of age." I commit this to memory, my experience of the world has been enriched. Another month I read in the same puzzling magazine, "The 19 Supreme and County Court rooms in Toronto's new courthouse have been panelled in teak from Burma and Siam, mahogany from Africa and Honduras, oak and walnut from the U.S. and English oak. No Canadian panelling was used."

Was this, I wondered, a snippet of dialogue from a new Harold Pinter play? No. It was hard fact. Meant to make me angry, I suppose. After all, why all that snobbish British oak and war-mongering American walnut in our courthouses? Was Canadian wood wormy or something?

The truth was, I decided, weeks before leaving for Montreal, I no longer understood the idiom. Doomed to always be a foreigner in England, I was now in danger of finding Canada foreign too. After thirteen almost uninterrupted years abroad, I now realized the move I had made with such certainty at the age of twenty-three had exacted a considerable price. Some foggy, depressing nights it seemed to me that I had come full circle. Many years ago my parents emigrated from Poland to Canada, to Montreal, where I grew up ashamed of their Yiddish accents. Now I had seemingly settled in London, where my own children (spoiled, ungrateful, enjoying an easier childhood than I had, etc. etc.) found my American accent just as embarrassing.

Still, being a Canadian writer abroad offers a writer a number of built-in perks. I have, through the years, been turning over a useful penny in the why-have-you-left-Canada interview, that is to say, once a year I make a fool of myself on TV for a fee.

Most recently a breathless girl from Toronto sat in my garden, crossed her legs distractingly as the TV cameras turned, smiled cutely, and said, "I've never read anything you've written but would you say you were part of the brain-drain?"

Sure, baby. I also assure her that I'm an Angry Young Man. A black humourist. A white Negro. Anything.

"But why did you leave Canada in the first place?"

I daren't tell her that I had no girl friends. That having been born dirty-minded I had thought in London maybe, in Paris certainly, the girls. . . . Instead, I say, "Well, it was a cultural desert, wasn't it? In London, I could see the Sadlers Wells Ballet, plays by Terence Rattigan. If overcome with a need to see the Popular Stars of Prague, I could hop on a plane and jolly well see them. *In their natural environment.*"

I arrived in Montreal late in June.

"QUEEN LEADS CELEBRATIONS," ran the July 1st headline in the

Montreal Star. "Canada is 100 years young today and Queen Elizabeth is doing her royal best to make it a real blast." Dominion Day, Prime Minister Pearson declared handsomely, belonged to all of us. "Every one of you, and every Canadian before you, has had some part, however humble and unsung, in building the magnificent structure that we honour and salute today."

Mr. Pearson, once feared to be an intellectual, showed himself a most regular (dare I say all-American?) guy in a recent interview with *Macleans*. Asked who was the greatest man he had ever met, he replied: "If you mean the man – leaving my father out – who made the greatest impression on me personally, it would be Mr. Downey, a teacher in my public school in Peterborough, when I was a boy."

"Can you recall anything that you're now ashamed of?"

"Considering that I've lived 70 years, I have a reasonable immunity from guilt. But I certainly have done some things I later regretted. I cheated in geography class once when I was in Grade 6 or 7, I think, and I've never forgotten it."

Canadians, notably reticent in the past, flooded the Dominion Day newspapers with self-congratulatory ads. Typical was the full page run by Eaton's, our largest department store chain, which asked, "WHO ARE YOU, CANADA?" Roaring back came the unastonishing answer, ". . . the young giant. The young giant of the North. . . ." Without a doubt, the most imaginative of the Dominion Day ads began:

> A GROWING NATION . . .
> A GROWING PROFESSION . . .
> A GROWING FIRM . . .
>
> In just 100 years, our nation has grown to assume a leading position in the world . . . a position of which all Canadians can be justifiably proud as we observe our Centennial.
> Canadian funeral service has grown, too, always keeping in step with changing times . . . And at D.A. Collins Funeral Homes, where we've been serving for 54 out of Canada's 100 years, progress . . .

Canada, 98 years without a flag, went so far as to commission a

Toronto ad agency to produce a Centennial song. "What we needed," an executive vice-president of the agency told a reporter, "was a grabber. A stirring flag-waver that would make everybody feel, 'Gee, this is a real good country.'" Bobby Gimby, a radio jingle writer, came up with the grabber which has been a fantastic success.

CA-NA-DA

(One little two little three Canadians)

WE LOVE THEE

(Now we are twenty million)

CA-NA-DA

(Four little five little six little Provinces)

PROUD AND FREE

(Now we are ten and the Territories – sea to sea)

North, South, East, West

There'll be happy times

Church bells will ring, ring, ring

It's the hundredth anniversary of

Con-fed-er-a-tion

Ev'-ry-bo-dy sing, to-geth-er

CA-NA-DA

(Un petit deux petit trois Canadiens)

NOTRE PAY-EE (Pays)

(Maintenant nous sommes vingt millions)

CA-NA-DA

(Quatre petites cinq petites six petites Provinces)

LON-GUE VIE

(Et nous sommes dix plus les Territoires – Lon-gue vie)

Hur-rah! Vive le Canada!

Three cheers, hip, hip, hooray!

Le Centenaire!

That's the order of the day

Frère Jacques, Frère Jacques

Merrily we roll along

To-geth-er, all the way.

1967 being our big year, there was a tendency to measure all things Canadian, and so the Canadian Authors' Association sent out a questionnaire to writers asking, among other things,

What contemporary prose writer(s) has the best chance of
still being read in 2000 A.D.? ....

How many words a year do you write? ....

How many words a year do you sell? ....

As a writer what do you most often wish for: inspiration, ideas,
better research facilities, an agent, a public relations man, more
markets, higher royalties, a grant, more hours to write, etc.
....

Note: Please answer only in terms of the Canadian scene in all
questions – whether specified or not.

Enclosed was a copy of *The Canadian Author and Bookman*, the
Association's quarterly, in which I found an ad for *Yarns of the
Yukon*, by Herman G. Swerdloff, with rave reviews from *Alaska
Highway News* and *R.C.M.P. Quarterly*; and a critical study of
Margaret Lawrence (*The Stone Angel, A Jest Of God*) that began
"Margaret (Wemyss) Lawrence was born with a pen in her hand
and a story in her heart." There was also a double page spread of
poems by expatriates with the corporate title HELLO CANADA. One
of the poems was "from homesick Maggie Dominic in New
York," who wrote "This year, 1966, as prompted by Premier
Joseph R. Smallwood, is Come Home Newfoundlander Year.
Being a Newfoundlander and a writer, I was asked to compose a
poem, commemorating C.H.Y./66 for Newfoundland ... I have
been published in the United States, Canada, and most recently
India."

The C.A.A. not only held its 1967 conference at Expo, but also
summoned a Congress of Universal Writers to "deal definitively
with the role of the author (creator of fiction, interpreter of
universal truth, ambassador of good-will, agitator, reformer, pro-
pagandist, inventor of language, etc. . .)." The U.S.S.R. sent
Alexander Chakovsky, editor of the Literary Gazette, and the
Reader's Digest (Canada) Ltd. shipped us James Michener.
Already gathered in Montreal were such Canadian writers as
Bluebell Phillips, Phoebe Erskine Hyde, Fanny Shulman, Grace
Scrimgeour, Una Wardelworth, and Madeline Kent de Espinosa.
Opening night, there was a party for Universal Writers, but
though it was sponsored by the largest of Canadian distilleries,

Seagram's, nothing more potent than coffee was served. At the meeting following the party, a friend reported, the ladies stood up one by one to announce how their branch regional histories were going. It was all very dull, my friend said, until suddenly, one lady rose to announce she had just finished a book called *Ripe and Ready*. As things turned out, the lady had not, to quote the *Bookman*, "prostituted her talent by writing sex-dripping prose." *Ripe And Ready* was in fact a history of apples.

"It's just great to be a Canadian this year," as John David Hamilton wrote in the *New Statesman*. "It's as if we suddenly turned on, in the hippie sense, when our hundredth birthday arrived . . . . At any rate, we are in the midst of an earthquake of national pride – for the first time in our history." Yes; and the quake has yielded a mountain of non-books, from the reasonably priced *Life* library-like Canadian Centennial Library (*Great Canadians, Great Canadian Writing, Great Canadian Sports Stories*, etc.), through a Beginning Reader's McGraw-Hill series on the 10 provinces, to the over-priced and exceedingly pretentious *To Everything There Is A Season*, a picture book by Roloff Beny (The Viking Press, $25). Mr. Beny introduces his book, somewhat grandiosely, with a quotation from Herman Hesse. "He looked around him as if seeing the world for the first time . . . ." And yet, *To Everything There Is A Season*, like all picture books I've seen on Canada, as well as many an old calendar, manages to contain all the clichés, albeit "poetically" seen. There is, for instance, the photograph of the age-old rocks beaten into egg-shape by the timeless sea; we are given the essential snow-shrouded tree; the ripe and ready apples rotting on the ground; the obligatory field of wild flowers; the autumnal woods; the Quebec churches etc. etc. etc. The truth is that though Mr. Beny is by trade a photographer, it is his prose style that singles his volume out for special interest. Comparing himself to a contemporary Ulysses, allowing that his collection of photographs is both "retrospective and prophetic," he writes that his was a personal odyssey, a voyage of discovery and rediscovery. Mr. Beny came to Canada via "Olympian heights," risking "the son et lumière of Wagnerian thunderstorms," which is to say, like most of us, he flew. His findings however were singular. ". . . the serene stretches of the St. Lawrence recalled the sacred Ganges; the South Saskatchewan . . . was the Tague River which loops the fabled city of El Greco – Toledo . . . Ottawa, its Gothic silhouette reflected in the river, was Mont Saint Michel . . . and Calgary . . . was Teheran, which boasts the same cool, dry climate and poplar trees."

The last time I was in Montreal, my home town, was in 1964. "Québec Libre" was freshly painted on many a wall, and students were fixing stickers that read "Québec Oui Ottawa Non" on car windows. Militant French-Canadian Separatism, and not Expo, was the talking point. I had returned to Montreal, as I wrote in *Encounter* at the time, on Queen Victoria's birthday, a national holiday in Canada. A thousand policemen were required to put down a French-Canadian Separatist demonstration. Flags were burnt, a defective bomb was planted on Victoria Bridge, and a wreath was laid at the *Monument aux Patriots* which marks the spot where twelve men were executed after the 1837-38 rebellion. The city was feverish. André Laurendeau, then editor of *Le Devoir*, developed the popular theory of "Roi Nègre," that is to say that the real rulers of Quebec (the English, represented by the Federal Government in Ottawa) used a French-Canadian chieftain (former, and once all powerful, Provincial Premier Duplessis) to govern the French, just as colonial powers used African puppets to keep their tribes in order. André Malraux, in town to open a "France in Canada" exhibition, told the City Council, "France needs you. We will build the next civilization together." Malraux added that he had brought a personal message from General de Gaulle. It was that "Montreal was France's second city. He wanted this message to reach you. . . . You are not aware of the meaning you have for France. There is nowhere in the world where the spirit of France works so movingly as it does in the province of Quebec."

Naturally, this made for an uproar, so that the next day at a hastily summoned press conference Malraux said, "The mere thought that French Canada could become politically or otherwise dependent on France is a dangerous and even ridiculous one."

Since then, as we all know, De Gaulle himself has been and gone, shouting the Separatist slogan, "Vive le Québec libre!" from the balcony of Montreal City Hall, and Prime Minister Pearson, rising to the occasion for once, declared that this was "unacceptable" to the Canadian Government. I doubt that De Gaulle's outburst, enjoyable as it was to *all* French Canadians, will make more than a momentary Separatist resurgence, but it is worth noting that France has not always been so enamoured of Quebec, a province which was largely pro-Vichy in sentiment during the war, and whose flag is still the *fleur de lis*.

In the summer of 1964, André d'Allemagne, one of the leaders of the RIN (*Le Parti Républican du Québec*) told me that in his struggle for an independent state of Quebec he was opposed to violence, but, should his party be outlawed, he might be obliged to turn to it. "Like the *maquis*." D'Allemagne looked to the next Quebec provincial election in 1966 as the big test – and he wasn't the only one.

But, in 1966, the RIN which claimed 8,500 militant members, failed to win a seat. Quebec, to almost everyone's astonishment, veered to the right again. Jean Lesage's reform Liberal Government, which worked fairly well with Lester Pearson's Federal Government, also Liberal, was squeezed out and the *Union Nationale*, the late Maurice Duplessis's graft-ridden toy for so many years, was returned, with a majority of two, under Daniel Johnson, largely because Lesage was moving too quickly for the backwoods villages and townships.

This summer I returned to Montreal in time for the St. Jean Baptiste parade on June 23. St. Jean Baptiste is the patron saint of Quebec. In 1964, for the first time, he was no longer played by a boy in the annual parade. Instead, he was represented by an adult, and the sheep that had accompanied him in former years was tossed out. This summer's St. Jean Baptiste parade was a dull, tepid affair. Minor officials and French-Canadian *vedettes* riding in open cars were followed by a seemingly endless run of unimaginative floats. Certainly the mood a week before De Gaulle's visit was not one to make for double-locks in Westmount Mansions, where Montreal's richest WASPS live. If only three years ago

English-speaking Canadians were running scared, then this summer, whenever the so-called "Quiet Revolution" came up, it was as a joke. "Have you heard the one about the Pepsi (French Canadian), watching hockey on TV, who lost a hundred dollars on a Toronto goal against Montreal?" "No." "He lost fifty dollars on the goal. And another fifty on the replay." (The replay being the instant TV re-run of the goal just scored.)

In the early Sixties, French Canadians justifiably complained that while it was necessary for them to speak fluent English to qualify for most jobs, English-speaking Canadians were not obliged to know French. English Canada's haste to remedy this imbalance by hiring French Canadians, sometimes indiscriminately, has spawned another joke. A man sitting by a pool sees a lady drowning. "Help, help," she cries. The man rushes over to the French-Canadian lifeguard and shouts, "Aren't you going to do anything?" "I can't swim," he says. "What! You're a life-guard and you can't swim?" "I don't have to. I'm bilingual."

Then newly elected Quebec Premier Daniel Johnson, eager to demonstrate that he is his people's champion, has put through a decree that will make the use of French obligatory in all·inscriptions of packaged foods and tins . . . which has led to speculation among Jews about the labels on next year's matzohs.

Montreal has always seemed to me an unusually handsome and lively city, but in recent months the mounting hyperbole in Expo-inspired articles in American and British publications had made me apprehensive. A case in point is the London *Sunday Times*, whose colour supplement on Canada included a piece with the title, "Montreal: Canada's Answer to Paris, London and New York." In the same issue, Penelope Mortimer, back from a flying trip to Montreal, wrote that she had just been able "to observe the customs of some of the most lively, uninhibited, civilized, humane, and adventurous people in the world today – the Canadians. . . ." I also had serious doubts about Expo itself. If it was ludicrous but somehow touching that Canada, after ninety-eight years and an endlessly embarrassing debate in Ottawa, had voted itself a flag, it seemed exceedingly late in the day to bet 800 million dollars on so unsophisticated an idea as a world's fair dedicated to the theme of "Man and His World" (*Terres des Hommes*). Let me say at once, then, that Expo is, as they say, awfully good fun and in the best possible taste.

Even more impressive to an old Montrealer, perhaps, are the changes that Expo has wrought on the city itself. On earlier visits to Montreal, during the past twelve years, I was asked again and again if I could "recognize" the city, and of course I always could. But this time, after an absence of only three years, I was in fact overwhelmed by the difference. Suddenly, all the ambitious building of twelve years, the high-rise apartments, the downtown skyscrapers, the slum clearance projects, the elegant new metro, the Place Ville Marie, the Place des Arts, the new network of express highways, the new hotels, have added up to another city. If, for many years, the choice open to me (and other Canadian writers, painters, and film-makers living abroad) was whether to suffer home or remain an expatriate, the truth quite simply is that the choice no longer exists. Home has been pulverized, bulldozed and spilled into the St. Lawrence to create an artificial island: Isle Notre-Dame. Home, suddenly, is terrifyingly affluent. Montreal is the richest-looking city I've seen in years.

Many of the new skyscrapers, it's true, are of the familiar biscuit-box variety, but there has also been a heartening drive to restore the old quarter, Bonsecours Market, the narrow cobblestone streets that surround it, and the baroque City Hall. The antique market is booming. Montreal even publishes its very own fervent right-wing magazine, *Canada Month*. In the most recent issue, Irving Layton, the country's best known "most outspoken, exuberant and controversial" poet, came out for American policy in Vietnam. "I think the Americans are fighting this war, not because they want to overthrow Chinese communism, or for that matter, even the communism of Uncle Ho-Ho"; rather, he felt, America's sole interest was its own territorial security.

I've been in Montreal twice this year: the first time just a week before Expo opened, and it was then that I first visited the American pavilion, Buckminster Fuller's transparent geodesic sphere, which is still, to my mind, the most fascinating structure at Expo. The sphere, 20 stories high, 250 feet in diameter, the plastic skin held together by a network of triangulated aluminum tubes, is a delight to the eye seen from any angle, inside or out; and in fact dominates the Expo grounds. The lighthearted stuff on display inside had been severly criticized by the time I visited the sphere a second time, late in June, and the PR man who escorted me, explained: "We try to tell all our colleagues in the media that this is not an exhibition. It's only meant to show the spirit symbolic of – well, you know."

Camp, he might have said. There are enormous stills of vintage Hollywood stars (Bogart, Gable, Joan Crawford) and a screen that runs great scenes from past movies, such as the chariot race from *Ben Hur*. On the next floor there is a display of pop art (Dine, Lichtenstein, Johns, Warhol), some pictures running as much as ten stories high. The highest floor is taken up with the inevitable display of spacecraft and paraphernalia. Briefly, it is the softest of all possible sells, radiating self-confidence.

The chunky British pavilion, designed by Sir Basil Spence is meant to be self-mocking, and so it is, sometimes unintentionally. Embossed in concrete on an outside wall stands "BRITAIN," pointedly without the "GREAT," though the French inscription reads "GRANDE BRETAGNE." Inside, the glossy scenes of contemporary British life suggest what Malcolm Muggeridge has called Sunday Supplement living taken into the third dimension. The pretty hostesses, as I'm sure you've read elsewhere, are mini-skirted and carry Union Jack handbags. If the declared theme is "The Challenge of Change" then, endearingly, it reveals how this challenge has been met. Wall charts of British geniuses list numbered photographs (Dickens, 12; Turner, 82), and before each chart there stands a computer. Theoretically, one should be able to press a number on the computer and come up with a card crammed with information. In practice, at Expo as in contemporary Britain itself, all the computers were marked TEMPORARILY OUT OF ORDER.

With other, larger powers usurping Canada's traditional self-effacing stance, it has fallen on the host nation to play it straight. Outside the Canadian pavilion there is a decidedly non-joke mountie on horseback, a sitting duck for camera-laden tourists in Bermuda shorts, who pose their children before him endlessly. Nearby stands Canada's People Tree. "As its name implies, the People Tree symbolizes the people of Canada. A stylized maple soaring to a height of 66 feet . . . it reflects the personal, occupational, and recreational activities of more than 20 million individuals. . . ." Briefly, a multi-coloured, illuminated magazine cover tree.

At the Tundra, the Canadian pavilion restaurant, it is possible to order Buffalo bouchées or whale steak. Robert Fulford of the Toronto *Star* has written that if the pavilion bar were really to represent Canada it would have to be "a pit of Muzak-drenched darkness . . . or, perhaps one of those sour-smelling enamel rooms in which waiters, wearing change aprons, slop glasses of draught beer all over the tables and patrons." Instead, it is well-lit and handsomely designed, with authentic Eskimo murals.

The most truculent of the pavilions is the small one representing embattled Cuba, plastered with photographs of the revolution and headlines that run to ATOMIC BLACKMAIL, DEATH, LSD, CIA, NAPALM. Outside the Czech pavilion, the most popular at Expo, the queues wind round and round, whole families waiting submissively in the sun for two, sometimes three, hours. Actually, none of the pavilion interiors is so gratifying as the gay Expo site itself, where I spent my most exhilarating hours simply strolling about. The improbable, even zany, pavilions are such a welcome change from the urban landscape we are all accustomed to: there are almost no cars, and the streets are astonishingly clean and quiet. Expo, only ten minutes from downtown Montreal by road or metro, lies on the island of Montreal proper, St. Helen's Island, and the artificially created island of Notre-Dame. In the early forties, when I was a boy in Montreal, St. Helen's Island was the untamed and gritty place to which working-class kids escaped for picnics and swims on sweltering summer days. There was, and still is, an old fort on the island. In 1940, Mayor Camillien Houde, a corrupt but engaging French-Canadian politician of Louisiana dimensions, was briefly interned there for advising young French Canadians not to register for conscription in a British imperialist war. Houde's companions included communists, also rounded up by the RCMP, and baffled Jewish-German refugees, sent over from England where they had been classified as enemy aliens. Now the island is tricked out with lagoons, fountains, canals, and artificial lakes.

In the months before Expo opened, probably no individual structure was more highly publicized than Habitat 67, Moshe Safdie's prefabricated design for cheap, high-density housing, the novelty being that the roof of one apartment would serve as the garden terrace of another, and that the entire unit, looking rather like a haphazard pile of children's blocks, could be assembled by a crane slipped into place alongside. Without a doubt, this angular concrete block has no place in Montreal with its long and bitter winters. Habitat 67, projecting out of a green hill in a tropical climate, could be something else again.

In any event, I think Expo is more likely to be remembered for its films rather than any particular building, save Buckminster Fuller's geodesic sphere. Films charge at you everywhere, from multiple and wrap-around screens, bounced off floors, stone walls, mirrors, and what-not. Alas, the pyrotechnics, the dazzling techniques, conceal, for the most part, nothing more than old-fashioned documentaries about life in Ontario, Czechoslovakia, Mod England, etc. The most highly touted and ambitious of these films, the Canadian National Film Board's *Labyrinth*, is also the most popular individual exhibit at Expo, its queues waiting as long as four hours.

Produced by Roman Kroiter, an undoubtedly talented filmmaker, housed in a specially constructed building, *Labyrinth* took more than two years and four and a half million dollars to make. Based on the legend of the Minotaur, *Labyrinth* is actually two films. The first, seen from multi-levelled galleries, is projected on two whopping big screens: one on a wall, the other on a sunken floor bed. At its most successful, it is tricky (child seen on wall screen throws a pebble *which lands with a splash* in a pool on floor screen) or aims at creating vertigo (suddenly, we are looking straight down a missile chute). From here, viewers grope their way through a spook-house type maze into a multi-screened theatre, wherein we learn that man comes into this world bloody and wailing and leaves in a coffin. Unfortunately, in this case it would seem that it is life that is long and art that's short. En route to the grave, we are instructed that all men are brothers (black, white, and yellow men, popping to life, simultaneously on the multi-screen) and are treated to an occasional brilliant sequence such as the crocodile hunt. But two years in the making, four and a half million dollars spent . . . the return seems both portentous and inadequate.

Finally Expo has done more for Canada's self-confidence than anything within memory. "By God, we did it! And generally we did it well," Pierre Berton wrote in *Macleans*.

"We're on the map," a friend told me. "They know who we are in New York now."

Hugo McPherson, professor of Canadian and American studies at the University of Western Ontario until recently and now head of the National Film Board, said in an interview: "We have our own 'scene' in Canada now. . . . It's no longer fashionable, the way it used to be, for Canadians to knock everything Canadian. Perhaps Expo will be the event we'll all remember as the roadmark. I think it's going to be a vast Canadianizing force, not only in Quebec but all across the country. There's a new feeling of national gaiety and pride at Expo. . . ."

Others go even further, demanding an alarmingly high emotional return from what is after all only a world's fair. A good one, maybe even the most enjoyable one ever. However, within it there lies merely the stuff of a future nostalgic musical, not the myth out of which a nation is forged. Unless it is to be a Good Taste Disneyland.

the great
comic book
heroes

"QUIET! A REVOLUTION IS BREWING," begins a recent advertisement for the *New Book of Knowledge.* "This is Gary. Age 11. He's a new breed of student. A result of the 'quiet revolution' in our schools. He's spent happy hours on his project. Away from TV. Away from horror comics. Completely absorbed. Learning! Reading about cacoons, larvae, butterfles. . . ."

No, no, Gary is no new breed. I recognize him. In my day he always did his homework immediately he came home from school. He never ate with his elbows on the table. Or peeked at his sister in the bath. Or shoplifted. Or sent unwanted pianos, ambulances, firemen, and bust developers to the class teacher, the unspeakable Miss Ornstein, who made us suffer creative games, like Information Please or Increasing Your Word Power with the *Reader's Digest.* Gary ate his spinach. He was made president of the Junior Red Cross Club and pinned The Ten Rules of Hygiene over his sink. He didn't sweat, he perspired. And he certainly never swiped a hard earned dime from his father's trousers, the price of a brand-new comic book. Oh, the smell of those new comic books! The sheer, the glossy feel! *Tip-Top, Action, Detective,* and *Famous Funnies.*

Each generation its own nostalgia, its own endearing fantasy-figures. For my generation, born into the depression, beginning to encourage and count pubic hairs during World War II, there was nothing quite like the comic books. While bigger, more mature men were cunningly turning road signs to point in the wrong direction in Sussex, standing firm at Tobruk, Sending For More Japs, holding out at Stalingrad, making atomic bombs, burning Jews and gassing Gypsies; while General ("Old Blood and Guts") Patton was opening the Anglo-American service club in London, saying, "The idea of these clubs could not be better because undoubtedly it is the destiny of the English and American people to rule the world. . . ." and Admiral William F. ("Bull") Halsey was saying off-the-record, "I hate Japs. I'm telling you men that if I met a pregnant Japanese woman, I'd kick her in the belly."; we, the young, the hope of the world, were being corrupted by the violence in comic books. Ask Dr. Frederic Wertham, who wrote in *Seduction Of the Innocent*:

". . . . a ten-year-old girl . . . asked me why I thought it was harmful to read Wonder Woman. . . . She saw in her home many good books and I took that as a starting point, explaining to her what good stories and novels were. 'Supposing,' I told her, 'you get used to eating sandwiches made with very strong seasonings, with onions and peppers and highly spiced mustard. You will lose your taste for simple bread and butter and for finer food. The same is true for reading strong comic books. If later you want to read a good novel it may describe how a young boy and girl sit together and watch the rain falling. They talk about themselves and the pages of the book describe what their innermost little thoughts are. This is what is called literature. But you will never be able to appreciate that if in comic book fashion you expect that any minute someone will appear and pitch both of them out of the window.' "

Or Kingsley Martin, who wrote that Superman was blond and saw in him the nefarious prototype of the Aryan Nazi. Never mind that Superman, the inspired creation of two Jewish boys, Jerome Siegal and Joe Shuster, was neither blond nor Aryan. It was a good theory. We were also being warped by Captain Marvel, The Human Torch, The Flash, Sheena, Queen of the Jungle, Hawkman, Plastic Man, Sub Mariner, and the Batman and Robin. Our champions; our revenge figures against what seemed a gratuitously cruel adult world.

This is not to say our street was without intellectual dissent. After all social realism was the thing, then.

"There's Tarzan in the jungle, week in and week out," Solly said, "and he never once has to shit. It's not true to life."

"What about Wonder Woman?"

"Wonder Woman's a dame, you schmock."

Wonder Woman was also a waste of time. Uncouth. Like ketchup in chicken soup. Or lighting up cigarette butts retrieved from the gutter. Reading was for improving the mind, my Aunt Ida said, and to that end she recommended *King's Row* or anything by John Gunther. Wonder Woman, according to Dr. Wertham, was a dyke as well. For boys, a frightening image. For girls, a morbid ideal. Yes, Yes, but as Jules Feiffer observes in his nostalgic *The Great Comic Book Heroes*, "Whether Wonder Woman was a lesbian's dream I do not know, but I know for a fact she was every Jewish boy's unfantasied picture of the world as it really was. You mean men weren't wicked and weak? . . . You mean women didn't have to be *stronger* than men to survive in the world? Not in my house!"

The Batman and Robin, the unsparing Dr. Wertham wrote, were also kinky. "Sometimes Batman ends up in bed injured and young Robin is shown sitting next to him. At home they lead an idyllic life. They are Bruce Wayne and 'Dick' Grayson. Bruce Wayne is described as a 'socialite' and the official relationship is that Dick is Bruce's ward. They live in sumptuous quarters with beautiful flowers in large vases. . . . Batman is sometimes shown in a dressing gown. . . . It is like a wish dream of two homosexuals living together."

Unfortunately I cannot personally vouch for the sexual proclivities of 'socialites', but I don't see anything necessarily homosexual in "beautiful flowers in large vases." This strikes me as witch-hunting. Sexual McCarthyism. Unless the aforesaid flowers were pansies, which would, I admit, just about clinch the good doctor's case. As, however, he does not specify pansies, we may reasonably assume they were another variety of flora. If so, what? Satyric rambling roses? Jewy yellow daffodils? Droopy impotent peonies? Communist-front orchids? More evidence, please.

Of more significance, perhaps, what Dr. Wertham fails to grasp is that we were already happily clued in on the sex life of our comic book heroes. As far back as 1939, publishers (less fastidious than the redoubtable Captain Maxwell) were offering, at fifty cents each, crude black and white comics which improvised pornographically on the nocturnal, even orgiastic, adventures of our champions. I speak here of GASOLINE ALLEY GANG BANG, DICK TRACY'S NIGHT OUT, BLIND DATE WITH THE DRAGON LADY, and the shocking but liberating CAPTAIN AMERICA MEETS WONDER WOMAN, all of which have long since become collector's items. It is worth pointing out, however, that I never came across anything juicy about Superman and Lois Lane, not even gossip, until dirty-minded intellectuals and Nazis had their say.

Item: Richard Kluger writes (Partisan Review, Winter 1966): "He could, of course, ravage any woman on earth (not excluding Wonder Woman, I daresay).... Beyond this, there is a tantalising if somewhat clinical and highly speculative theory about why Superman never bedded down with Lois, never really let himself get hotted up over her; Superman, remember, was the Man of Steel. Consider the consequences of supercoitus and the pursuit of The Perfect Orgasm at the highest level. So Supe, a nice guy, had to sublimate...."

Item: When Whiteman, one of the many Superman derivatives, this one published by the American Nazi Party, is asked whatever became of the original Superman, he replies: "Old Supey succumbed to the influence of Jew pornography.... It seems Superman was putting his X-ray vision to immoral use and was picked up by the vice squad as a Peeping Tom."

Superman of course was the original superhero. "Just before the doomed planet Krypton exploded to fragments, a scientist placed his infant son within an experimental rocketship, launching it toward earth!" Here Superman was discovered and finally adopted by the Kents, who gave him the name Clark. When they died "it strengthened a determination that had been growing in his mind. Clark decided he must turn his titanic strength into channels that would benefit mankind. And so was created . . . SUPERMAN, champion of the oppressed, the physical marvel, who had sworn to devote his existence to helping those in need." Because Superman was invincible, he soon became something of a bore. . . . until Mort Weisinger, a National Periodical Publications vice-president who has edited the strip since 1941, thought up an Achilles' heel for him. When exposed to fragments from the planet Krypton, Superman is shorn of his powers and reduced to mere earthly capabilities. A smooth touch, but the fact is the real Superman controversy has always centred on his assumed identity of Clark Kent, a decidely faint-hearted reporter. Kent adores Lois Lane, who has no time for him. Lois is nutty for Superman, who in true aw shucks tradition has no time for any woman. "The truth may be," Jules Feiffer writes, "that Kent existed not for purposes of the story but the reader. He is Superman's opinion of the rest of us, a pointed caricature of what we, the non-criminal element, were really like. His fake identity is our real one." Well, yes, but I'm bound to reveal there's more to it than that. Feiffer, like so many before him, has overlooked a most significant factor: The Canadian psyche.

Yes. Superman was conceived by Toronto-born Joe Shuster who originally worked not for the Daily Planet but for a newspaper called The Star, modelled on the Toronto Star. This makes his assumed identity of bland Clark Kent not merely understandable, but artistically inevitable. Kent is the archetypal middle-class Canadian WASP, superficially nice, self-effacing, but within whom there burns a hate-ball, a would-be avenger with superhuman powers, a smasher of bridges, a breaker of skyscrapers, a potential ravager of wonder women. And (may those who have scoffed at Canadian culture in the past, please take note) a universal hero. Superman, first drawn by Shuster in 1938, now appears in twenty languages. This spring, God willing, Lois Lane, who has pined for him all these years, will be married off to a reformed mad scientist,

Dr. Lex Luther. I am indebted to another aficionado, Alexander Ross, a *Maclean's* editor, for all this information. Last March Ross went to visit Joe Shuster, fifty and still single ("I have never met a girl who matched up to Lois Lane," he has said), at Forest Hills, Long Island, where he lives with his aged mother. Shuster, sadly, never did own the rights on his creation. It is the property of NPP, who say that by 1948 the legendary Shuster was no longer able to draw the strip because of failing eyesight. He was discharged and now earns a living of sorts as a free-lance cartoonist. "He is trying," Ross writes, "to paint pop art – serious comic strips – and hopes eventually to promote a one-man show in some chic Manhattan gallery." Such, Ross might have added, is the inevitable fate of the artistic innovator under capitalism.

If Superman, written and drawn by a hard-faced committee with 20-20 vision these days, continues to flourish, so do the imitations; and here it is worth noting how uncomfortably the parodies of the anarchistic left and broad Jewish humour have come to resemble the earnestly-meant propaganda of the lunatic right.

On the left, *The Realist* has for some time now been running a comic strip about Leroi Jones called Supercoon. Little Leroi becomes mighty Supercoon, threat to the virtue of white women everywhere, by uttering the magic curse, "Mother-fucker." Jones, I'm told, was so taken with this parody that he wrote the script for an animated cartoon called Supercoon which he wished to have made and released with the film version of his play *Dutchman*. It has, however, yet to be produced. On a more inane level, *Kosher Comics*, a one-shot parody, published in New York, which runs strips called The Lone Arranger (with the masked marriage broker and Tante) Tishman of the Apes, and Dick Shamus, also includes Supermax, who is called upon to defeat invaders from the planet Blech. The invaders are crazy for matzoh balls.

Meanwhile, back at American Nazi headquarters in Arlington, Va., the *Stormtrooper* magazine has recently given us Whiteman. "Jew Commies Tremble . . . Nigger Criminals Quake In Fear…Liberals Head For The Hills…Here Comes Whiteman." In his first adventure, Whiteman, whose costume is a duplicate of Supey's, except that the emblem on his chest is a swastika rather than an S, "fights an interplanetary duel with a diabolical fiend. . . . THE JEW FROM OUTER SPACE." He also does battle with SUPERCOON. In real life, Whiteman is a milkman named Lew Cor (Rockwell spelt backwards, for Nazi Commander George Lincoln Rockwell) and is transformed into Whiteman by speaking the secret words, "Lieh Geis!" "With my super-vision," Whiteman says, "I can see three niggers have been caught in the act of trying to burn down a Negro church. If they had not been caught in the act, some poor southern white man would have been blamed for it." He soon beats up the Negro arsonists ("Sweet dreams, Jigaboo."), but meanwhile, inside a mysterious spacecraft, MIGHTY MOTZA is creating SUPERCOON with an atomic reverse-ray gun. The emblem on Supercoon's chest, incidentally, is a half-peeled banana, and naturally he is no match for Whiteman, who quickly eliminates him. "So long, Supercoon! You just couldn't make the grade with your second-class brain. With my white man intelligence, I have reduced you to a super-revolting protoplasmic slime. Ugh! Looks like a vile jellyfish."

In the past, comic strips, or derivatives thereof, have been put to less extreme political purpose. All of us, I'm sure, remember the late Vicky's Supermac. Parralax, publishers of *Kosher Comics*, have also brought out *Great Society Comics*, with Super LBJ and Wonderbird; and *Bobman and Teddy Comics*, featuring the Kennedy brothers. Then day by day, in the Paris edition of *New York Herald Tribune*, *Washington Post* and hundreds of other newspapers, Steve Canyon and Buzz Sawyer risk their lives for us in Vietnam. Canyon, a more politically-conscious type than Sawyer, has recently had some sour things to say about dove-like congressmen and student peace-niks: neither fighter has yet had anything to say about Whiteman. If and when the crunch comes on the Mekong Delta, it remains an open question whether or not Buzz and Steve would accept Whiteman's support.

Canyon's political past, incidentally, is not unblemished. When he came to serve at a U.S. Air Force base in northern Canada in 1960, the Peterborough, Ont., *Examiner* took umbrage. "We have become disturbed by the political implications of the strip. The hero and his friends were on what was obviously Canadian soil, but it seemed to be entirely under the domination of American troops who were there as a first-line defence against the Russians." There was only one manly answer possible; Canadian-made strips such as Larry Brannon, a non-starter, who was to glamourize the face of Canada. In his first adventure, Brannon visited "Toronto, focus of the future, channel for the untold wealth of the north, communications centre of a vast, rich hinterland, metropolis of rare and precious metals." The last time we were asked to make do with Canadian comics was during the war years when in order to protect our balance of payments the government stopped the import of American comic books. The Canadian comic books hastily published to fill the gap were simply awful. We wouldn't have them. Banning American comic books was a typically unimaginative measure, for whatever pittance the government made up in u.s. currency, it lost in home front morale. Comics, as Feiffer has written, were our junk. Our fix. And before long a street corner black market in *Detective* and *Action* comics began to flourish. Just as we had come to the support of Americans during the prohibition years, thereby founding more than one Canadian family fortune, so the Americans now saw that we didn't go without. Customs barriers erected against a free exchange of ideas never work.

I have no quarrel with Feiffer's selection from the comics for his *The Great Comic Book Heroes*, but his text, the grammar and punctuation quirky, seemed to me somewhat thin. Feiffer is most knowledgeable, a veritable Rashi, on the origins and history of the comic books. He is at his most absorbing when he writes about his own experience as a comic book artist. He learned to draw in the schlock houses, the art schools of the business. "We were a generation," he writes. "We thought of ourselves the way the men who began the movies must have." And indeed they went to see *Citizen Kane* again and again, to study Welles's use of angle shots. Rumours spread that Welles in his turn had read and learned from the comic books. Fellini was certainly a devotee.

In the schlock houses, Feiffer writes, "Artists sat lumped in crowded rooms, knocking it out for a page rate. Pencilling, inking, lettering in the balloons for ten dollars a page, sometimes less. . . ."; decadence setting in during the war. The best men, Feiffer writes, went off to fight, hacks sprouting up everywhere. "The business stopped being thought of as a life's work and became a stepping stone. Five years in it at best, then on to better things: a daily strip, or illustrating for the *Saturday Evening Post*, or getting a job with an advertising agency. . . . By the end of the war, the men who had been colouring our childhood fantasies had become archetypes of the grown-ups who made us need to have fantasies in the first place.

But it was Dr. Wertham, with his *Seduction Of The Innocent*, who really brought an end to an era. His book led to the formation of a busybody review board and an insufferable code that amounted to the emasculation of comic books as we had known them.

1. Respect for parents, the moral code, and for honourable behaviour, shall be fostered.
2. Policemen, judges, government officials and respected institutions shall never be presented in such a way as to create disrespect for established authority.
3. In every instance, good shall triumph over evil and the criminal punished for his misdeeds.

To be fair, there were uplifting, mind-improving side-effects. Culture came to the news stands in the shape of *True Comics*, *Bible Comics*, and the unforgettable series of *Classic Comics* from which Feiffer quotes the death scene from Hamlet.

> Fear not, queen mother!
> It was Leartes
> And he shall die at my hands!
> . . . Alas! I have been poisoned
> And now I, too go
> To join my deceased father!
> I, too – I – AGGGRRRAA!

Today, men in their thirties and forties trade old comic books with other addicts and buy first issues of *Superman* and *Batman* for fifty dollars or more. Although the original boyhood appeal of the comic books was all but irresistible to my generation, I have not gone into the reasons until now for they seemed to me obvious. Superman, The Flash, The Human Torch, even Captain Marvel, were our golems. They were invulnerable, all-conquering, whereas we were puny, miserable, and defeated. They were also infinitely more reliable than real-life champions. Max Schmeling could take Joe Louis. Mickey Owen might drop that third strike. The Nazi Rats could bypass the Maginot Line, and the Yellow-Belly Japs could take Singapore, but neither dared mix it up with Captain America, the original John Bircher, endlessly decorated by FBI head J. Arthur Grover, and sponsor of the Sentinels of Liberty, to which we could all belong (regardless of race, colour or creed) by sending a dime to Timely Publications, 330 West 42nd St., N.Y., and signing a pledge (the original loyalty oath?) that read: "I solemnly pledge to uphold the principals of the Sentinels of Liberty and assist Captain America in his war against spies in the U.S.A."

Finally, many of our heroes were made of paltry stuff. The World's Mightiest Man, Powerful Champion of Justice, Captain Marvel was mere Billy Batson, newsboy, until he uttered the magic word, "Shazam!" The Flash is another case in point.

"Faster than the streak of lightning in the sky . . . Swifter than the speed of light itself . . . Fleeter than the rapidity of thought . . . is The Flash, reincarnation of the winged Mercury . . . His speed is the dismay of scientists, the joy of the oppressed — And the open mouthed wonder of the multitudes!"

Originally however he was as weak as you or I. A decidedly forlorn figure. He was Jay Garrick, "an unknown student at a midwestern university . . ." and, for my money, a Jew. The creators of The Flash, Gardner Fox and Harry Lampert, even like Arthur Miller, wrote at a time, remember, when Jews were still thinly disguised as Gentiles on the stage, in novels, and comic books. There is no doubt, for instance, that The Green Lantern has its origin in Hassidic mythology. Will Eisner's The Spirit, so much admired by Feiffer, is given to cabalistic superstitions and speaking in parables. With *The Flash,* however, we are on the brink of a new era, a liberated era. Jay Garrick is Jewish, but Reform. Semi-assimilated. In the opening frame, lovely Joan (significantly blonde) won't date him, because he is only a scrub on the university football team while Bull Tyron is already a captain. "A man of your build and brains," she says, "could be a star. . . . A scrub is just an old washwoman! You won't put your mind to football. . . !" Jay, naturally, is intellectually inclined. Probably he is taking freshman English with Leslie Fiedler. An eye-opener! Huck Finn and Nigger Jim, like Batman and Robin, are fags. Jay, however, spends most of the time in the lab with his professor. Then one day an experiment with hard water goes "Wrong." Jay, overcome by fumes, lurches forward. ("It's . . . it's . . . too much for me. . . .") He lies between life and death for weeks, coming out of it endowed with superhuman powers. "Science," the doctor explains, "knows that hard water makes a person act much quicker than ordinarily. . . . By an intake of its gases, Jay can walk, talk, run and think swifter than thought. . . . He will probably be able to outrace a bullet!! He is a freak of science!" Briefly, he is now The Flash.

How puerile, how unimaginative, today's comic strips seem by comparison. Take Rex Morgan, M.D., for instance. In my day, to be a doctor was to be surrounded by hissing test tubes and vile green gases. It was to be either a cackling villain with a secret formula that would reduce Gotham City to the size of a postage stamp or to be a noble genius, creator of behemoths who would bring hope to the oppressed multitudes. The best that can be expected of the loquacious Dr. Morgan is that he will lecture us on the hidden dangers of medicare. Or save a student from LSD addiction. There's no magic in him. He's commonplace. A bore.

writing
for
the movies

Once, it was ruled that any serious novelist or playwright who tried his hand at film-writing was a sellout. Indeed, many a novelist-turned-screenwriter next proffered a self-justifying, lid-lifting novel about Hollywood, wherein the most masculine stars were surreptitiously (not to say gratifyingly) queer, the most glamorous girls were empty inside, deep inside, but lo and behold, the writer, on the last page, had left the dream palace, fresh winds rippling through his untamed hair, to write the book-of-the-month you had just finished reading. Later, the novelist returned to Hollywood, but on *his own terms*, to do the screenplay of his novel. It was filmed frankly, outspokenly, and everybody felt better inside, deep inside.

Hollywood is one thing, London another. No better than the archetypal boss's son, I started out at the bottom in films. I got work as a reader for a studio script department. For two quid, in 1955, a reader was expected to write a ten page synopsis of a book followed by a shrewd evaluation of its film potential. Like Harold Robbin's visual, but Proust isn't. Experts, I discovered, managed to zip through and report on as many as four books a day. I never got to be an expert. One day a script editor handed me a book for which, she said, I would be paid a double fee. It was Brecht's *Mother Courage*. "The play's only sixty pages," I said. "Why can't the producer read it himself?"

I did not yet know that it was no more expected of most producers to actually read books than it was, say, of Walter O'Malley to chop down trees to make baseball bats. So I took the play home, wrote a synopsis, and mailed it off. The next morning the script editor phoned me, outraged. "But you haven't said whether or not you think it would make a good film," she said.

That ended my career as a reader, but shortly afterwards I was hired to write a script for the TV serial mill. The hero of the series was a freelance sea captain (tough, fearless, jaunty), and my script took him to Spain for some smuggling. The producer didn't like it one bit. "You call this a script? What's this here? Two guys talking. *Talking?* Yak-yak-yak for two whole pages. Where's the action?"

I bought a book with three screenplays in it by Graham Greene and set to work again. I made absolutely no plot or dialogue changes, but, whereas, a page of my first draft script read,

CARLOS: Things are very quiet here tonight. I do not like it, Nick.
 NICK: I was just wondering ...

my revised, professional version, read,

CARLOS: Things are very quiet here tonight. I do not like it, Nick.
 SOUND: *It is very quiet.*
  «CUT TO CU NICK. *He lights a cigarette. He inhales.*»
 NICK:«with a far-off, wondering look» I was just wondering ...

I had arrived. Another writer, hired to do two half-hour comedies, pilots for a possible series for Peter Sellers (Sellers, at the time, had made only one feature-length film, *The Lady Killers*), made me his collaborator. He wanted company. He executed all the routines meant for Sellers. I learned to say, "Why, that's swell. A great gag." I did the typing and brewed the tea. Eventually, we were summoned to a script conference. Present were Sellers, the director, the producer, two assistants, my collaborator, and I. We sat solemnly round an enormous table in a board room overlooking Hyde Park. Before each of us there was a pad, a pencil, and a glass of water. The producer, a tiny wizened man with pebble-glasses, told us, "Gentlemen, we are here to exchange ideas. To my right is our director. Need I say, a great talent. A talent I have engaged, I might say, for a pretty penny."

The director, who hadn't worked in years, said "I consider this series a challenge."

The rest of us were fulsomely introduced. "Now about the script. . . ." Squinting, the producer held the script no more than two inches from his face. "Page twenty-nine, boys. We've slowed down here. We need a gimmick. Well, if you saw *Love Happy* with the Marx Brothers you will recall there was a great scene in that picture. Harpo is leaning against a wall. Groucho comes by and says, what are you doing, holding up the building? Harpo nods. He moves away and the building collapses."

Sellers was silent.

"Now, boys, ours is a small budget film. What I think we could do on page twenty-nine is this. Instead of a building Mr. Sellers could be leaning against a lamp post. When he moves away," the producer said, already beginning to break up with laughter, "the lamp post falls down."

Sellers lit one cigarette off another.

"Page thirty-two, boys. Have you ever had the good fortune to see Mr. Danny Kaye, a great comedian, in *Up in Arms*?"

To my astonishment, the two films were made and distributed. I never saw them, but within months I was working on my first feature film, a mediocre thriller that required rewrites. The director wasn't jumpy, he was panic-stricken, and he insisted that I work with him at his flat every day. Together we raked each scene over and over again.

"Mn," he'd say, reading a page just ripped out of the typewriter, "jolly good. . . . Well, not bad. But would he say *that*? Is it really in character for him to say 'thank you' at that moment?"

I'd look pensive. Wearily I'd say, "I think you're on to something, you know. It *is* out of character. I think he'd say 'thanks', not 'thank you'."

"But isn't that too American-y?"

"Exactly. But that's the point. *He's American-oriented.*"

The director sometimes kept me all day without doing any writing. Nervously, he would dig out his copy of *Spotlight*, a catalogue with photographs of almost every actor and actress in the country, and solicit my opinion on casting. My opinion was worthless and, if you figured it at a day's pay, worthless and expensive.

"What would you think of John Mills?"

"He's all right."

"What do you mean all right? Are you holding something back? Do you know something?"

I swore I didn't.

"What about Jack Hawkins?"

"Sure."

"If you don't like Jack Hawkins, tell me. This is very important."

Like most novelists, I am conditioned to working for months on material I discuss with nobody, because to talk about it is to risk losing it. To adjust from that to script writing, where you are bound to meet once a week with a director or producer or both to discuss work in shaky first-draft form and work yet to be done, is more than unnerving, it's indecent. It is too much like what Truman Capote once described as group sports.

Here it is necessary to make a sharp distinction between the entertainment and the so-called art film, each presenting the novelist-turned-scriptwriter with special problems. I'd like to deal with the entertainment first because it's simpler, a straightforward street corner deal. Money is time, and writing an entertainment can buy a novelist a very sweet chunk of it.

As a general rule, the writer who adapts a thriller or a best-seller for the screen is the most lowly and expendable of technicians; in fact most take-charge, can-do producers don't feel secure until they've hired and fired one writer after another, licking the script into shape, as they say. Once I was summoned by a producer who had already hired a writer for an adventure film he was going to make. Although the writer had not yet begun work, the producer wanted to know if I could take over within twelve weeks. "What," I asked, "if the man you've got turns in a script that doesn't require more work?"

"Don't worry," the producer replied immediately, "he can only go seven innings."

Traditionally, producers are the butt of most film jokes, but in my limited dealings I've found many of them engaging and surprisingly forthright about their needs. At the moment, too, they are running touchingly scared. Commercial producers are baffled by the new films, they don't understand their success. Arty directors, writers, and actors, whom the big production units have been shunning for years, are not only making pix but some of their pix are making money. Wowsy in Denver, boffo in Cincy. Suddenly art is good biz. So now the call is out for no-saying playwrights, black humourists, and dirty-minded novelists. Only the producers still want the same old stuff, the good old stuff, but tarted up, modishly done, with frozen frames, action speeded up here, slowed down there, clichés shot through a brandy glass or as seen reflected in a cat's eye, and performers talking directly to the audience. It's much as if, instead of printing the best take, they've now begun to print the take before the last, the one wherein the actors sent up the film, including jokes that were hitherto private, limited to the studio unit. Which, incidentally, often brings the bewildered producers full circle, right back to where many of them started out years and years ago, making Robert Benchley and Edgar Kennedy shorts.

The problems involved in writing a screenplay for a seriously meant film are at once more intricate and perplexing, assuming that you are adapting somebody else's novel or play. To begin with, there's your relationship with the director. A talented director does not eat a batch of interchangeable writers; he seeks out, and is prepared to wait for, the writer he wants and who he feels, will see a screenplay through from beginning to end. He will treat a writer well, protecting him from prying, nervy producers, stars who want a peek at the script-in-progress, and other occupational hazards; but in return he demands that you do your best for him. Let me put it another way. He has actually read your novels, not your screenplays, and that's why he wants you.

Flattering. But how far do you go with such a director? How many of your own original ideas do you contribute to an adaptation of somebody else's work? I have, for instance, twice worked for Jack Clayton, on the final script for *Room At The Top* and doing the screenplay for John Le Carre's *The Looking Glass War*. I've also worked with Ted Kotcheff, writing the screenplay for *Life At The Top*. In each case, as a novelist myself, with split loyalties, I couldn't help feeling that no matter what I added to Braine or Le Carre the written work remained essentially theirs, justifiably so. Why, then, do more than adapt? Why turn in a scene or an idea or a character you've been hoarding and can very nicely use in one of your own novels?

Ideally, I used to believe the thing would be to get yourself commissioned to write an original screenplay, but I no longer think so, if only because even under the most ideal circumstances film is not a writer's medium. Film-making belongs more than anything to the writer-director, say Fellini, and, failing that, to the truly gifted director, always remembering that the director, no matter how inspired, who cannot write his own scripts is an incomplete artist.

One comes away from film-making with an increasing respect for the serious director, one who needs somebody else for the script. I speak here of the director who will not make any film, even any worthwhile film, unless it touches him. To watch him between films, devouring novels and plays, reading scripts, is to witness the anguish of a sadly dependent man. Why wait for novels or plays, then, why not get something of his own going? Sometimes he does, but the sort of writer such a director would like to commission to write an original screenplay is also the kind who presents the most difficulties. In the nature of things, he won't or can't submit an idiotic four-page synopsis to be sent on to a producer for financing. More seriously, he is loath to write an original screenplay because his ego, like the director's, tends to be discomfortingly large, and the same concept committed to a novel remains in his control.

Even given an admirable screenplay, my sympathies remain with the director. The writer leads a comparatively sheltered life, everything happens in his room. The director, equally proud and sensitive, if you like, is almost always on. Performing. Not only must he be able to con producers and flatter actors, but, ultimately, he has to be up to making his mistakes in public. The writer, having done a scene badly, rips it out of his typewriter and tries again or goes out to shoot pool for the rest of the day. Nobody knows. The director, botching a scene, does it before a crowd. His off-days are shared and possibly savoured by an entire studio unit and there may not be time or money left to re-do the scene.

As recently as 1962, Daniel Fuchs was driven to defending his abandoning fiction for the movies. "Generations to come," he wrote in Commentary, "looking back over the years, are bound to find that the best, the most solid creative effort of our decades was spent in the movies, and it's time someone came clean and said so."

Today no apologies are asked for or given. The movies have become increasingly, almost insufferably modish, especially among writers, intellectuals and students. In fact, the sort of student who once used to help put out a little magazine is nowadays more likely to be making a movie with a hand-held camera. His mentors are Antonioni, Resnais, Godard, Losey, Bergman, Fellini, Polanski, etc. He also studies corny old movies, resuscitated as camp.

This is not to say that in our student days, in the Forties, we did not cut morning lectures to watch the Marx Brothers or guffaw at inspirational war films. Say, The Pride of the Marines with John Garfield. In an early scene, as I recall it, Garfield has a Jap grenade explode smack in his face, but he continues to fire his machine gun heroically with Dane Clark's help. Shipped back to a military hospital in San Francisco, blinded but unscarred(!),

Garfield dictates a letter to his sweetheart saying he never wants to see her again, he's found somebody else. The truth is Garfield is too proud to become a burden to such a nice girl as Eleanor Parker. He tells Dane Clark bitterly, "Nobody will give a blind man a job," and Clark replies, if I remember correctly, "*I've* always had that problem. My name is Shapiro."

This era of treacly, brother-loving films, in which so many of the good guys were Jews or Negroes and nearly all the shits were WASPS, broke up with the coming of McCarthyism. Ultimately Senator McCarthy – so despicable in his time, seen to be such a buffoon in retrospect – may come to be appreciated as the most effective of cultural brooms. He did more than *Cahiers du Cinema* or *Sight & Sound* to clean the liberal hacks as well as some talented men out of Hollywood.

But the point I was really trying to make here was that we, too, laughed at jingoism, bad taste, and enjoyed slapstick: however, as we took this to be altogether unexceptionable, we did not go on and on about it. We did not enshrine it, calling it camp. I should add, incidently, that we also went in for screwing in the afternoon. Or, as a thought-provoking *Time* essayist might put it, we had sex without love. But we did not think for a minute that this made us revolutionaries. Or alienated. Or that it was happening for the first time. We put it down to being horny, that's all.

I throw this in because so much that is praised in the new, serious films is dependent on an appallingly ignorant, mistaken belief that things are happening for the first time. The truth is they are only happening for the first time on film. But I'll return to this later. First I'd like to deal with camp.

Camp, the old Batman serials revived, Randolph Scott westerns, need not detain us long. In passing, however, I must say one can only pity the American middle-class. Excoriated by a generation of novelists for being Babbits, jeered at for years for preferring the Andrew Sisters to Vivadli, A.J. Cronin to Marcel Proust, and Norman Rockwell to Picasso, they are now being howled at for giving in. While they were doing their cultural home-work (going to listen to John Mason Brown when he was in town, gobbling up

Clifton Fadiman anthologies), Vivaldi, Picasso, and Proust have gone out of style. Artists, sensing encirclement by a middle class with a newly found leisure time, have abandoned that space on the cultural board, pronouncing it square, and scampered round to attack sneakily from the rear. Now they are telling the striving middle class that there is nothing to beat the crap the self-improvers left behind them.

Well, I, too, can enjoy Monogram Pictures and other old trash, in limited quantities, but I strongly object to the new sub-literature on old pop films, if only because it is so awesomely serious and self-inflated. A case in point is *An Illustrated History of Horror Films* by Carlos Clarens, wherein the author writes, "Unlike the Western, the horror film has not attracted sufficient critical attention . . . . What seems to put the reviewers off horror films, what prevents them from surrendering their critical resistance, is the frequent – and necessary – depiction of the fantastic. But do we dismiss a painting by Fra Angelico or Max Ernst because we don't, simply won't, believe in angels and sphinxes? Is it indispensable that one be a Christian to read Saint John in Patmos?" This shaky, utterly unacceptable analogy is, I'm afraid, typical of the "critical attention" Mr. Clarens and others focus on a thin subject. Elsewhere, Mr. Clarens is obvious or superficial. "A supremely violent age like ours," he writes, "calls for an unprecedented violence in its aesthetic manifestations . . . ." But the violence of horror films is not of this age at all, but dependent on the vampire and other myths of a much earlier age and the gothic novels and ghost stories of a time we have come to look back on as enviably more secure than ours.

There are two opposite, but equally tiresome, equally humourless, ways to approach the subject of horror films: to condemn them as harmful to children, as Dr. Frederic Wertham does in his book, *Seduction of the Innocent*; or, like the unblinking Carlos Clarens, to unearth in them "hidden" sexual meanings (driving stakes into beautiful, bosomy blondes?), a necessary release, catharsis.

Mr. Clarens's History, in common with so many other books

of film criticism, is more of a catalogue than an illumination: it bulges with lists of titles and credits, plot synopsis spilling over plot synopsis. Here, for instance, you may discover that *Abbott and Costello Meet Dr. Jekyll and Mr. Hyde* was made by Universal in 1953, directed by Charles Lamont, written by Leo Leob and John Grant, photographed by George Robinson, and among the cast were Craig Stevens, John Dierkes, and Reginald Denny. *Red Planet Mars*, on the other hand, was made in 1952 by United Artists-Veiller-Hyde, directed by Harry Horner, with music by David Chudnow, and a cast that included Morris Ankrum, House Peters, and Gene Roth . . . . Such incriminating information should, perhaps, more decently be limited to friends, very good friends, and agents, but if you want it, here it is.

The main point about horror, however, is that it is more suited to literature than film, for the truly horrifying is the unseen. Monsters from outer space, vampires, cat women, Frankensteins, and zombies scare us only so long as they are off screen. Once perceived, they are comic or endearing. King Kong, for example, was a honey. The film made of King Kong was technically brilliant, but it is Mr. Clarens's error, shared with too many other writers on film, to confuse special effects, cutting-room wizardry, and other mechanical advances, with art.

The sometimes stupefying, but undeniably formative, effect years of movie-going has had on all of us has yielded at least one good comic novel, Walker Percy's *The Moviegoer*, and, more recently, what I take to be a trend-setting film, *Morgan*, wherein the hero – no, no, the anti-hero – identifies with King Kong and Tarzan.

Morgan, the work of an intelligent director and a talented writer, Karel Reisz and David Mercer respectively, was occasionally very funny indeed. It introduced Vanessa Redgrave to movie-goers, something we should all be grateful for. But the film's underlying premise was surprisingly reactionary and could not but fortify smug middlebrow clichés about the artist. Morgan is endearing, outrageous, cute, inventive, but essentially a child, an intellectual Dagwood, dependent on his wife, unable to manage his own affairs, and clearly too kooky to pronounce on politics. None of Morgan's declared fantasies are as worrying as the unspoken daydream, integral to his character, that the working-class artist is such a lovable child that the girl-with-the-Rolls-Royce, should she only meet him, would find him irresistible and take care of him for evermore. Then in *Morgan,* as in other new films, there has been a curious displacement. In earlier serious cinema, say *Brief Encounter,* the working-class was introduced as comic relief. In *Morgan* it is the middle-class that is used to do the funny bits between. There has been no broadening of vision; rather, a change in focus.

This change in focus can be traced back to *Room At The Top,* generally agreed to be such a breakthrough in British film-making. Like so many cinema break-throughs, however, it was actually a reverberation of a literary eruption.

In 1955 the last of the British colonies, the indigenous working-class, rebelled again, this time demanding not free medical care and pension schemes, already torn from the state by their elders, but a commanding voice in the arts and letters. Briefly, a new style in architecture.

At its best, this gave us Alan Sillitoe and, at its most hilarious, a reputable publisher's ad promising a new book with "all grammatical errors intact, not one spelling mistake corrected." We were also offered Braine, Wesker, Delaney, Colin Wilson and, above all, Joan Littlewood.

I come from a continent justly accused, I think, of having often confused vitality with art, but in England, for a while, it seemed to be a new rule. Joan Littlewood was a case in point.

To begin with, there was the schmaltzy, romantic notion that a working-class district would support a theatre that truly reflected the conditions of its own life. One, to my way of looking, the Theatre Workshop never did reflect these conditions truthfully, and two, to make the long dreary trip out to Stratford East was to see all your Hampstead, Swiss Cottage, and even Chelsea friends. Most of the young working-class boys I did see at the Theatre

Royal came, it seemed to me, in exactly the same spirit as I used to go to the theatre when I was a boy, that is to see some "hot stuff." Miss Littlewood – shrewdly, I think – did not disappoint. What I saw at the Theatre Royal was plenty of vitality as well as the most boorish, reactionary attitudes remembered from my childhood. By this token, to present an artist on stage is to reveal an outlandish queer (the interior decorator in *Fings Ain't Wot They Used t'Be*); the poor are warm, funny, and hate the middle-class; and, turning a West End cliché on its head, the panty straps of all the girls of Kensington Gore melt at the thought of a navvy's hot hand.

This somewhat condescending, decidedly romantic interpretation of the working-class infected *Room At The Top*, the break-through film, and the spate of "frank, outspoken" films that followed. *Saturday Night and Sunday Morning*, *A Taste of Honey*, *A Kind of Loving*, etc. etc. Six years after Jack Clayton's *Room At The Top*, in 1964, the same story was retold as comedy for the first time in *Nothing But The Best*, a bridging film that prepared us for *Morgan* and *Georgy Girl*.

In *Room At The Top*, a gritty venture, Joe Lampton (out of Balzac by way of Dreiser) had to choose between love and money, and when he opted for the latter, a moral judgement was implied. Joe had become corrupt and for this he would suffer. In *Nothing But The Best*, Jimmy Brewster, a real estate clerk with a lower middle-class background, has made his choice before the picture even begins. He's corrupt, but *gleefully* corrupt. He will not suffer soulfully for it in later life because, let's face it, we all stink. Brewster is Lampton looked at through another, more contemporary lens. While *Room At The Top* sprang from a climate of anger, Osborne, Suez and CND, *Nothing But The Best* was typical of another wind of change. It came after *Beyond The Fringe*, through *TW3* and *Private Eye* and the James Bond books.

If Lampton reaches the top by marrying the boss's daughter, he is filled with anguish at the wedding because he feels responsible for the suicide of his mistress. Brewster, who has also married into wealth, feels no such remorse because he has been obliged to murder his brother-in-law en route. All that worries him is the possibility of his crime being inconveniently discovered. With *Morgan*, we move beyond guilt or even practical fears. He, too, has found freedom by marrying a rich girl, but in a world where everybody's insane, it's the lunatic who is the sainted child. Nothing bothers Morgan.

Yet *Morgan*, whatever its shortcomings, was not without wit and did not insult the intelligence. It is clearly one of those films meant, when we hear it argued, as I imagine we have all heard it argued, that films have finally displaced the novel. To some extent, this is true. Fellini's *I Vitelloni* was not only first-rate, but a new departure. For the first time, as far as I know, a conventional first novel (young man, disgusted with values of a provincial town, leaves for the capital) was not written but instead brilliantly composed for film.

In recent years, it is fair to say that films have become less juvenile, more intelligent. An increasing number of good, satisfying films have come from Europe. There have been two or three that are arguably great. But, by and large, I am convinced that the new films are not nearly so good as they are cracked up to be, their seriousness is often spurious and half-educated, and they are being critically oversold. A major trouble is we are so grateful for even a modicum of originality on the screen, we are so flattered to be addressed directly, we seldom realize that the so-called serious film is, for the most part, shamelessly derivative, taking up a position abandoned by novelists years ago.

Meanwhile, film reviewers continue to gush. Unmissable! Electrifying! Breath-taking! Beautiful! Once-in-a-lifetime! One of those rare . . . .! Raw with genius! To open up a London or New York newspaper at the cinema pages is to discover masterpieces held over for the third month everywhere. Film masterpieces are minted at least twice a month. No other art form, as they say, can make that claim. However, it is equally true that the masterpieces in no other art form are so relentlessly up-to-date. Or date so quickly.

Before turning to consider a recent masterpiece, *Blow-Up*, it might be instructive to recall that *Brief Encounter* was once hailed as a breakthrough. So, come to think of it, was *The Best Years of Our Lives*. They seemed frank and outspoken in their sociological time, just as more recent masterpieces pull no punches in our infinitely more sizzling, sexy time.

Ads for *Blow-Up* pointedly exploited sex. They showed Vanessa Redgrave stripped to the waist, arms crossed over her breasts. "Antonioni's camera," the copy ran, "never flinches. At love without meaning. At murder without guilt. At the dazzle and the madness of London today. SHE'S DARING! EXCITING! PROVOCATIVE IN. . . ."

Cut the cake any way you like. Modern life is empty, experience is meaningless, sex deadening, but when we lined up for *Blow-Up* we knew, in our hearts, exactly what we hoped to see. A tit show. Not only that. In the scene where the anti-hero romps with two nude girls on his studio floor, there was supposed to be a crotch shot, pubic hairs that would not titillate but were indicative of our spiritual malaise, the sick times we live in, etc. etc. etc.

In these heady, permissive times, the movies have it all over your adult sex novel. The four-letter words, all spelled the same, soon pall on us, not so the breasts and private parts of stars and starlets, especially when we can ogle in the name of art, with no guilt attached, as there would be coming out into the sun after an afternoon at the nudies.

The fact is a number of so-called serious film directors have been able to con the censor, getting away with a good deal of windy talk on the subject of sex as a profound comment on our Godless time, when it is merely salacious. Not that I'm against nudity in films; it gives me a charge. Why, I am even grateful that the orgy scene has become as integral a part of so many adult films (*La Dolce Vita*, *Darling*, *The Loved One*) as freckled kids and dogs with wagging tails were to Walt Disney. What I do object to is the hot stuff going by another name.

Sydney Lumet, for instance, was able to argue successfully for a bare-breasted shot of a coloured prostitute in his ponderous, prosaic *The Pawnbroker*, claiming high purpose and, incidentally, acquiring a lot of useful publicity. Most likely, Lumet believed the shot necessary to the film, just as he obviously considered it powerful stuff to show a nude, sexy Jewish wife waiting for her SS man on her concentration camp bed. If so, he is a man of integrity who suffers, alas, from a failure of taste and imagination.

In any event, I would give a lot to sit with Jack Valenti and his bunch, or the Catholic Legion of Decency, as they deliberate – loftily, I'm sure – on whose breasts are edifying, whose lascivious. On their curious, decidedly prudish scale of values, I rather imagine Ingrid Bergman's breasts are the cleanest, whereas Raquel Welch's big boobs would come at the bottom of the scale, the very nipples being dirty-minded.

Anyway, *Blow-Up*, unflinching camera and all, promises rather more than it fulfills. Miss Redgrave, in her big scene, does cavort bare to the waist, arms uncrossed, but she always has her broad back to us. Like the supposedly torrid paperbacks of my high school days, *Blow-Up* is a tease. This is fair comment because Antonioni's film is not a flawed work of art, which would command respect, but a good commercial idea, badly realized.

The good commercial idea buried within *Blow-Up* is also its only plot thread. An immensely rich and successful photographer (David Hemmings), wandering through a London park one day, begins to snap pictures of a girl (Vanessa Redgrave) and a man romping lyrically in the distance. The girl urgently demands the film. He refuses. She goes so far as to visit his studio and offer to sleep with him. His curiosity aroused, the photographer develops the film and notices an ambiguous blur in the bushes. In *Blow-Up*'s central sequence, he enlarges this area of the print again and again, until he thinks he can identify a dead body. Has he seen a murder? The photographer returns to the park and finds the body still lying there. Back at his studio, however, he discovers that his enlargements have been stolen. At the park once more, he discovers that the body has now disappeared as well. Has he seen a murder or not? Is what we – any of us – see, true?

Within this modish framework, Antonioni has contrived to

tip his modish hat at most, if not all, "cool" concerns. The Bomb. Pot. Alienation. Queers. And joyless sexual connections, if, that is, you are willing to accept that for a young bachelor to make love to two pretty young girls on his studio floor is more Angst-ridden than fun-filled.

The thin plot aside, everything else in Blow-Up, the sequence of other events, follows an arbitrary pattern. If a fragmentary meeting in a restaurant comes after a modelling scene, then the order of the two scenes could just as easily be reversed. Sensational experiences wash over our anti-hero, but being uninvolved or cool, he never gets wet. Neither, come to think of it, does he act. "An actor," Antonioni recently said," is only one element – perhaps sometimes the most important. But the director is the only person who understands the composition. If an actor thinks he understands, he becomes the director himself, which is a great disaster."

In the same interview, with Francis Wyndham of the London Sunday Times, he went on to say:

"Life is irregular – sometimes fast, sometimes slow. It is ridiculous to impose a rhythm, as films did before the war: it may be a perfect rhythm, but it is false. Simplicity can have a place in art – but never for its own sake. There are some complicated things in life, and it is a sort of betrayal to simplify them. Today, with scientific progress teaching us to see things in a more subtle way, there is much in the world that we can't explain. We are victims of this problem, this effort to represent them.

Man is complicated. Everything has been tried, studied, analysed, cut into pieces. One could perhaps understand the moon, the universe, even the horizons of life – but man himself remains mysterious. Life is difficult. My films are true."

Yes, yes, life is irregular, sometimes fast, sometimes slow, but Blow-Up struck me as simplified and untrue. It is about attitudes, not people. Antonioni, reacting strongly to a tiresome cliché of adult films (and middlebrow stage plays and novels) of twenty years ago has not moved beyond it: he has inverted it. In the bad old days, for instance, nobody ever did anything in scene B that hadn't been motivated, "psychologically motivated," and signaled!

in scene A. Or, to look at a concrete variation of this hackneyed, mechanical approach, if our adult hero in scene A was shown to be a lousy anti-Semite, we instantly flashed back to his childhood, scene B, wherein Dr. Hymie Hymovitch overcharges his unemployed father. It was once a convention that armed with a Marxist slide rule and Freudian binoculars, there were no more mysteries, all behaviour could be explained, as (to borrow from the stage) in *Death of a Salesman*. This was oversimplified, a distortion. But it is also oversimplified and distorted to say that nothing whatsoever can be explained and all action is unmotivated and therefore meaningless. It is false and in *Blow-Up* it is taken as a licence to improvise capriciously. If God is dead, the director is lawful. Anything goes. Furthermore, we tend at first to believe in Hemming's reactions and behavior, because we actually see it. Obviously, we do not resist film as skeptically as we do books.

Which brings me to another problem; the film writer's problem. Film writing, even under the most astute director, seldom calls for the highest order of invention. On the contrary. It is usually an invitation to laziness and sleight of hand. In a novel, for example, one really must avoid the banal. I love you, she says, I love you too, he says, simply won't do. Writing for a film, however, one knows that when she (say, Monica Vitti, Julie Christie or Jane Fonda) says, I love you, she will be undoing her bra straps or, already nude, she will set to licking his ear. Then when he (say Belmondo, Michael Caine or Albert Finney) replies, I love you too, his hand will be fondling a breast or running up a leg. Who's listening? Not me, certainly. There's too much that's juicy to look at.

Similarly, stuck on an expositional scene, an obligatory scene, it is cleverness not imagination that's called for. For example, if he is explaining to her, When I was six years old my mother . . . you write into the script that this essentially boring scene should be shot while they are both in the shower or on a ferris wheel or as seen through a jagged mirror with a stripteaser reflected in it.

In recent years there has also been a substitution of art film clichés for entertainment ones, so that if once we knew that a girl who wore pearls and a cashmere twin set (Joan Fontaine, Dorothy McGuire) couldn't be immoral no matter what suspicions aroused by Hitchcock, we now grasp that any girl with a propensity for walking barefoot or in the rain or especially amid falling autumn leaves (Jeanne Moreau, Monica Vitti) can't be all bad. Similarly, David Hemmings, with his mop of curly blond hair, big sensitive eyes, and Carnaby Street clothes, can't be as boorish as his behaviour suggests. Like Belmondo, Finney, and Terence Stamp, he is the anti-hero type. Most films, no matter how supposedly serious, have failed to progress beyond asking us to identify only with the handsome and the lovely, sometimes to the utter ruination of the story, other times to the salvation of a decidedly sordid little tale.

In John Fowles' novel, *The Collector*, for instance, an unattractive young man, a pinched embittered bank clerk, wins the football pools, buys a country house, catches a beautiful girl and makes her his love prisoner. In the film the pinched young man is played by irresistible, beautiful Terence Stamp, and it is no longer credible that his love prisoner would find his advances repugnant. In *Georgy Girl*, on the other hand, we are asked to find engaging a girl who sleeps with her best friend's lover on the night she is having his baby and then marries a man twice her age for money. We find her endearing only because she is played by Lynn Redgrave, who, incidently, doesn't for a minute, as she says of herself in one scene, look like the wrong end of a bus.

Anti-heroes and heroines may be unconventionally handsome or beautiful, but handsome and beautiful they still are. Terence Stamp and David Hemmings, who look uncannily alike, currently filling the dubious office of hipsters' Andy Hardys. Meanwhile love, except as comic relief, between a short fat man and a flatchested girl is still beyond the limits of the movies.

"Perhaps Londoners won't like it," Antonioni has said of *Blow-Up*, "as they see their city in another way. It could be set in Paris or New York without losing truth. But I think London is the best place. Fashion photographers here belong to this moment. And they are without background; one doesn't know where they come from. Like the girl in my film – one never knows anything about her, not even who she is."

Blow-Up was certainly not set in the London I or my friends know, but a prettified city, a mannered place. One would not object, one would cheer in fact, if it weren't London as say Kafka's *Amerika* wasn't America, but neither does the film capture the essence of . . . well, "swinging" London, the invention of American magazines in the first place. There wasn't one exterior sequence in the film that wasn't obviously set up and strained at that. If, for example, two queers stroll down the street, walking a poodle, then they are the only two people on the street, and they are not seen in passing: attention is called, not once, but twice, putting them in italics as it were. Elsewhere, passers-by are Africans in colourful robes or nuns. Again and again, it is the stunning picture, the arresting image, that is of primary importance, just as in a musical. The scenes in *Blow-Up* which had made it such a commercial success are the sexy ones, and though I enjoyed them because they were lingered on, they could not have been lingered on for any valid artistic reason. If *Blow-Up* is a failure, it is a glossy, commercial one, not a work of art gone sadly wrong. Like too many other new "serious" films – the love scenes, frank and outspoken, the dialogue daring, as compared to earlier films – it flirts with contemporary concerns without having anything fresh to say.

the catskills

Any account of the Catskill Mountains must begin with Grossinger's. The G. On either side of the highway out of New York and into Sullivan County, a two hour drive north, one is assailed by billboards. DO A JERRY LEWIS – COME TO BROWN'S. CHANGE TO THE FLAGLER. I FOUND A HUSBAND AT THE WALDEMERE. THE RALEIGH IS ICIER, NICIER, AND SPICIER. All the Borscht Belt billboards are criss-crossed with lists of attractions, each hotel claiming the ultimate in golf courses, the latest indoor and outdoor pools, and the most tantalizing parade of stars. The countryside between the signs is ordinary, without charm. Bush land and small hills. And then finally one comes to the Grossinger billboard. All it says, *sotto voce*, is GROSSINGER'S HAS EVERYTHING.

"On a day in August, 1914, that was to take its place among the red-letter days of all history," begins a booklet published to commemorate Grossinger's 50th anniversary, "a war broke out in Europe. Its fires seared the world. . . . On a summer day of that same year, a small boarding house was opened in the Town of Liberty." The farm house was opened by Selig and Malke Grossinger to take in nine people at nine dollars a week. Fresh air for factory workers, respite for tenement dwellers. Now Grossinger's, spread over a thousand acres, can accommodate fifteen hundred guests. It represents an investment of fifteen million dollars. But to crib once more from the anniversary booklet, "The greatness of any institution cannot be measured by material size alone. The Taj Mahal cost a king's ransom but money in its intrinsic form is not a part of that structure's unequalled beauty."

Grossinger's, on first sight, looks like the consummate kibbutz. Even in the absence of arabs there is a security guard at the gate. It has its own water supply, a main building – in this case Sullivan County Tudor with picture windows – and a spill of outlying lodges named after immortals of the first Catskill Aliya, like Eddie Cantor and Milton Berle.

I checked in on a Friday afternoon in summer and crossing the terrace to my quarters stumbled on a Grossinger's Forum Of The Air in progress. Previous distinguished speakers – a reflection, as one magazine put it, of Jennie Grossinger, in whom the traditional reverence for learning remains undimmed – have included Max Lerner and Norman Cousins. This time out the lecturer was resident hypnotist Nat Fleischer, who was taking a stab at CAN LOVE SURVIVE MARRIAGE? "I have a degree in psychology," Fleischer told me, "and am now working on my doctorate."

"Where?"

"I'd rather not say."

There were about a hundred and fifty potential hecklers on the terrace. All waiting to pounce. Cigar-chumpers in Bermuda shorts and ladies ready with an alternative of the New York *Post* on their laps. "Men are past their peak at twenty-five," Fleischer shouted into the microphone, "but ladies reach theirs much later and stay on a plateau, *while the men are tobogganing downhill.*" One man hooted, another guffawed, but many ladies clapped approval. "You think," Fleischer said, "the love of the baby for his momma is natural – *no!*" A man, holding a silver foil sun reflector to his face, dozed off. The lady beside him fanned herself with *From Russia, With Love.* "In order to remain sane," Fleischer continued, "what do we need? ALL OF US. Even at sixty and seventy. LOVE. A little bit of love. If you've been married for twenty-five years you shouldn't take your wife for granted. Be considerate."

A lady under a tangle of curlers bounced up and said, "I've

been married twenty-nine years and my husband doesn't take me for granted."

This alarmed a sunken-bellied man in the back row. He didn't join in the warm applause. Instead he stood up to peer at the lady. "I'd like to meet her husband." Sitting down again, he added, "The shmock."

There was to be a get-together for singles in the evening, but the prospects did not look dazzling. A truculent man sitting beside me in the bar said, "I dunno. I swim this morning. I swim this afternoon – indoors, outdoors – my God, what a collection! When are all the beauties checking in?"

I decided to take a stroll before dinner. The five lobbies at Grossinger's are nicely panelled in pine, but the effect is somewhat undermined by the presence of plastic plants everywhere. There is plastic sweet corn for sale in the shop beside the Olympic-size outdoor pool and plastic grapes are available in the Mon Ami Gift and Sundry Shop in the main building. Among those whose pictures hang on The Wall Of Fame are Cardinal Spellman and Yogi Berra, Irving Berlin, Governors Harriman and Rockefeller, Ralph Bunche, Zero Mostel, and Herman Wouk. The indoor pool, stunningly simple in design, still smelled so strongly of disinfectants that I was reminded of the more modest "Y" pool of my boyhood. I fled. Grossinger's has its own post office and is able to stamp all mail "Grossinger, N.Y." There is also Grossinger Lake, "for your tranquil togetherness"; and 18-hole golf course; stables; an outdoor artificial ice rink; a ski trail and toboggan run; a His'n Her's health club; and of course a landing strip adjoining the hotel, the Jennie Grossinger Field.

The ladies had transformed themselves for dinner. Gone were the curlers, out came the minks. "Jewish security blankets," a guest, watching the parade with me, called the wraps, but fondly, with that sense of self-ridicule that redeems Grossinger's and, incidentally, makes it the most slippery of places to write about.

I suppose it would be easiest, and not unjustified, to present the Catskills as a cartoon. A Disneyland with knishes. After all, everywhere you turn the detail is bizarre. At the Concord, for instance, a long hall of picture windows overlooks a parking lot. There are rooms that come with two adjoining bathrooms. ("It's a gimmick. People like it. They talk about it.") All the leading hotels now have indoor ice skating rinks because, as the lady who runs The Laurels told me, our guests find it too cold to skate outside. True, they have not yet poured concrete into the natural lakes to build artificial filtered pools above, but, short of that, every new convenience conspires to protect guests from the countryside. Most large hotels, for instance, link outlying lodges to the main building through a system of glassed-in and sometimes even subterranean passages, all in the costly cause of protecting people from the not notoriously fierce Catskills outdoors.

What I'm getting at is that by a none too cunning process of selected detail one can make Grossinger's, the Catskills, and the people who go there, appear totally grotesque. One doesn't, because there's more to it than that. Nothing, on the other hand, can prevent Sullivan County from seeming outlandish, for outlandish it certainly is, and it would be condescending, the most suspect sort of liberalism, to overlook this and instead celebrate, say, Jennie Grossinger's maudlin "warmth" or "traditional reverence" for bogus learning.

Something else. The archetypal Grossinger's guest belongs to the most frequently fired at class of American Jews. Even as Commentary sends out another patrol of short story writers the Partisan Review irregulars are waiting in the bushes, bayonets drawn. Saul Bellow is watching, Alfred Kazin is ruminating, Norman Mailer is ready with his flick-knife, and who knows what manner of trip wires the next generation of Jewish writers is laying out at this very moment. Was there ever a group so pursued by such an unsentimental platoon of chroniclers? So plagued by moralists? So blamed for making money? Before them came the luftmensh, the impecunious dreamers – tailors, cutters, corner grocers – so adored by Bernard Malamud. After them came Phillip Roth's confident college boys on the trot, Americans who just happen to have had a Jewish upbringing. But this generation between, this unlovely spiky bunch that climbed with the rest of middle-class America out of the depression into a pot of prosperity, is the least liked by literary Jews. In a Clifford Odets' play they were the rotters. The rent-collectors. Next Jerome Weidman carved them up and then along came Budd Schulberg and Irwin Shaw. In fact in all this time only Herman Wouk, armed with but a slingshot of clichés, has come to their defense. More of an embarrassment, I'd say, than a shield.

Well now here they are at Grossinger's, sitting ducks for satire. Manna for sociologists. Here they are, breathless, but at play, so to speak, suffering sour stomach and cancer scares, one Israeli bond drive after another, unmarriageable daughters and sons gone off to help the Negroes overcome in Mississippi. Grossinger's is their dream of plenty realized, but if you find it funny, larger than life, then so do the regulars. In fact there is no deflating remark I could make about minks or match-making that has not already been made by visiting comedians or guests. Furthermore, for an innocent goy to even think some of the things said at Grossinger's would be to invite the wrath of the B'nai Brith Anti-Defamation League.

At Grossinger's, guests are offered the traditional foods, but in super-abundance, which may not have been the case for many of them in the early years. Here, too, are the big TV comics, only this is their real audience and they appreciate it. They reveal the authentic joke behind the bland story they had to tell on TV because Yiddish punch-lines do not make for happy Neilson ratings.

The "ole swimmin' hole," as one Catskill ad says, was never like this. Or to quote from an ad for Kutsher's Country Club, "You wouldn't have liked The Garden of Eden anyway – it didn't have a golf course. Kutsher's, on the other hand. . . ." There are all the knishes a man can eat and, at Brown's Hotel, they are made more palatable by being called "Roulade of Fresh Chicken Livers. In the same spirit, the familiar chicken soup with *lockshen* has been reborn "essence of chicken broth with fine noodles" on yet another menu.

The food at Grossinger's, the best I ate in the Catskills, is delicious if you like traditional kosher cooking. But entering the vast dining room, which seats some 1600 guests, creates an agonizing moment for singles. "The older men want young girls," David Geivel, the head waiter told me, "and the girls want presentable men. They want to line up a date for New York where they sit alone all week. They've only got two days, you know, so they've got to make it fast. After each meal they're always wanting to switch tables. The standard complaint from the men runs... 'even when the girls are talking to me, they're looking over my shoulder to the dentist at the next table. Why should I ask her for a date, such an eye-roamer.' "

I picked up a copy of the daily *Tattler* at my table and saw how, given one bewitching trip through the hotel Gestetner, the painfully shy old maid and the flat-chested girl and the good-natured lump were transformed into "sparkling, captivating" Barbara, Ida, "the fun-loving frolicker"; and Miriam, "a charm-laden lass who makes a visit to table 20F a must." I also noted that among other "typewriter boys" who had stayed at "the G." there was Paddy Chayefsky and Paul Gallico. Dore Schary was a former editor of the *Tattler* and Shelley Winters, Betty Garrett, and Robert Alda had all once worked on the special staff. Students from all over the United States still compete for jobs at the hotel. They can clear as much as a hundred and fifty dollars a week and, as they say at the G., be nice to your bus boy, next year when he graduates he may treat your ulcer. My companions at the table included two forlorn bachelors, a teenager with a flirtatious aunt, and a bejeweled and wizened widow in her sixties. "I hate to waste all this food," the widow said, "it's such a crime. My dog should be here he'd have a wonderful time."

"Where is he?"

"Dead," she said, false eyelashes fluttering, just as the loud-speaker crackled and the get-together for singles was announced. "Single people only, please."

The teenager turned on her aunt. "Are you going to dance with Ray again?"

"Why not? He's excellent."

"Sure, sure. Only he's a *faigele*." A homosexual.

"Did you see the girl in the Mexican squaw blanket? She told her mother, 'I'm going to the singles. If I don't come back to the room tonight you'll know I'm engaged.' What an optimist!"

The singles get-together was thinly attended. A disaster. Bachelors looked in, muttered, pulled faces, and departed in pairs. The ladies in their finery were abandoned in the vast ballroom to the flatteries of staff members, twisting in turn with the hair dresser and the dance teacher, each of whom had an eye for tomorrow's trade. My truculent friend of the afternoon had resumed his station at the bar. "Hey," he said, turning on a "G-man" (a staff member), "where'd you get all those dogs? You got a contract with New York City maybe they send you all the losers?"

The G-man, his manner reverent, told me that this bar was the very place where Eddie Cantor had discovered Eddie Fisher, who was then just another unknown singing with the band. "If you had told me in those days that Fisher would get within even ten feet of Elizabeth Taylor –" He stopped short, overcome. "The rest," he said, "is history."

Ladies began to file into the Terrace Room, the husbands trailing after them with the mink stoles now slung nonchalantly over their arms. Another All-Star Friday Nite Revue had finished in the Playhouse.

"What was it like?" somebody asked.

"Aw. It goes with the *gefilte* fish."

Now the spotlight was turned on the Prentice Minner Four. Minner, a talented and militant Negro, began with a rousing civil liberties song. He sang, "From San Francisco to New York Island, this is your land and mine."

"Do you know Shadrack?" somebody called out.

"Old Man River?"

"What about Tzena Tzena?"

Minner compromised. He sang Tzena Tzena, a hora, but with new lyrics. CORE lyrics.

A G-man went over to talk to my truculent friend at the bar.

"You can't sit down at a table," he said, "and say to a lady you've just met that she's, um, well-stacked. It's not refined." He was told he would have to change his table again.

"Alright. o.k. I like women. So that makes me a louse."

I retired early, with my g. fact sheets. More than 700,000 gallons of water, I read, are required to fill the outdoor pool. g. dancing masters, Tony and Lucille, introduced the mambo to this country. Henry Cabot Lodge has, as they say, graced the g. roster. So has Robert Kennedy. Others I might have rubbed shoulders with are Baron Edmund de Rothschild and Rocky Marciano. It was Damon Runyon who first called Grossinger's "Lindy's with trees." Nine world boxing champions have trained for title bouts at the hotel. Barney Ross, who was surely the first othodox Jew to become lightweight champion, "scrupulously abjured the general frolicsome air that pervaded his camp" in 1934. Not so goy-boy, Ingemar Johansson, the last champ to train at Grossinger's.

In the morning I decided to forgo the recommended early riser's appetizer, a baked Idaho potato; I also passed up herring baked and fried, waffles and watermelon, blueberries, strawberries, bagels and lox, and French toast. I settled for orange juice and coffee and slipped outside for a fast cigarette. (Smoking is forbidden on the sabbath, from sunset Friday to sundown Saturday, in the dining room and the main lobbies.) Lou Goldstein, Director of Daytime Social Activities, was running his famous game of Simon Says on the terrace. There were at least a hundred eager players and twice as many hecklers. "Simon says put up your hands. Simon says bend forward from the waist. The *waist*, lady. You got one? oi. *That's* bending? What's your name?"

"Mn Mn," through buttoned lips.

"Alright. Simon says what's your name?"

"Sylvia."

"Now that's a good Jewish name. The names they have these days. Désirée. Drexel. Where are you from?"

"Philadelphia."

"Out."

A man cupped his hands to his mouth and called out, "Tell us the one about the two *goyim*."

"We don't use that word here. There are people of every faith at Grossinger's. In fact, we get all kinds here. (Alright, lady. Sit down. We saw the outfit.) Last year a lady stands here and I say to her what do you think of sex. Sex, she says, it's a fine department store." Goldstein announced a horse shoe toss for the men, but there were no takers. "Listen here," he said, "at Grossinger's you don't work. You toss the horse shoe but a member of our staff picks it up. Also you throw downhill. Alright, athletes, follow me."

I stayed behind for a demonstration on how to apply make-up. A volunteer was called for, a plump matron stepped forward, and was helped on to a make-shift platform by the beautician. "Now," he began, "I know that some of you are worried about the expression lines round your mouth. Well, this putty if applied correctly will fill all the crevices. . . . There, notice the difference on the right side of the lady's face?"

"No."

"*I'm* sure the ladies in the first four rows can notice."

Grossinger's has everything – and a myth. The myth of Jennie, LIVING SYMBOL "HOTEL WITH A HEART" runs a typical Grossinger News headline. There are photographs everywhere of Jennie with celebrities. "A local landmark," says a Grossinger's brochure, "is the famous smile of the beloved Jennie." A romantic but mediocre oil painting of Jennie hangs in the main lobby. There has been a song called Jennie and she has appeared on This Is Your Life, an occasion so thrilling that as a special treat on rainy days guests are sometimes allowed to watch a rerun of the tape. But Jennie, now in her seventies, can no longer personally bless all the honeymoon couples who come to the hotel. Neither can she "drift serenely" through the vast dining room as often as she used to, and so a younger lady, Mrs. Sylvia Jacobs, now fills many of Jennie's offices. Mrs. Jacobs, in charge of Guest Relations, is seldom caught without a smile. "Jennie," she told me, "loves all human beings, regardless of race, colour, or creed. Nobody else has her vision and charm. She personifies the grace and dignity of a great lady."

Jennie herself picked Mrs. Jacobs to succeed her as hostess at the G.

"God, I think, gives people certain gifts – God-given things like a voice," Mrs. Jacobs said. "Well, I was born into this business. In fifty years I am the one who comes closest to personifying the vision of Jennie Grossinger. The proof of the pudding is my identification here." Just in case further proof was required, Mrs. Jacobs showed me letters from guests, tributes to her match-making and joy-spreading powers. You are, one letter testified, T-E-R-R-I-F-I-C. You have an atomic personality. "There's tradition," she said, "and natural beauty and panoramic views in abundance here. We don't need Milton Berle. At Grossinger's, a seventy-five dollar a week stenographer can rub shoulders with a millionaire. This is an important facet of our activities, you know."

"Do you deal with many complaints?" I asked.

Mrs. Jacobs melted me with a smile. "A complaint isn't a problem – it's a challenge. I thank people for their complaints."

Mrs. Jacobs took me on a tour of Jennie's house, Joy Cottage, which is next door to Millionaire's Cottage and across the road from Pop's Cottage. A signed photograph of Chaim Weizmann, first president of Israel, rested on the piano, and a photograph of Jack Benny, also autographed, stood on the table alongside. One wall was covered from ceiling to floor with plaques. Inter-faith awards and woman-of-the-year citations, including The Noble Woman of the Year Award from the Baltimore Noble Ladies' Aid Society. There was also a Certificate of Honour from *Wisdom* magazine. "Jennie," Mrs. Jacobs said, "is such a modest woman. She is always studying, an hour a day, and if she meets a woman with a degree she is simply overcome. . . ." Jennie has only one degree of her own. An Honorary Doctor of Humanities awarded to her by Wilberforce University, Ohio, in 1959. "I've never seen Jennie so moved," Mrs. Jacobs said, "as when she was awarded that degree."

Mrs. Jacobs offered me a box of cookies to sustain me for my fifteen minute drive to "over there" – *dorten*, as they say in Yiddish – the Concord.

If Jennie Grossinger is the Dr. Schweitzer of the Catskills then Arthur Winarick must be counted its Dr. Strangelove. Winarick, once a barber, made his fortune with Jeris Hair Tonic, acquired the Concord for $10,000 in 1935, and is still, as they say, its guiding genuis. He is in his seventies. On first meeting I was foolish enough to ask him if he had ever been to any of Europe's luxury resorts. "Garages with drapes," he said. "Warehouses."

A guest intruded; he wore a baseball cap with sunglasses fastened to the peak. "What's the matter, Winarick, you only put up one new building this year?"

"Three."

One of them is that "exciting new sno-time rendezvous," King Arthur's Court, "where every boy is a Galahad or a Lancelot and every damsel a Guinevere or a fair Elaine." Winarick, an obsessive builder, once asked comedian Zero Mostel, "What else can I do? What more can I add?"

"An indoor jungle, Arthur. Hunting for tigers under glass. On *shabus* the hunters could wear *yarmulkas*." Skullcaps.

It is unlikely, however, that anyone at the Concord would ever wear a skullcap, for to drive from the G. to *dorten* is to leap a Jewish generation; it is to quit a *haimeshe* (homey) place, however schmaltzy, for chrome and concrete. The sweet but professional people-lovers of one hotel yield to the computer-like efficiency of another. The Concord, for instance, also has a problem with singles, but I would guess that there is less table-changing. Singles and marrieds, youngs and olds, are identified by different coloured pins plugged into a war plan of the dining room.

The Concord is the largest and most opulent of the Catskill resorts. "Today," Walter Winchell recently wrote, "it does 30 million Bux a year." It's a fantastic place. A luxury liner permanently in dry dock. Nine storeys high with an enormous lobby, a sweep of red-carpeted stairway, and endless corridors leading here, there, and everywhere, the Concord can cope with 2,500 guests who can, I'm assured, consume 9,000 *latkas* and ten tons of meat a day. Ornate chandeliers drip from the ceiling of the main lobby. The largest of the hotel's three nightclubs, the Imperial Room, seats 2,500 people. But it is dangerous to attempt a physical description of the hotel. For even as I checked in, the main dining room was making way for a still larger one, and it is just possible that since I left, the five inter-connecting convention halls have been opened up and converted into an indoor spring training camp for the Mets. Nothing's impossible. "Years ago," a staff member told me, "a guest told Winarick you call this a room, at home I have a toilet nicer than such a room. And Winarick saw that he was right and began to build. 'We're going to give them city living in the country,' he said. Look at it this way. Everybody has the sun. Where do we go from there?"

Where they went was to build three golf courses, the last with 18 holes; hire five orchestras and initiate a big-name nightclub policy (Milton Berle, Sammy Davis Jr., Judy Garland, Jimmy Durante, etc.); install a resident graphologist in one lobby ("Larry Hilton needs no introduction for his humorous Chalk-talks. . . .") and a security officer, with revolver and bullet belt, to sit tall on his air-cushion before the barred vault in another; hire the most in life-guards, Director of Water Activities, Buster Crabbe ("This magnificent outdoor pool," Crabbe recently wrote, "makes all other pools look like the swimming hole I used to take Jane and the chimps to. . . ."); buy a machine, the first in the Catskills, to spew artificial and multi-coloured snow on the ski runs ("We had to cut out the coloured stuff, some people were allergic to it."); and construct a shopping arcade, known as Little Fifth Avenue, in the lower lobby.

Mac Kinsbrunner, the genial resident manager, took me on a tour beginning with the shopping arcade. A sign read:

SHOW YOUR TALENT
Everyone's Doing It
PAINT A PICTURE YOURSELF
The Spin Art Shop
50 cents
5 x 7 oil painting
Only Non Allergic Paints Used

Next door, Tony and Marcia promised you could walk in and dance out doing the twist or the bossanova or pachanga or cha-cha.

"We've got five million bucks worth of stuff under construction here right now. People don't come to the mountains for a rest any more," Kinsbrunner said, "they want *tummel*."

Tummel in Yiddish means noise and the old-time non-stop Catskill comics were known as *tummlers* or noise-makers.

"In the old days, you know, we used to go in for calisthenics, but no more. People are older. Golf, O.K., but – well I'll tell you something – in these hotels we cater to what I call food-cholics. Anyway I used to run it – the calisthenics – one day I'm illustrating the pump, the bicycle pump exercise for fat people – you know, in-out, in-out – zoom – her guts come spilling out. A fat lady. Right out. There went one year's profits, no more calisthenics."

We went to take a look at the health club. THRU THESE PORTALS, a sign read, Pass The Cleanest People In The World. "I had that put up," Kinsbrunner said. "I used to be a school teacher."

Another sign read:

FENCE FOR FUN
Mons. Octave Ponchez
Develop Poise – Grace – Physical Fitness

In the club for singles, Kinsbrunner said, "Sure they're trouble. If a single doesn't hook up here she goes back to New York and says the food was bad. She doesn't say she's a dog. Me, I always tell them you should have been here last weekend. Boy."

The Concord, indeed most of the Catskill resorts, now do a considerable out-of-season convention business. While I was staying at the hotel a group of insurance agents and their wives, coming from just about every state in the union, was whooping it up. *Their* theme-sign read:

ALL THAT GLITTERS
IS NOT GOLD
EXCEPT ANNUITIES

Groups representing different sales areas got into gay costumes to march into the dining room for dinner. The men wore cardboard moustaches and Panama hats at rakish angles, and their wives wiggled shyly in hula skirts. Once inside the dining room they all rose to sing a punchy sales song to the tune of "Mac the Knife", from *The Threepenny Opera* by Bertold Brecht and Kurt Weill. It began, "We're behind you/Old Jack Regan/To make Mutual number one. . . ."Then they bowed their heads in prayer for the company and held up lit sparklers for the singing of the national anthem.

The Concord is surrounded by a wire fence. It employs some thirty security men. But MacKinsbrunner, for one, is in favour of allowing outsiders to stroll through the hotel on Sundays. "Lots of them," he told me "can't afford the Concord yet. People come up in the world they want to show it, you know. They want other people to know they can afford it here. So let them come and look. It gives them something to work toward, something to look up to."

The Concord must loom tallest from any one of a thousand *kochaleins* (literally "cook-alone's") and bungalow colonies that still operate in Sullivan County. Like Itzik's Rooms or the Bon-Repos or Altman's Cottages. Altman's is run by Ephraim Weisse, a most engaging man, a refugee, who has survived four concentration camps. "The air is the only thing that's good in the Catskills," Ephraim said. "Business? It's murder. I need this bungalow colony like I need a hole in the head." He shrugged, grinning. "I survived Hitler, I'll outlast the Catskills."

Other large hotels, not as celebrated as Grossinger's or the Concord, tend to specialize. The Raleigh, for instance, has five bands and goes in for young couples. LIVE 'LA DOLCE VITA' (the sweet life), the ads run, AT THE RALEIGH. "We got the young swingers here," the proprietor told me.

Brown's, another opulent place, is more of a family hotel. Jerry Lewis was once on their social staff and he still figures in most of their advertisements. Brown's is very publicity-conscious. Instead of playing Simon Says or the Concord variation, Simon

Sez, they play Brown's Says. In fact as I entered the hotel lobby a member of the social staff was entertaining a group of ladies. "The name of the game," he called out, "is not bingo. It's BROWN's. You win you yell out BROWN's."

Mrs. Brown told me that many distinguished people had stayed at her hotel. "Among them, Jayne Mansfield and Mr. Haggerty." Bernie Miller, tummler-in-residence, took me to see the hotel's pride, The Jerry Lewis Theatre-Club. "Lots of big stars were embryos here," he said.

Of all the hotels I visited in the Catskills only The Laurels does not serve kosher food and is actually built on a lake. Sackett Lake. But, oddly enough, neither the dining room nor the most expensive bedrooms overlook the lake, and, as at the other leading resorts, there are pools inside and out, a skating rink, a health club, and a nightclub or two. "People won't make their own fun any more," said Arlene Damen, the young lady who runs the hotel with her husband. "Years ago, the young people here used to go in for midnight swims, now they're afraid it might ruin their hairdos. Today nobody lives like it's the mountains."

Finally, two lingering memories of the Sullivan County Catskills.

As I left the Laurels I actually saw a young couple lying under a sun lamp by the heated indoor pool on a day that was nice enough for swimming in the lake outside the picture window.

At Brown's, where THERE'S MORE OF EVERYTHING, a considerable number of guests ignored the endless run of facilities to sit on the balcony that overlooked the highway and watch the cars go by, the people come and go. Obviously, there's still nothing like the front-door stoop as long as passers-by know that you don't have to sit there, that you can afford everything inside.

this year
in
jerusalem

AN ISRAELI JOURNAL
MARCH 31, 1962

Outside, it was balmy, marvelously bright and blue; and what with London's sodden skies and bone-chilling damp only eight hours behind me, I began to feel elated. The shuttlebus to Tel Aviv, a Volkswagen, was driven by a rotund Ethiopian Jew. "How do you like it in Israel?" he asked immediately.

"I only just got here," I said.

The other passenger in the bus, an American boy with buck-teeth, said, "I've been here for three days. Leaving tomorrow. Tonight I'm going to see *Breakfast At Tiffany's*."

"Did you come all this way to see movies?" I asked.

"But it's a very good movie. I'm on a world tour, you know."

On the Allenby Road, boys and girls in uniform, kids with transistors clapped to their ears, lottery-ticket sellers, youngsters wearing tiny knitted skullcaps fastened to their heads with a bobby pin, passed to and fro. At the corner of Ben Yehudah, a young man leaned against an MG spitting out poppy seeds. The wizened street vendors, the fruit juice and bagel men, all looked Arabic to me. Actually, most of them were North African Jews. Two American ladies with winged sunglasses and gaily-patterned skirts passed with a click-clack of bracelets.

"But have you heard their English yet, Sadie?"

"No."

"So help me, they speak better than us. They speak like the British."

The Yiddish restaurant I stopped at was typical of its kind anywhere. Wine-stained linen tablecloths and toothpicks in brandy glasses, the familiar sour shuffling old waiter with his shirt-tail hanging out, and here and there satisfied men sucking their teeth absently. "Sit down," somebody said. It was Mr. Berman, who had sat immediately in front of me on the flight from London. "This is your first time in Israel?"

"Yes it is," I said, excited.

"All cities are the same, you know. A main street . . . hotels, restaurants . . . and everybody out to clip you. Here they're champion clippers. Me, I'm in sporting goods. I sell guns, sleeping bags, tents." He laughed, wiped his spoon on the edge of the tablecloth, and began to chop his strawberries in sour cream. "You'd never catch me spending a night in a sleeping bag. People are crazy. I should complain." Mr. Berman told me he was leaving for Tokyo tomorrow. "The girls in Tokyo are the best. They're ugly but you can get used to them. Used to them? It's easy. They wait on you hand and foot."

Bill Arad, an Israeli acquaintance, took me to the California, a café favoured by young journalists and artists. I told him I intended to look up Uri Avnery, the editor of *Ha'Olem Haze*.

"He's a pornographer," Arad said. "Clever, but irresponsible. Don't believe anything he tells you about Israel."

Arad introduced me to another journalist. Shlomo. "Do you really call yourself 'Mordecai' in Canada?" Shlomo asked, making it sound like an act of defiance.

"But it's my name," I said, feeling stupid.

"Really? In Canada! Isn't that nice!"

The American boy with buck teeth was waiting at the bus stop. "How was the movie?" I asked.

"It was really something. I'm on a world tour, you know."

"You told me."

"I leave for Bombay at three o'clock tomorrow afternoon."

What's playing in Bombay, man? But I didn't say it. Instead, I said, "Enjoy yourself."

"I'll only be there overnight."

It was not yet midnight; I decided to give the Hotel Avia's Jet Club, Open Nightly, a whirl. The bartender turned out to be a painter and an admirer of Uri Avnery. "The government," he said, "would rather hang him than Eichmann. Shimon Peres hates him."

Peres, then Assistant Minister of Defence, was one of Avnery's targets. It was Ha'Olem Haze (This World) that first revealed Israeli-made guns were being used by the Portuguese against the natives in Angola. The bartender was distressed because, to his mind, Israel had become identified in the Middle East with repressive colonial powers. "Uri," he said, "was the only journalist here with guts enough to come out for an independent Algeria. The other papers stuck by France and the alliance."

The bartender assured me that Israel kept a cultural attaché in Stockholm whose sole purpose was to lobby for a Nobel Prize for S. Y. Agnon. "Buber would have got one last year," he said, "but Hammerskjold died as he was translating him."

Each country its own cultural problems. Retiring to my room, I read in the Herald-Tribune that Chicago had taken Montreal in the third game of the Stanley Cup semi-finals. Mikita had figured in four goals, Beliveau had done nothing.

It was extremely hot. I considered taking a bath, but the sign over my sink restrained me.

> HELP US TO IRRIGATE THE NEGEV!
> SAVE WATER!
> Public Committee For Water Saving

I couldn't sleep, so thrilled was I to be in Israel. Eretz Yisrael. Even the tourist office handout, A Visitor's Guide To Israel, had a characteristic warmth to it. "Let's hope not, but should you require medical attention such services are easily obtainable. . . ." All my life I seem to have been heading for, and postponing, my trip to Israel. In 1936, when I was five years old, my maternal grandfather, a hasidic rabbi, bought land in Holy Jerusalem. He

166

intended for all of us to immigrate. He died, we didn't go. When I was in high school I joined Habonim, the Labour-Zionist youth movement. On Friday evenings we listened to impassioned speeches about soil redemption, we saw movies glorifying life on the kibbutz, and danced the hora until our bodies ached. Early Sunday mornings we were out ringing doorbells for the Jewish National Fund, shaking tin boxes under uprooted sleepy faces, righteously demanding quarters, dimes, and nickels to help reclaim our desert in Eretz. Our choir sung stirring songs at fundraising rallies. In the summertime we went to a camp in a mosquito-ridden Laurentian valley, heard more speakers, studied Hebrew and, in the absence of Arabs, watched out for fishy-looking French Canadians.

When fighting broke out in Israel, following the Proclamation of Independence on May 14, 1948, I lied about my age and joined the Canadian Reserve Army, thinking how rich it would be to have Canada train me to fight the British in Eretz, but in the end I decided to finish high school instead.

If I could put what I felt about Israel into one image I would say the news photo of Ben-Gurion, taken on his arrival in Canada. It shows that grumpy knot of a Polish Jew reviewing an honour guard of Canadian Grenadier Guards. The Guards are standing rigidly at attention; Ben-Gurion's tangle of white hair hardly comes up to their chests. I have held on to that photograph because of the immense satisfaction it gives me.

Driving into Tel Aviv the next morning we slowed down for donkey-carts and motorcycle trucks, weaving through streets of machine shops and junk yards, where I saw rusty wheels and dilapidated bedsteads, all being thriftily reclaimed. It was hot, oppressively hot, and most people, very sensibly, I thought, were informally dressed. Not so the hasidic Jews, who clung to costumes more appropriate to their East European origins; streimels and kaftans and heavy woolen sweaters. Beggars lolled in the shade of the municipal synagogue. There was a man with his trousers hitched up to reveal his artificial legs and another with a hideously gnarled face.

I stopped at a cafe on Ahad Ha-Am Street. Ahad Ha-Am ("one of the people") was the pseudonym of Asher Zvi Ginsberg, an original Zionist thinker. When he settled in Tel Aviv in his later years, the street on which he lived was named after him and even closed off during his afternoon rest hours. Ahad Ha-Am died in 1927 and today his street is a busy commercial one. Suddenly I was caught up in a swirl of shrieking newspaper vendors. "M'ariv! M'ariv!" I bought a copy of the *Jerusalem Post*, and was immediately struck by a boxed notice on page one.

> We have lost our crowning glory!
>   The great rabbi
>   Nissim Benjamin Phanna
> Chief Rabbi of the City of Haifa and its
> environs, has been taken by his maker
>
> Funeral cortège will leave the Rothschild
> Hospital, Haifa (April 1, 1962) 11 A.M.
>   THE BEREAVED FAMILY

Once, impassioned Russian and Polish Jews, who were determined to settle in Palestine, made up the bulk of the country's Jewish population. Now each immigrant group presents Israel with a ready-made issue. It is accepted, for instance, that many of the new arrivals from Eastern Europe were not so anxious to come to Israel as to quit the communist states. Israel is often only a transit station for them in the yearned-for trip to America. In recent years the racial structure of the country has altered drastically. Today Kurds, North Africans, and Yemenites, who were forced – or, if you accept the Arab argument, urged by Zionist agents – to leave their homelands, account for more than a third of the population, many of them having been literally lifted – "upon eagled wings," as in the Yemenite prophecy – from one age slap into another. The oriental Jews create Israel's thorniest social problem. Many are unskilled. Others become quickly embittered.

For there's no doubt that almost all high offices in the land are filled by Western Jews. They are the managers and executives and government officials. The Kurds, Moroccans, and Yemenites tend to become labourers, army non-coms, and clerks. The army, by mixing young people of all origins into the same units, hopes to break down suspicion and prejudice, but there is already a colour problem in Israel.

Arad and I talked about the problem as we strolled toward the new Hagana Museum. "I'm paying for it," he said. "We might as well look inside."

Like most men of his generation, Arad fought first alongside the British, in World War II, and then against them in the Israeli War of Independence. We saw Orde Wingate's uniform on display in the museum. We also looked at many of the devices that were used to conceal arms in the run to Jerusalem during the seige: an oxygen tank, three rifles inside, a boiler stuffed with a machine gun, and other seemingly innocuous agricultural equipment, all used to hide arms. I also saw my first Davidka.

When morale in Jerusalem was possibly at its lowest, as the shelling of the Holy City reached such a pitch that the projectiles were falling at the rate of one every two minutes and the Jews inside had nothing to reply with, a young engineer, David Leibovitch, invented a home-made weapon that came to be known as the Davidka. Dov Joseph, in *The Faithful City*, writes, "It was basically a kind of mortar that used a six-inch drainpipe. It fired a bomb of nails and metal scrap which exploded with some force and – what was more important – with tremendous noise and fury. It's effect on the Arabs was sometimes considerable . . . its noise frightened them almost as much as its projectiles hurt them, and it gave great heart to the people of Jerusalem when real artillery shells were falling on them."

On Sunday I moved to the Garden Hotel in Ramat Aviv. On the way to my bungalow I passed the pool, where lots of foot-weary, middle-aged tourists were sunning themselves.

"The ones I saw in Jerusalem they're poor kids," a lady said.

"They don't even know what a handkerchief is, should I chase them away? They're sneezing and blowing and coughing all the time."

A card player looked up from under his baseball cap long enough to say he was taking the tour to Eilat tomorrow.

"If you're constipated," Mr. Ginsburg told him, "the water is good for you, if not – pardon me the expression – you'll get the diarrhoea."

Mr. Ginsburg questioned each new arrival at the hotel. Shooing flies away with his rolled newspaper, pondering his toes as he curled and uncurled them, he'd ask, "And where are you from? Ah ha . . . . How long you here for? I see . . . . Longer you couldn't stay? . . . And tell me, Mr. Richler, you came over here on one of our planes, you like it? You were impressed?"

"They're Boeing 707's, you know. American-made."

"And the pilots? Eh? . . . This country it's a miracle. . . . So? The only thing I got a complaint is the hotel keepers they make the monkey business. I been here seven years ago and what they done since it's remarkable. . . . I'm not a millionaire, Mr. Richler, and I'm not poor. I spend? It's the children's money. . . . Do I want to be the richest man in the cemetery? The less I leave, the less the children have to fight over, God bless them. So, Mr. Richler, you're enjoying here?"

Sitting on the terrace of a café on the Dizengoff Street in the afternoon, I saw a crazed young man pass reading aloud from a Hebrew prayer book. Drifting up and down there was the inevitable spill of young officers and smart-looking girls in uniform. An elderly hassid shuffled from table to table, selling plastic combs, toothbrushes, and religious articles. Later, Bill Arad joined me. He told me of how success had changed the kibbutzim. Once, he said, there had been fierce ideological arguments as to whether it was a bourgeois corruption to replace the benches with chairs in the communal dining hall. Now people took their evening meal in the privacy of their own cabins. The kibbutz movement was dying, very few new ones were being started.

Arad and I drifted to the California, where we fell in with two young architects. One of them felt that the Eichmann trial was a mistake. "It dragged on and on, cheapening things."

"But we had to have a trial to educate the young. They have no respect. They don't understand why the Jews in Europe didn't rebel."

"We're a new kind of Jew here," the other architect said. "What do you think?"

The other side of Ramla, our bus began the slow winding rise and fall, rise and fall, through the bony, densely cultivated mountains. Arab villages jutted natural and ravaged as rock out of the hills. The gutted shells of armoured trucks lay overturned round bends in the narrow steepening road. Here a dried wreath hung on a charred chassis; elsewhere mounds of stone marked where a driver, trapped in the cab of his burning truck, had died an excruciating death. These ruins, spilling along the roadside, were a memorial to those who had been killed running the blockade into Jerusalem in April, 1948, when the Arabs held the vital heights of Bab el Wad and Kastel, an ancient Roman encampment and crusaders' castle which dominate the closest approaches to the city.

I took a taxi to the Hebrew University. On the way, we passed a prison block. "Today he's in there," the driver said.

"Who?"

"The Eichmann."

With Yizhok, a law clerk who had just completed a month's military duty on the Jerusalem frontier, I climbed a stony hill to an abandoned courtyard where the Israelis and Jordanians occupied sandbagged positions about a hundred yards apart. "When I served here," Yizhok said, "we used to gossip every morning and throw fruit back and forth."

From the lookout at Ramat Chen, Yizhok pointed out Mount Zion, the road to Bethlehem, the hill where Solomon's Tomb is supposed to be and, baking in the distance, the Old City of Jerusalem.

Mr. Ginsburg was lying in wait for me in the lobby of the Garden Hotel.

"Tell me, Mr. Richler, is it right I have donated so much to build this country . . . it costs a man thousands to come here . . . is it right they should charge me extra if I want a cup tea after my dinner?"

I assured him hotel keepers were the same everywhere. They would charge him extra for his tea in Italy too.

"Italy," he said, disgusted.

I told Uri Avnery about Mr. Ginsburg. "He feels unwanted in Israel," I said.

Avnery replied, "But for the middle-aged tourists from America, the old-time Zionists, this has to be paradise and no criticism is possible. They come here as to heaven on earth and they want it pure, not filled with quarreling human beings. Those old men would cut off their fingers for Israel. It's true they wouldn't settle here, but they will pay for it. They are, in a sense, the backbone of the Israeli economy." Yet, he felt, many Israelis were anti-Jewish. "As far as most people are concerned your middle-aged tourists are shirkers for living abroad. They come here to be delighted by Jewish cops, a Jewish army, well, they have to pay for it."

Avnery's office was bombed twice. He has been beaten up. He described his weekly, Ha'Olem Haze, as one-third sex and sensation, one-third Time-style, and another third modelled on l'Expresse. "Ours is the only true opposition paper," he said.

When Ha'Olem Haze revealed that Israeli arms were being used in Angola, the report was denied by the government. But Avnery insisted and other, more reputable journals were obliged to investigate the claim. They came back with concrete proof that a number of Israeli-made arms were in fact being used in Angola. "The government," Avnery said, "then explained they had sold the arms to Germany and had no idea where or how they would be used. That much is true. But what is also true is they must have known Germany had no need whatsoever for Israeli arms. . . . They buy them for show, out of guilt. . . . Also they are too clever to send their own arms for use in a dirty colonial war. So," he said, "once more we get the worst of both worlds."

We drove past Ben-Gurion's house. Ben-Gurion, who was then still prime minister, had three homes. An official residence in Jerusalem, his own house in Tel Aviv, and his desert retreat. "He really hates the desert," Avnery said, "but he is a man with a rare sense of style. If he is going to be interviewed on American TV. he flies out to the desert by helicopter a half hour before the camera crew. A half hour after they've left he's back in Tel Aviv." Avnery spoke of Ben-Gurion with warmth. "Nobody here can touch him politically."

The Israeli economy, Avnery argued, was totally unrealistic. It was based on continued help from Zionists outside the country, international loans, and German reparation money. "Israel insists on behaving as if it was not a Middle Eastern country. The Jews will continue to pretend they are a Western power. Nobody is really interested in what goes on in Alexandria and Beirut, so close by, but they will go rushing off to New York and London, where they can parade as heroes in the Jewish communities. . . . From the beginning, going back to the days of the earliest settlements, there has never been an attempt to assimilate with the Arabs."

Finally, Avnery said, "You know I love it here." He had to laugh at himself. "In London, where you live, everything's been done. Here, we'll see."

Hadera, a sun-baked industrial town on the coastal plain had the rare distinction, for Israel, of not being listed as "a place of interest" in any official guide book I'd seen. Only an hour's run from Tel Aviv along the coastal plain, the town is built on sand dunes. My cousin Shmul lived there.

I had not seen Shmul since we had both been kids together in Montreal, more than twenty years ago. Shmul's shop, the Hadera Locksmithy, was shut down. He wasn't home, either. But his wife, Sarah, let me into their apartment. Sarah was a New Yorker. She and Shmul kept a strictly orthodox home. They had met on a kibbutz, on their first trip to Israel some years ago, and then again in New York, where they were married and had a child. Shmul had learnt his locksmith's trade in New York, bought equipment on credit, and returned to scttle in Hadera with his family. I asked Sarah about the Moroccan Jews I had seen on the street.

"A problem? Wherever you have black and white there's a problem. With the least excuse," she said, "they take out a knife.... The worst are the ones from the Atlas Mountains. They've just come out of the caves."

Sarah went next door to phone another cousin of mine, Benjy, who taught at a school in Parness Channa, close-by. I hadn't seen Benjy since his bar mitzvah, eight years ago. He had grown into a tall thin introverted boy. A knitted skullcap was clasped to his head with a bobby pin; he wore a beard. Benjy explained why he had quit Canada. "I would always think that one day I'd have to leave, all the Jews would have to leave. It's not our country."

Benjy took me to a liquor store where I could buy a bottle of cognac to take back to Shmul's house. Benjy interrupted the transaction. "Is this bottle kosher?" he demanded of the shopkeeper.

"Don't worry," the shopkeeper said impatiently, "it's kosher, it's kosher."

Orthodox Jews are not enormously popular in Israel. They are considered a throwback to the ghetto. I asked Benjy if he thought the religious community had an influence out of proportion to its numbers on the secular life in the country. "Elsewhere," he said, "I would be for a separation of church and state, but this is Israel. If civil marriage was allowed there would eventually be two nations."

Sarah, like so many of the Americans and Canadians I met who had settled in Israel, retained a reserve of arrogance about the gesture. "Don't forget we didn't have to come here. Like the European Jews."

My Cousin Shmul no longer called himself Herscovitch. He had, following a popular immigrant practice, given his name a clearer Israeli ring. He was known as Shmul Shimshoni.

"When I first came to Hadera," he said, "the locals thought I was crazy. For forty years, they said, there has never been a locksmith in town, what do we need one now for? Then, out of sympathy for a new man, one by one they looked for something in their attics to bring into my shop. My first customer brought me an old suitcase, the case was locked and the key was lost, he asked if I could open it and make him a new key. When I did it for him, he was amazed. He had to go home to get money to pay me. . . . Over here, we believe in letting the other man live. As long as you're not a pig, everybody helps out. "

I returned to Jerusalem on Friday to assemble with two hundred others to hear a lecture by Y. Freiman and join the synagogue tour to Mea Shearim. Our group, predominantly American, was comprised of gaudily made-up middle-aged women and their cigar-biting men, harnessed with cameras, light meters, filters, and binoculars. Freiman, speaking above a jangle of bracelets and winding cameras, reminded us that in ancient times the priests and levites, dressed in white, used to make the pilgrimage to Jerusalem at just this time of year, between Purim and Passover. The tradition of a sabbath eve visit to Jerusalem went back to the time of Solomon's Temple.

Only Yiddish is spoken in Mea Shearim; Hebrew, the holy language, being restricted to prayers. The devout Jews of Jerusalem used to live in the Old City, close-by the Wailing Wall, but after the war in 1948 they were forced to take up residence in Mea Shearim, outside the Old City walls. The predominant influence in the quarter is Polish, but other, equally devout groups are of Persian, Yemenite, and North African extraction. Rivalry is fierce. Yemenites will not eat meat slaughtered by Polish hassids, and vice versa. One might expect that all groups were at least united by dint of their shared wait for the Messiah, but even here there is cause for dispute. The Yemenites are sure that when the Messiah comes he will be a dark Jew; the Poles insist he will surely be white, like themselves. The Jews of Mea Shearim are agreed on only one issue: none of them recognizes the state of Israel. In a typically virulent sermon Rabbi Binyamin Mendelson said, "Zionism and nationalism were responsible for the Nazi holocaust. Zionism prevented the coming of the Messiah, which would have saved Jewry."

Following Mr. Freiman's lecture we set out in buses for the narrow, squalid streets of Mea Shearim. It was an unusually hot afternoon. Poor men with glazed eyes watched as our group shuffled past, others slammed their doors as we approached. You could hardly blame them. More than once a tourist would stop, push open the door to somebody else's home, and beckon to his wife, "Look, Sylvia, it's not so bad inside."

A man clad in dirty pyjamas sat on a stone outside his house, muttering to himself. Another man, more spritely, hurried from street to street, blowing on a horn to announce the approach of the sabbath. One of our number, a fat lady with sunglasses, poked our guide with a dimpled elbow and pointed to an olive-skinned little girl playing on a square. "Is that one Jewish?" she demanded.

"Oh, yes," the guide said. "She's from Persia."

"Isn't that nice, Irving?"

Irving stopped, grinned at the retreating child, and called out, "*Shabbat shalom.*"

As we twisted up yet another cramped, narrow alley, a man said to his wife, "I'll bet you couldn't buy a lot here for any price."

"Who wants one?" she replied.

Inside one small dank synagogue, God's name was spelled out in neon lights over the Holy Ark. In the Yemenite *shul,* the last one we visited, the guide announced, "In this synagogue, the rabbi will come out and bless *all of you.*"

A decrepit old man, wearing a fez, came out and muttered a prayer.

"*You have now been blessed,*" the guide said. "Anybody who wants to shake hands with the rabbi is now free to do so. One further announcement. Please do not rush for the buses. There are enough seats for everybody."

Tovia Shlonsky, a young lecturer at the Hebrew University, told me how much he admired Bellow, Malamud, Roth. "Unfortunately, they are not much read here." He laughed, embarrassed. "The young think of them as ghetto writers."

Tovia picked me up at noon Saturday and we went to visit a

young couple he knew who had just built a house in Abu-Tor, on the frontier with Jordan, overlooking an Arab village on the mountainside and the walled Old City. As we sat on the terrace, sipping Turkish coffee, we could hear the Arabs on the other side of the frontier being summoned to prayer. "At night we can listen to their drummers," Miriam said. "Children often stray across the frontier. The Arabs are very good about it. They always give the kids candy, treat them well, and return them. But if an adult wanders across, he's beaten up. Not gratuitously," she added. "For information."

Miriam, like most intellectuals I met, wanted more traffic with the Arabs. She missed her old Moslem neighbours and regretted that Jerusalem had not been made an international city.

A youth group, wearing blue hats, neckerchiefs, shorts, and carrying packs, marched past below, singing vigorously. "Just consider our splendid view," Miriam said. "We can see the Old City, the Arabs . . . but the poor Arabs," she said, indicating the singing group below, "this is all they can see."

"I'm putting up the finest hotel in Israel," Raphael Elan told me, "the biggest hotel in the desert. It's in Beersheba – the Desert Inn. We're going to have a golf course, hot springs – the works. I'm even organizing a secret international society to be called Sons of the Desert."

Elan was a squat, thrusting man in his late thirties. His project was backed by Canadian and American capital. "It isn't charity, it's business. Either we show a profit or die."

Elan came round early Monday morning in an American station wagon to drive me to Beersheba. With him were a Lieutenant-Colonel in the Air Force, Mischa Keren, and two hotel employees, a Mrs. Raphaeli and a Mr. Gordon. About a half hour out of Tel Aviv, we wheeled inland into a lush cultivated belt. "When I used to fly over this area in 48-49," Keren said, "it was almost impossible to navigate. It was all desert. Look how green it is now."

Elan, an endless run of statistics at his command, went on and on about irrigation, reclamation, and crops. He was tiresome; but

177

the accomplishment was clearly impressive, especially once we started into the desert proper and I could see how desolate the greenery had once been.

"You have no idea what a pleasure it is for me," Keren said, "to see women and children walking casually along the highway." Before the Sinai campaign, he said, it was impossible, for this was the area where the fedayin used to strike regularly.

We started into the tribal hills of Sheik Suleiman, an encampment that went on for miles, darkened here and there by long low black tents made from sheepskins. Suleiman, a Bedouin chief, was loyal to Israel during the war, and for this he had been rewarded with tractors, land grants, and other aid: he had also become something of a standing joke in the country. The Bedouin land, on one side of the highway, looked parched, compared to the kibbutz fields on the other. "The Bedouins," Elan said, "are not interested in irrigation, which can take years to pay off. Instead of investing in the land they bury their money in jars in the earth." As we cut deeper into a landscape of blowing sands, gritty shrubs and dunes, Keren added, "This must be our breadbasket one day. This is where our country is widest."

We rocked to a stop on the outskirts of Beersheba. Protecting my face against windblown sand, I saw an enormous roadhouse rising abruptly out of the desert. "This is it," Elan said. "Later we'll have the biggest neon sign in Israel – THE DESERT INN – and you'll be able to spot us from miles away."

A chauffered car was parked alongside us. The foreman was showing a middle-aged American couple through the inn. "More stockholders," Elan said, irritated. But once he caught up with Dr. and Mrs. Edelson he was ready with a smile. "Hi."

"Say, you've got quite a baby here."

"Have you seen anything like it anywhere in Israel?"

"Quite a baby, I'd say."

"On the execution side and the investment side," Elan said, "this is the most modern hotel in Israel. The best."

We moved out of the blowing sand into a litter of planks, piping and puddles, that was to be the dining room. "The sweeping suspended stairway, the only one of its kind in Israel, will be right here."

Dr. Edelson walked to the edge to look.

"Oh, I can see you could sell anything," Mrs. Edelson said, "but it's quite a baby, isn't it, Henry?"

"It's my baby I'm selling."

"Don't you worry. You know how they say 'Next Year in Jerusalem?' Well, we'll be saying 'Next year at the Desert Inn', won't we, Henry?"

Sidestepping wet cement and exposed nails, Elan led us inside an unfinished suite. "*Shalom, shalom,*" Dr. Edelson sang out warmly to the men at work. Then, turning to Elan, he said, "They don't seem to work very fast here, do they?" Mrs. Edelson stopped, her brow wrinkled, before some nudes that had been drawn in pencil on the framework of the bathroom door. "I suppose," she said, "this does come off . . . ?"

"Sure, sure, like to see the roof?" As he led us through more muck into the second wing of the inn, Elan said, "We were not going to build this wing for another two years, then the demand for reservations was so high – "

"You hear, Henry?"

" – that we decided it would be best to *build big* before another hotel opened across the road."

We emerged in front of the inn again.

"I'm going to have a doorman with a long sword standing here. The waitresses will wear veils."

Elan took us to see the unfinished Sheik's Suite.

"You know what it says up there," Mrs. Edelson said with a smile. "It says reserved for Dr. and Mrs. Edelson."

"Want to make reservations. Speak to Mrs. Raphaeli."

"Oh, good . . . em, what will stockholders have to pay when you open up?"

"Stockholders will be allowed to sign for one month's credit. Like to see our kitchens?"

"We want to see *everything.* But . . . em, what will stockholders have to pay?"

Dr. Edelson pretended to be winding his camera.

"In the United States," Mrs. Edelson continued, "if you bring a guest and you're a stockholder, well, once a month the guest is free. . . . It's very nice, you know. It makes for good-will."

At last, Elan led the Edelsons to their car.

"Well, I'm sure you'll want to put out the red carpet for us when you open, won't you, Mr. Elan?"

"Sure will."

"Next year at the Desert Inn."

We stopped at a Rumanian restaurant in Beersheba for lunch. Lieutenant-Colonel Keren, who had flown for the Red Air Force in World War II, told me that as a young man in Russia he had hardly known or cared that he was a Jew. "When I came home after the war I found that all my family was dead. Sudden outbursts of anti-semitism here and there made me feel uncomfortable. I decided to get out. Israel was an accident, though. I might just as easily have gone to America. But I came here and I feel good. I did not feel good in Russia. I'm not what you would call a Zionist, but I feel good here."

I asked Keren about the Arabs.

"We're only twenty miles wide. Either we live in Israel or we drown in the sea. So we will fight very hard and they must know it." Still, he was troubled about the refugees on the Gaza Strip. "The way they live; it's terrible. But we have only twenty miles and then the sea. Why can't Nasser help them? We help our refugees. You saw the houses we built for them."

Mr. Gordon and Mrs. Raphaeli had other problems.

"It will be difficult for us to hire waiters," Mrs. Raphaeli said.

I asked why.

"Jews don't want to be waiters. Head waiters yes."

"Maybe some Yemenites," Mrs. Raphaeli suggested.

"We're going to have trouble."

Finally, we drove off. As we passed Shiek Suleiman's camp once more, Elan said, "I've got quite a deal with Suleiman. I'm going to take the Sons of the Desert for treks into his camp at night. They'll see Bedouin dances, eat in tents – the works. Only trouble is the camp is too close. I'll have to lead the Sons in circles on the back roads to make them think they've come a long way."

Returning to Tel Aviv, we drove through Rishon-le-Zion, the first agricultural settlement in Israel founded by the Bilu pioneers late in the 19th century.

"My grandfather was a Bilu," Elan said.

"A real Mayflower type, our Elan," Mr. Gordon said.

We had to gear down to a crawl as we approached the big, brilliantly-lit sprawl of Tel Aviv. "Well, well, well," Mrs. Raphaeli said, "I can still remember when Tel Aviv was only a street."

"Even when I first came here," Elan said, "we were just a family. Today we're a nation."

Of all the places I had seen in Israel, I came to feel most at ease in Tel Aviv. It was not nearly as beautiful as Haifa. It hadn't, like Jerusalem, a halo of history suspended above. Tel Aviv was a dirty, grubby Mediterranean city, but livelier and with more spirit than any other place I had been to in the country.

One evening, a couple of weeks after I arrived in Israel, I was invited to a dinner party in honour of a celebrated left-wing theatre director from London and the Ambassador from Ghana. Racial relations took an embarrassing turn early – the director, her eyes brimful of love, told the ambassador, "Your people are natural actors" – then broke down completely when the director asked the ambassador "to sing us a song."

Retreating hastily to another room I fell in with Migdal. Migdal, a thin severe man in his sixties, came of a French-Jewish family. A graduate in engineering from the Ecole Polytechnique, he first came to Palestine with the Foreign Legion in the twenties. There he met and married a Canadian girl, quit the Legion, and swiftly established himself as a consultant engineer and agent for British firms in Palestine, Transjordan and Syria. Migdal was equally at ease in French, Hebrew, English and four Arabic tongues. He returned to France in 1939, fought first with the French army and then with the British as a colonel. Still later he commanded a sector of Jerusalem during the seige.

Migdal turned out to dislike American Jews more vehemently

than most. "This country," he said, "restored Jewish pride with the defence of Jerusalem and then bartered it for American-Jewish aid. We can do without the fancy new Hebrew University, we didn't need the hideous Rabbinate building in Jerusalem. We could wait another ten years for such things, until we could properly afford them."

Migdal was full of contempt for the hassids of Mea Shearim.

"No sooner had the Arabs attacked than they were ready with the white flag. You'll find we're a new kind of Jew here. We don't cringe."

"I didn't come all the way to Israel," I said, "to hear that familiar anti-semitic argument. The Jews in Canada didn't cringe, either, when it was time to go to war."

"There are only two possibilities for the Jew," Migdal said. "Assimilate or come to Israel. Nothing else will do."

I asked Migdal if it was possible that the concept of a nation-state, with all it entailed, was contrary to the real Jewish tradition.

"If you mean," he said, "that we have compromised our lousy Jewish souls here then you're right. This state deals, lies, and cheats, just like any other. But we have restored Jewish pride. It's worth it."

Mr. Ginsburg was back. He had been to Haifa for a couple of days. "So, Mr. Richler, walk, walk, see, see. Quite a country, eh?"

"Mr. Ginsburg," I said, "we're surrounded by anti-semites here."

"Ah ha. So you drink a little, Richler?"

"Yes. But we're surrounded by anti-semites all the same. Ever read Koestler?"

"Who?"

"Darkness At Noon. When Rubashov is in prison, as they march him up and down the yard for afternoon exercise, the crazed man behind him, another old Bolshevik, repeats over and over again, 'This could never happen in a socialist country.' Rubashov hasn't the heart to tell him they're actually in Russia."

"Very interesting. But this . . . Koestler; he's a communist?"

"He used to sell lemonade right here in Tel Aviv."

"Oh, that's something else. That's different."

Following the example of the tourists who had come to see heaven on earth and wanted it pure, not filled with quarreling human beings. I often did not go out but lay exhausted by the poolside. Half-asleep, I used to hear their voices.

"If I send a letter to my Stuart in Toronto do I have to write 'Canada' too?"

"What are you wearing tonight – the long sleeves or the short?"

From another nest of canvas chairs.

"Do you know how long this hotel would last in Miami?"

"What?"

"Six days – and, boom, bankrupt. The waiter didn't even bring me a glass of water with my meal."

These people, not surprisingly soured by an accumulation of strange bed, bumpy drives, haggling tourist agents, and unaccustomed foods; these people, clearly dejected because not flowers but scorn was thrown in their path in Israel, had, it suddenly occurred to me, done more real good than I ever had. Tiresome, vulgar, rude they might be, but the flawed reality of Israel was a testimony to their generosity. Evidence of their achievement was everywhere. Hospitals, factories, forests, libraries, schools, mostly paid for out of tin boxes in corner groceries as well as the big donations pledged in the heady atmosphere of the country club.

Tovia Shlonsky had once said, "Why shouldn't they pay for Israel? Their money is ill-begotten anyway."

If it's ill-begotten, why accept it? And ill-begotten or not there was no reason why they had to give the money to Israel. Whatever their motives – community pressure, the need for prestige, tax exemptions – the result was the same; and they could just as easily have blown the money on a fling.

One afternoon an old settler said to me, "Why should we feel obligated because of American-Jewish patronage? It's blood money they give us. We risk our lives here. They're paying off their guilt for not coming here."

"We need Anglo-Saxons urgently," Mr. Chaifetz said, at the

annual dinner of the Association of Americans and Canadians in Israel, at the Sheraton Hotel.

It is one of the smaller ironies of Israeli life that immigrants from Canada, England, and the U.S.A., who often left their countries because the Anglo-Saxons there made them feel unwanted, are, in Israel, called Anglo-Saxons themselves. All Canadians and American settlers can and generally do retain dual citizenship – a possible out in hard times that has antagonized other Israelis. Canadian and American settlers are in fact regarded with skepticism. Too many return when they find the going difficult.

One afternoon I called on Murray Greenfield, director of the Association of Americans and Canadians in Israel. Greenfield, an explosively energetic man of thirty-six, came to Israel in 1947 to serve with Hagana, and now, his work for the Association apart, he ran two art galleries and was active in real estate. "Half the Canadians and Americans who come here leave after two-three years," he said. "If they stay longer they're hooked. Why do they quit? They think it's all going to be orange picking and dancing the hora. They go to a kibbutz and want to dance round a tree after one bushel's been picked. Another reason so many go home is, let's face it, most of them come from middle-class homes and coming here means a big drop in their standard of living. Not everybody can take it. Many others miss their close family ties. Momma."

In recent years, Aliyah from Canada and the U.S.A. had dropped to a trickle; it could be measured in hundreds.

"I'm a big fish in a small pond," Greenfield said, "and I like it. You know, my picture's in the papers here, everybody knows who I am. I'm taking part in something. In America who knows me? Who would care?"

Greenfield, along with other Anglo-Saxon settlers, including Meyer Levin, was trying to start a reform synagogue in Tel Aviv: his group was worried about anti-Americanism in the country. "This could still become an independent non-Jewish sort of state rather than a centre for world Judaism."

At Greenfield's art gallery, in the Sheraton Hotel, we ran into the fabulous Brother John, a California millionaire whose hold-ings included a vast cattle ranch, uranium mines and chemical plants. Brother John was one of a breed of Bible-reading Gentiles who wanted to take part in the rebirth of the Holy Land.

Brother John came of a long tradition. In 1844, the United States sent its first representative to Palestine, accrediting Mr. Warden Cressen as first U.S. Consul to the Turkish Court and "All The Holy Land." Cressen established himself in Jerusalem and a year later embraced Judaism and changed his name to Michael Boaz Israel. In 1847, Israel founded an agricultural colony, "God's Vineyard," on the outskirts of Jerusalem. Employ-ing the bible as a text and his own farming experience as a guide, Israel printed pamphlets and sought volunteers for his project. Within four years two hundred Americans joined him, fifty-two were Jewish and the others converts to Judaism or Protestants. The colony, born before its time, sunk into oblivion, but not the tradition.

Brother John, the most engaging of tycoons, had made it his personal mission to replenish the zoos of the Holy Land, flying in once or twice a year with the gift of a giraffe or perhaps an ele-phant. He had already dropped thousands in zany Israeli invest-ments, but he was not dismayed. "I have just earned my first Israeli dividend." Brother John, a prodigious bible student, had invested in a new chemical plant in an unpromising area because he remembered Moses had said, "Judah will dig riches from the earth here." Brother John banged his gold-tipped walking stick against a chair, he waved his stock certificate at us. "And by George they have, they sure have!"

Greenfield and I retired to the MacCabean Room at the Sheraton Hotel, where a quartet was playing a cha-cha-cha. "We're living too high in Israel these days. It's unrealistic. But this is a crazy, lucky country. When the United Jewish Appeal money began to dry up, German reparations began."

"What happens when that ends?"

"Another miracle, I suppose. Ask Brother John."

On the short flight to Eilat, we flew first over the green cultivated belt so recently torn from the desert; then Beersheba. Between Beersheba and Eilat there was only sand and rock. The
Negev. A desolate, ghostly landscape of dunes and red mountains
and hills laced together with dessicated river beds. Just before
Eilat there came Beer Ora and the copper mines that went back
to King Solomon's time.

The Hotel Eilat was managed by a young Canadian, Harvey
Goodman, thirty-one, who was brought up on Clark Street in
Montreal, just around the corner from where I used to live. Good-
man had been in Israel for ten years. "All Jews should come here.
We're hated everywhere."

I protested.

"Come on. How can you feel comfortable in Canada – with
them? They don't want us. Me, I'm always nervous in their company. Fuck 'em."

"Aren't you curious about Clark Street? Wouldn't you like to
see it again?"

"The ghetto? Yiddish mommas? The hell."

A pale, stooping old man approached our table timidly. It was
only a day before Passover, the man was a monitor from the rab-
binical council, and he had come to see whether the dietary laws
were being observed. "I could do without him," Goodman said.
"I'd like to toss him into the sea. The bastards who come here
from America don't keep kosher at home, but when they're in the
Holy Land the expect us to do it for them."

I went to watch the bronzed young fishermen haul in their
nets, which were heavy with gasping, struggling Blue Fish. The
fish kicked up a violent spray; soon the sea was red with their
blood.

The bartender at the Hotel Eilat was a Jew from Tangier.
"One day," he said, "I served a Spaniard here. A rich man. He
told me that in Madrid he was an anti-semite. He said, I didn't
believe these Jews could ever build a country so I thought I'd see
for myself. Well, now I've seen the country, he said, and it's
marvellous. It wouldn't surprise me if you people had the atom

bomb in five years and took over the Middle East in ten. But you're not Jews; you're different. You've fought for your land, you've spilled blood for it, and you have pride. The Jews in Spain would only fight for their families and their businesses. You're different here, he said," the bartender repeated proudly.

In all the bars I had been to in Israel I had never encountered anybody who had had too much to drink, so running into glassy-eyed Bernard, a local fisherman, was something of an occasion. Unfortunately, we did not hit it off. Clapping me on the back as he ordered another round, Bernard said, "I'm not personal, but I always speak frank. I don't like Canadians ... Canada is a big country, it's as small as Lichtenstein. Understand?"

"I understand. Goodman doesn't like Canada either. They hate him there."

"You know why I live here?"

"Don't tell me. It's because you're a new kind of Jew," I said, glaring at the bartender.

"I'm not Tolstoi, I'm not Christ," Bernard said. "I'm just a stinking Jew, but I like my smell."

"You smell like a lousy fisherman to me."

Bernard slapped me on the back again. "I'm a Jew," he bellowed. "Like Freud. Like Einstein."

"The hell you are. You're not a Jew like Freud or a fisherman like St. Peter. You're a fisherman like a fisherman, Bernard."

"I've never liked Canadians."

"Well, I'm a Canadian. Like Maurice Richard."

"You're a stinking Jew. Like me."

"I'm a Canadian Jew. That means I'll fight for my family and my business, if I had one, but not for my country."

"I didn't say the Spaniard was right," the bartender said. "I only work here."

"You tell your rich Spanish friend that the Jews in Canada have not only fought for their country – some of them even fought for Spain."

"You're an assimilationist," Bernard said.

"The truth is, I'm one of the Elders of Zion."

I ended an altogether unsatisfactory evening in Eilat's one nightclub, The End of the World. A busload of Swedes had preceeded me. They sat around drinking beer as two young Israeli folksingers, wearing Yemenite shirts, sang 'Take Me Back To The Red River Valley' in Hebrew.

The Anglo-Saxon kibbutz of Gesher Haziv lies in the foothills of the Galilee, a mile from the Mediterranean, five miles from the Lebanese border: it is at the opposite end of the country from Eilat. Before flying to Eilat I had booked a taxi driver in Tel Aviv to meet my return flight and drive me to the kibbutz, eighty odd miles away, as I would be travelling on the eve of Passover, not unlike the Christmas rush in Canada. "How much do you want?" I asked the driver.

"Are we getting married? Do we need a rabbi? We'll settle a price tomorrow."

We settled there and then for £50 Israeli; about seventeen dollars.

"In Canada," the driver said as we started out the next morning, "you must have your own airplane."

"I'm afraid not."

"But many Canadians have private planes," he said, affronted. "Say, one in ten."

"Not even one in ten thousand."

"You think I'd charge more?" His was the usual old, battered DeSoto with shattered windows and dented fenders. "Next to Japan," he said proudly, "we have the highest accident rate in the world."

I whistled, impressed.

"And that," he added, "is without benefit of drunken drivers. So, in Canada, you drive a Jaguar I'm sure."

"In Canada, I once drove a taxi too. Just like you."

"Can I pick up other people on the road? We could go partners."

"No."

Gesher Haziv, at first glance, suggested a summer camp in the Laurentians. A main dining hall, other administration and communal buildings, and shaded paths leading off to the cabins. The kibbutz was built on the site of an old British army rest camp in 1949 by Habonim members, drawn from Canada and the United States, in association with forty sabras. I was taken to the home of a Canadian family, Meyer and Deborah Shlossberg, where I was immediately made welcome. Capable Deborah, mother of three boys, wore trousers and men's shoes. Meyer, who was in charge of the turkey farm, came in, exhausted. "We're expecting more than a hundred guests for the seder," he said.

Passover celebrates our liberation from Egypt. At the seder, the father of the family reads aloud from the Hagadah, beginning, "We were slaves in Egypt. . . ." Traditionally, the youngest member of the family asks four questions, starting with, "Why is this night different from any other night?" For years now the kibbutz movement has been experimenting with a more militant Hagada, a revised version which includes new Israeli songs and more recent history. But kibbutzniks have found this increasingly unsatisfactory and are gradually lapsing back towards the traditional Hagada.

The seder, at Gesher Haziv, was conducted admirably by Bill Kofsky of Montreal. After the meal, there was an hour's break, allowing the children to be put to bed and the tables to be cleared. I was invited to an American couple's cabin for coffee and cake. David's wife said, "Some things you can't modernize. You know what I miss? I miss my father's jokes."

David and his wife work extremely hard. I asked them if they weren't resentful of visiting freeloaders, like me.

"As long as they don't take moving pictures in the dining room like last year we don't mind. We're not monkeys in a zoo here."

Bill Kofsky, a reserved, intelligent man in his mid-thirties, has been at Gesher Haziv since it was founded in 1949. His wife's American; they have two children. In Gesher Haziv, children live with their families, which is a radical departure in kibbutz living, an experiment that has been closely watched by other communal farms. "Originally," Kofsky said, "it was felt that we were going to create a new man for a new society and so it was necessary to protect the kids from the ghetto mentality of their parents. We might unconsciously taint them. It was best to leave them to their teachers. But somehow," Kofsky said, fondling the child on his lap, "it just didn't work out. Other kibbutzim would like to follow us, but it means rebuilding, they'd have to add extra rooms to the cabins, and there isn't always money."

The one hundred and twenty founders of Gesher Haziv lived in tents for the first year. The next year, whilst they were still clearing the fields and as yet had no income, they moved into temporary shacks, and the following year they borrowed money to build their permanent dwellings. "That was how our financial troubles started," Deborah said. "We're still paying interest on these houses."

When the young, unproven kibbutz wanted to borrow money they had to resort to the black market, where interest rates were as high as thirty per cent. Further loans have been negotiated to buy equipment and against the occasional crop failure. "The result," Kofsky said, "is that we now put in a fifth of our working day just to pay off interest."

Debts aside, the problems of Gesher Haziv were considerable. "First of all," Kofsky said, "there's the big turnover in people. Let's say a new guy comes out here with a wife and kids, maybe we build a house for him, we certainly clothe and school his kids. It takes a new guy six months before he's any good in the fields, and all that time we lose the labour of another man, the guy who's training him. Well, O.K. But maybe six months later the guy ups and returns to Canada or moves to the city. . . . Or let's say, we decide to go in for cotton. We train a guy, he becomes our cotton expert, and a year later he moves off and we're in trouble with cotton."

The practice of even modified socialism on the kibbutz exacts a toll. As everybody is theoretically equal on the kibbutz all members are elected to offices of authority (secretary, farm supervisor) for limited periods only. This is supposed to make for a built-in safeguard against the development of two classes: the workers and the bosses. "But the result," Kofsky said, "is not altogether satisfactory. It takes six months to train a secretary, a year passes, and we have to train another. We lose a lot in efficiency. Also, in spite of our efforts, we find the same personalities turning up again and again in the bigger, responsible jobs."

Gesher Haziv, like many other kibbutzim, has been unable to make a financial success of agriculture, an industry somewhat dependent on cheap labour at harvest time, so the kibbutz was feeling its way into industry and would even hire casual labour, a definite break with kibbutz dogma. One Anglo-Saxon kibbutz, Urim, had built a knife factory: Gesher Haziv was going to manufacture turkey sausage and was hopefully building a tourist hotel. HAVE AN UNUSUAL HOLIDAY – SEE LIFE ON A KIBBUTZ.

Kibbutzniks were distressed by their decline in status. "At one time," Deborah said, "you could walk into town just as you are, and people would point you out with envy and pride. There goes a kibbutznik. . . . But not today. Today we're looked at as characters. We don't dare go into town without dressing up and putting on make-up."

Kofsky said, "Once we were considered the élite, today we're looked on as hayseeds. In town they say we've abdicated our worries. You work eight hours a day, they say, you have your food and security, and others worry for you."

Life on a struggling kibbutz can be spartan. The chaverim work hard, very hard. Their farms generally have an alterior purpose too. They are usually dug into thinly populated areas, where it is in the strategic interest of Israel to have settlements.

Kofsky had little curiousity about the Canada he had left behind him.

"What's happening in Montreal? It's gotten bigger, that's all. All my friends are in Israel anyway. I guess we must seem very chauvinistic to you here. We're curious about everything in this country, it's ours, and we want to know all there is to know. The names of the different flowers and birds; and all the history."

The day after the seder Gesher Haziv celebrated the Omer. Chaverim, guests and children crowded on to tractor wagons that had been decked out with flowers and started out on a bumpy ride that took us through all the fields of Gesher Haziv. As the group sang rousing songs we wheeled over wheat and cotton fields, the banana plantation, past workshops and the cemetery, finally pulling up at a field where the first wheat of the year was to be ceremoniously cut. The festivities had a forced folksy air to it, I'm afraid. The visiting Habonim Youth Group, Americans wearing Yemenite shirts, mounted a platform to perform harvest dances to the tune of a solitary flute. The rustic gesture clashed somewhat with the University of Syracuse sweatshirts and Bermuda shorts other youngsters were wearing, and the whirr of cameras as they avidly took moving pictures of one another.

Nobody at Gesher Haziv felt that the tourist motel, rapidly nearing completion, was a herald of decadence.

"We are a curiosity. Why shouldn't people come to see how we live?"

Two young boys shared the room next to mine. One of them, a twenty-two year old, had given up his American citizenship to become an Israeli.

"Why? Because I'm a Jew. I feel better here with my brothers the Yemenites. I have more in common with Iraqi and African Jews than I do with Irishmen in my home town."

"Why didn't you settle on a Yemenite kibbutz, then?"

"I just sort of ended up here. Besides, the Yemenites hardly ever form kibbutzim. They're the sort who like the jingle of money in their pockets."

Everywhere I went in Israel I asked about the Arabs.

Harvey Goodman, manager of the Eilat Hotel, said, "It's got to be one thing or another. Either we develop a more enlightened Arab policy or we go to war and teach them a lesson. Next time we could take Cairo, set up a pro-Israeli government and move out again. They hate us, you know. They sit by the radios in their villages, listening to venemous broadcasts from Cairo. They stone our police cars and even tear down Israeli flags." Goodman explained what he meant by a more enlightened policy. "Educate them. We could integrate them and teach them that it's not such a bad thing to be an Arab in Israel."

"Or a Jew in Canada?" I asked.

"No, sir. Never. You're always a Jew there. You know, there's actually no such thing as an 'Arab'. What, for instance, has an Arab in Cairo in common with a Bedouin from Iraq?"

"What have I got in common with a Yemenite Jew?"

"Jerusalem. All that the Arabs have in common is the fact that they're Moslem. Look here, the Americans could force them to sign a peace treaty with us any time they want to. They won't, though. We've been betrayed by the oil lobby in Washington."

"Why don't the Arabs themselves want peace?"

"Because they need to maintain a war feeling within their own countries to keep the people's minds off their own miserable state."

Bill Kofsky said, "The trouble with the Arabs is they won't mix. They're private. They stick to their own people and areas. Another thing, you know, is they have loyalties outside the country."

On the Mediterranean shore, at the foot of Gesher Haziv, lies the abandoned Arab village of Haziv. The fishermen of Haziv fled during the war. Now an enterprising young Israeli lived in the village; he had made a museum and hopefully built a hostel and opened a nightclub. Haziv is mentioned in the Old Testament; Arab fishermen lived there even then. Wandering through its ruins two thousand years later one cannot help but feel guilty. This land belongs to the Arabs too.

The Arab settlements I visited in Israel were characterised by children with rickets, old men with tracoma, and ignorance and squalor everywhere. Take Ako, for instance. Once a Phoenician port, later a famous crusader stronghold, Ako is surrounded by a sea wall and towering fortifications. Barefoot kids scamper over the crumbling ramparts, leathery old men fish off the stone steps. Occasionally there was the surprise of a cool, delightful square with a fountain in the middle, but, for the most part, there was only the stinking narrow streets. Donkeys, chickens and other animals wandered somnolently through the maze of stalls in the marketplace. Barefoot boys flitted freely through the muck of decaying refuse and turds. The wares the vendors had to offer were pathetic. Rusty ancient locks, faded cotton dresses and split boots reclaimed from junk piles. Flies were everywhere.

Bill Kofsky had little patience with Ako. "You think they're poor? Those guys own property everywhere. They have plenty of money."

The souvenir shop I stopped at in Nazareth dealt in the usual bogus articles, water from Mary's Well, and so forth. The enterprising Arab proprieter, however, also sold little bags of earth; half of them labelled "Earth from the Holy Land, Nazareth," the printing superimposed over a cross; the others reading "Earth from the Holy Land, Israel," a blue Star of David fixed above. I laughed. The Arab laughed. And it was with this shrewd irreverent Arab that the land of Israel came full circle for me. This Arab's gift for survival and self-evident humour seemed profoundly Jewish to me, more Jewish than the sabra. I could identify with him.

A lawyer I met in Jerusalem told me that he had served on the Gaza Strip when Israel had occupied the zone in 1956. "Don't forget they've been there for fourteen years. Many have died out and others are not proper refugees at all. They were born in Gaza, they've never even seen Israel. The figure of one million is an inflated one too. When a man dies they don't hand in his ration book, but go on claiming his food."

"But, surely," I said, "if the Jews are entitled to come 'home' after two thousand years then the son of an Arab refugee is a Palestinian too?"

"All right. Conditions in their camps are deplorable. However, the conditions I lived under in Dachau were worse."